Praise for the Novels of Karen Kendall

Take Me If You Can

"A sexy, riveting read!"
—*New York Times* bestselling author Christina Dodd

"Flirty, fun, and fabulously original."
—*USA Today* bestselling author Julie Kenner

"Sexy, witty, fast-paced, and full of delicious plot twists."
—*USA Today* bestselling author Cherry Adair

"Sexy, charming, witty, and irresistible."
—National bestselling author Roxanne St. Claire

"If you're looking for a fun, entertaining read that will keep you on the edge of your seat, then look no further than *Take Me If You Can*. It will make you laugh, make you cry, and keep you glued to the very end."
—Romance Reviews Today

"A swift, smart, and sassy suspense with lots of romantic tension . . . reminiscent of smart, sexy movies like *The Thomas Crown Affair*. . . . A delight." —Fresh Fiction

continued...

Fit to Be Tied

"Sexy-hot delicious and laugh-out-loud delightful! Karen Kendall is my new favorite author!"

—*New York Times* bestselling author Nicole Jordan

"Kendall's lively tale about breaking up, making up, and shaking it up is funny and poignant. Fans of Lori Wilde, Susan Donovan, and Connie Lane will appreciate Kendall's humorous take on tying the knot."

—*Booklist*

"Kendall again presents a story that mixes humor with a more serious plot. The journey of the two main characters toward an awareness of what really matters, and secondary characters who make their own discoveries, give this lighthearted romance substance."

—*Romantic Times*

"This funny, sexy romance will keep you reading."

—Fresh Fiction

"Be prepared to laugh, cry, and feel some emotions for the characters and their plights . . . an unforgettable read."

—Romance Reviews Today

The Bridesmaid Chronicles

First Date

"Lighthearted comedy . . . the snappy talk keeps the plot in constant motion. . . . Something fun . . . to read on the beach."
—*Publishers Weekly*

"A sharp, sexy, and fun read with engaging characters who steal into your heart right away. Karen Kendall's newest romance contains all the ingredients required to make it a supersassy romp, and practically thrums with vibrant, snappy dialogue. Utterly delightful and very highly recommended!"
—The Best Reviews

"*First Date* is a magnificent, captivating read that will keep you totally entertained from the first page until the last."
—The Romance Readers Connection

First Dance

"Hilarious and downright sexy! Karen Kendall will delight you!"
—*New York Times* bestselling author Carly Phillips

"Kendall's sparkling third installment in [the] Bridesmaid Chronicles series offers both zany romance and serious probing of her protagonists' emotional depths. This witty, well-crafted entry bodes well for the final volume."
—*Publishers Weekly*

Also by Karen Kendall

Take Me Two Times
Take Me If You Can
Fit to Be Tied
First Date
First Dance

Karen Kendall

Take Me for a Ride

A SIGNET ECLIPSE BOOK

SIGNET ECLIPSE
Published by New American Library, a division of
Penguin Group (USA) Inc., 375 Hudson Street,
New York, New York 10014, USA
Penguin Group (Canada), 90 Eglinton Avenue East, Suite 700, Toronto,
Ontario M4P 2Y3, Canada (a division of Pearson Penguin Canada Inc.)
Penguin Books Ltd., 80 Strand, London WC2R 0RL, England
Penguin Ireland, 25 St. Stephen's Green, Dublin 2,
Ireland (a division of Penguin Books Ltd.)
Penguin Group (Australia), 250 Camberwell Road, Camberwell, Victoria 3124,
Australia (a division of Pearson Australia Group Pty. Ltd.)
Penguin Books India Pvt. Ltd., 11 Community Centre, Panchsheel Park,
New Delhi - 110 017, India
Penguin Group (NZ), 67 Apollo Drive, Rosedale, North Shore 0632,
New Zealand (a division of Pearson New Zealand Ltd.)
Penguin Books (South Africa) (Pty.) Ltd., 24 Sturdee Avenue,
Rosebank, Johannesburg 2196, South Africa

Penguin Books Ltd., Registered Offices:
80 Strand, London WC2R 0RL, England

First published by Signet Eclipse, an imprint of New American Library,
a division of Penguin Group (USA) Inc.

First Printing, November 2009
10 9 8 7 6 5 4 3 2 1

Printed in the United States of America

This one is dedicated to
the Penguin sales team. Without
you, I wouldn't be in print!
Thank you.

ACKNOWLEDGMENTS

A big thanks to my husband, friends, family, and critique partners for always catching the sky when it fell! I love you all.

And to Joanne, John, and Sue at Murder on the Beach bookstore.

One

Manhattan, September 2008

Some people steal money. Others steal cars, liquor, or big-ticket items like jewelry. Art recovery agent Eric McDougal stole women.

He did it with wit, style, passion—and guile . . . since they never knew they were missing in action until he returned them to reality.

McDougal took his women for a ride, and a good time was had by all. Afterward, he set them down gently on their own two feet; then he gave 'em a sweet smile, a wink from his Newman blue eyes, and a swat on the backside. How they handled things from there was not his problem. Well, not usually.

This evening, as he trained his gaze on the pretty target two blocks ahead, McDougal contemplated the horrifying memory of what a tasty, busty little psychopath had done to his Kawasaki Ninja ZX-14. He'd almost bitten through his own tongue when he saw it. Even now, three days later and a thousand miles from Miami, he winced.

Pink. She'd painted the Ninja *pink*. His jaw worked.

Why? He'd taken her to nice places. He'd never made any promises. He'd given her—if he did say so himself—the mother of all orgasms. And just because he hadn't called afterward . . .

Okay, so maybe he wasn't much of a gentleman. He'd never advertised himself as one. But . . .

Pink.

It was cold. Beyond cold. Vicious brutality without conscience was what it was. Carnage.

He was tempted to press charges. But then he pictured the cop's face as he filled out the report, and he deep-sixed that bright idea.

Focus, you bonehead.

Natalie Rosen, his mark this evening, had nothing to do with the destruction of his bike. An art restorer and probable thief, she lurched left on the crowded Manhattan sidewalk between Ninety-second and First. The door of Reif's opened and she vanished inside.

Reif's? She didn't look the type for a seedy old neighborhood bar run by three generations of Irish. Reif's was a blue-collar place in a now-affluent neighborhood. North of Ninety-sixth got dicey as it eased into Spanish Harlem, but south of Ninety-sixth had become gentrified. Still, there were a few old holdouts like Reif's, where electricians and plumbers mingled with white-collar yuppies and argued politics in a haze of dust mingled with decades of lingering stale cigarette smoke. The Yankees, the Mets, the mayor, the weather . . . those were typical topics.

Reif's was situated on the ground floor of a six-story apartment building. It smelled beer sodden and mildewy, but it was also homey and offered a sort of tobacco-stained comfort that suited McDougal . . . but not a girl like Natalie Rosen.

Natalie had dark, glossy, straight hair and dark, serious eyes that looked a little at odds with her snub, lightly freckled nose. She was cute in a repressed, academic sort of way. Not tweedy or preppy—more earnest and artsy. The chick wore a lot of black, but there was a difference between severe New York black and sultry Miami black.

New York black covered, while Miami black revealed. New York black involved tights, turtlenecks, scarves, and coats. Miami black involved thongs, skirt lengths just shy of illegal, spike heels, and fishnets—particularly on some of those little Brazilian hotties, with their bras clearly showing under skimpy tops. Oh, yeah. McDougal was a big fan of Miami black.

Focus. He frowned. What in the hell was a girl with an art degree from Carnegie Mellon doing in a beer-soaked joint like Reif's? Surely not unloading a $2 million necklace that had once belonged to Catherine the Great.

It was his job to find out, but he needed to hang back for a few. Let her get settled. Have a drink or two. He pegged her for the type that would walk into a dusty place like Reif's and order, say, white wine. A little naive. A little out of touch with reality.

Twenty minutes later, McDougal shoved his hands into his pockets, crossed the street, and entered Reif's. He glimpsed her immediately: Natalie perched on one of the old, backless wooden barstools, staring sightlessly into the dregs of a short glass of what looked like whiskey on the rocks.

His opinion of her went up a notch—at least she hadn't ordered a white Zinfandel in an Irish pub. Of course, his opinion of her didn't matter much—he'd get what he came for, regardless. He always did.

In all that black, Natalie looked as if she'd smell of sulfur or mothballs, but as she dug into her nylon messenger bag for a tissue, he caught a waft of fresh laundry detergent and a tinge of 4711, a cologne his sisters used to wear.

Over the bar hung a four-foot-by-eight-foot mirror that reflected, among other things, Natalie's drawn, downcast face. Something was on the lady's mind.

McDougal nodded to the bartender and mounted the stool next to hers. It was covered in cheap green vinyl and had seen better days, but the upside of worn was comfortable. It announced his presence by creaking under his solid 180 pounds, but Natalie didn't look at him.

Didn't matter. She would. Women always did, eventually—not that in every case they liked what they saw. Some of the smarter ones summed him up as a player in one glance and dismissed him. Others focused on the bare fourth finger of his left hand. The fun ones started shoveling verbal shit at him immediately. Which type was she?

As Eric casually ordered a Guinness, he watched her in the mirror. Watched as her pointed little chin came up and she pushed some hair out of her face and cut her eyes toward him, her lashes at half-mast.

Then came her first impression, the undercover evaluation of his six-foot-two frame, his muscular forearms sprinkled with freckles and golden hair, his denim-clad legs. She took in the brown leather jacket and the reddish brown stubble on his chin, then the grin that widened as he watched her.

That was when she realized that he'd seen her inspecting him in the mirror. Her gaze flew to his in the reflected surface and froze. A slow blush crept up her neck—a blush so fierce he could see it even in the dim light of Reif's.

"Hi," McDougal said, turning to face her with the full wattage of his grin.

She blinked, stared, then looked away as the blush intensified. She put a hand up to her neck as if to cool the skin off. "H-hi."

She was a babe in the woods . . . without mosquito repellent. He prepared to feast on her tender young naïveté.

"I didn't mean to embarrass you," McDougal said, taking his grin down a few notches, from wolfish to disarming.

She seemed to have no adequate response to that.

"It's very normal to check out the guy sitting next to you. He could be a vagrant, a pervert, or a serial killer."

She laughed reluctantly at that, and it transformed her face from mildly pretty to dazzling. She'd gone from librarian to . . . to . . . *Carla Bruni* in a half second flat. It was McDougal's turn to stare. The French First Lady had nothing on her.

"So, which one are you?" she asked, evidently emboldened.

"Me? I'm just a tourist, sweetheart. The only cereal killing I do involves a bowl of raisin bran or cornflakes."

That got a smile. "Where are you from?"

"Miami."

"Florida," she said, sounding wistful. "I'd love to be on a beach right now, not in the city."

"You work here?"

Natalie nodded. "I'm a restoration artist."

"A restoration artist," McDougal repeated. "As in, they call you to touch up the Sistine Chapel?" He nodded at the bartender and pointed to her glass.

"Something like that. But I specialize in rugs and tapestries, not painting." A wary expression crossed her face as the drink was set in front of her. "Um, I didn't order—"

"It's on me," McDougal said.

"Oh, but . . ."

"What's your name?"

She hesitated. "Natalie."

"Natalie, it's just a drink. Not a big deal. 'Kay?"

"Thank you," she said after a long pause. She curled her small but competent hand around the glass. "Actually, you have no idea how much I need this."

Yes, I do. First heist, honey? It always shreds your nerves. But all McDougal said was, "You're welcome. I'm Eric." And he proceeded to chat her up while she got tipsy on her second whiskey.

Really, he should be ashamed of himself.

Natalie Rosen's eyes had gone just a little fuzzy, her gestures loose and her posture relaxed. She'd also gotten wittier. "So, you said you're a tourist. Are you an accidental one?"

He smiled. "Nope. I do have a purpose. Are you an accidental barfly?"

"No." She averted her gaze, then looked down into her whiskey and murmured, "I'm an accidental thief."

"Do tell," McDougal said, showing his teeth and signaling the bartender again. If he had his wicked way, she'd soon be a naked thief.

Natalie took a sip of her third Jameson's whiskey and had a short debate with her smarter, more sober side. Hadn't her parents always told her not to talk to strangers? Not to accept candy—or whiskey—from them?

However, the drink had come straight from the hand of the bartender, so she knew there was nothing funny in it. And she desperately, urgently needed to talk to someone about the crisis she faced. She could pay a shrink . . . or she could talk to this startlingly good-looking stranger with the laser blue eyes. Not like she'd ever see the man again after tonight, which was kind of a shame.

Eric had a young Paul Newman's features but not his cool, distant countenance. Instead he possessed the freckles and warm mischief of Prince Harry. He also had the prince's ginger hair, but his skin was unusually bronzed for a redhead, rather than milk white. His looks bordered on irresistible, made even more so by his air of total confidence.

If Natalie was being honest, she didn't know whether she was slightly drunk on the stranger's looks or on the whiskey. Probably both. There he sat, one reddish eyebrow raised, looking intrigued and attracted—to her, of all people—and inviting her to tell her story. She had the sensation of acting out someone else's page in a script.

But for once she did have an unusual tale to tell, one

that set her apart from all the other worker bees swarming the concrete sidewalks of Manhattan.

"How can anyone be an accidental thief?" Eric asked. "Seems to me that you either are one or you aren't."

Natalie swirled the ice counterclockwise in her glass, which made a small rumble as its base rubbed against the worn wood of the bar. "Not true. Let's say that you borrowed something to show it to someone, but she refused to give it back."

Eric took a swig of the Guinness and eyed her reflectively. "Well, I personally would insist on its return."

"I tried," said Natalie.

"Failing that, I'd probably 'borrow' it back."

"What if the person has hidden it?"

"Then I'd think about using force."

Natalie sighed. "What if the person who won't give back what you borrowed is seventy years old and fragile?"

"Hmm," said Eric. "That does complicate things."

"And worse, what if she's your grandmother and she helped raise you?"

"I see your point. You're kind of screwed."

Natalie turned to him and spread her hands wide. "I am completely, utterly, totally screwed."

Those Newman eyes seemed to deepen in color, and the corner of his mouth quirked. Belatedly, she thought about the literal meaning of her words and had a sudden image of a bedspread pulled back in invitation. Her pulse quickened and she crossed her legs.

He took note of the movement, his gaze moving to her thighs, outlined under her skirt. A silken shame slid along her spine, and she shifted on the barstool.

"What am I supposed to do, knock her down?" Natalie continued. "She won't even open the door to me now." She took a large swallow of her whiskey.

"I'm a little confused," McDougal said. "Why don't you start from the beginning?"

Sexual attraction aside, decency and integrity seemed to shine out of his eyes. Deep blue. The color of truth. She wavered. "You have to promise not to tell anyone," she said, pushing the hair off her forehead.

"Scout's honor. Who am I going to tell? And you've shared only your first name. You're practically incognito."

That comforted her. In a city of eight million people, his not knowing her last name *was* like a cloak of invisibility.

"Talk to me, baby, won't you talk to me . . . ," he crooned cheesily, making her laugh.

"Fine," she said, and inhaled some more whiskey. "Three days ago, I went in to work, and there it was: the most unusual necklace I've ever seen . . ."

Two

Three days earlier . . .

The holidays had come and gone their merry way, leaving behind a lugubrious, definitely insalubrious early March in Manhattan. Luc Ricard Conservation and Restoration Associates, where Natalie worked, was housed in a dignified, if moody, old brownstone that seemed reluctant to suffer the company's presence inside it.

Nat wrapped her sweater more tightly around her body as a frigid draft blew under the windowsill at the second-floor landing. The draft seemed to have chosen just the moment when she walked by on her way to the kitchen on the first floor.

A fresh blast of arctic air assaulted her as she grimaced out at the gray, slushy daylight repressed by cranky, cumbersome clouds.

Tea. She needed some hot green tea and she needed a new set of eyeballs, since her current ones ached and had gone blurry under the strain of focusing on tiny embroidery stitches for hours on end.

The piece she was restoring was an eighteenth-century Susani tapestry, which was doing its best to disintegrate after generations of being carelessly draped over console tables and hung on smoky dining room walls. The tapestry was tired and worn. Her job was to rejuvenate it, smack some color back into its cheeks, and then mount it under Plexiglas for future generations to enjoy—or sell it at auction for a tidy profit.

Natalie yawned and then knelt down near the windowsill so that the next whoosh of freezing air would blow right into her face and wake her up. Below, on the street, a heavyset man in a dark wool coat looked behind him and then to the left as he rounded the corner of the building. Natalie heard the familiar light jangle of the bells at the door.

As she descended the stairs from the second floor to the first, she saw the heavyset man in conversation with her boss, Luc, and Selia Markovic, an associate who specialized in fine jewelry repair. Luc laughed a little too hard at something the bulky man said, and then nodded like a bobble-head. The bobble-head thing was very uncharacteristic, since Luc usually glided around in abstraction as if he were part of an alternate universe. He moved slowly, as if he were underwater.

Pinch-lipped Selia, who wore standard-issue white cotton gloves that protected valuable items from the oils and acids in the human hand, examined a piece lying on a bed of black velvet.

Natalie couldn't make out much about the piece except that it was gold in color. She kept going toward the kitchen, rounding the base of the stairs and walking under them in search of her green tea and, if she was lucky, an oatmeal cookie.

She set the old copper kettle to boil, ignoring the brand-new white plastic hot pot that Drake, their receptionist, had brought in. Nat refused to use it on the grounds that hot plastic was poison. She didn't like microwave ovens, either.

So she stood and tapped her foot for a good five minutes before the water even showed an inclination to steam, much less boil. Then she rooted around in the cabinet for the two oatmeal cookies she'd cleverly hidden between pieces of stale low-carb bread in the bread's original bag. Surely the food bandit wouldn't have found them there?

But the bag was suspiciously light. Natalie narrowed her eyes and untwisted the tie that sealed the mouth of it from the air. She looked inside, lifted the top piece of camouflage bread.

Gone.

Her cookies were gone.

How on earth had the food bandit thought to look in her bread bag? Natalie's stomach growled, adding insult to injury. Though they held little appeal, she removed the two slices of dry bread and tossed them into the toaster, not that there'd be any butter in the refrigerator.

She double-checked that, but her prediction was accurate. All she found was a lonely packet of duck sauce lurking behind someone's miraculously unfilched yogurt. Natalie grabbed the packet and squirted the contents onto one of the pieces of toast when it popped up. She sandwiched the other one on top of it and took a bite, just as the kettle whistled.

She poured boiling water into an oversize mug, added a tea bag, and kept munching, though as far as snacks went, this one was highly unsatisfactory. If she hadn't been the daughter of two professors who discouraged such language, she would have said it sucked. But she was, and she remembered all too well her mother's reaction when she'd used the word at age ten.

First they'd had to define the subject of the sentence, *this*, which Nat had used in reference to homemade sugar-free peanut butter. Then her mother had forced her to contemplate the missing object of the sentence. The peanut butter sucked what, exactly?

Well, gee, ten-year-old Natalie didn't know.

So they had to examine the origins of the verb and its missing object, follow the trail of the obscene slang. Once Nat had found out what, in actuality, *got* sucked, she'd made the mistake of saying she was completely "grossed out."

And by the time she'd closed the dictionary on the etymology of *that* term, Nat had resolved to just go mute for life—at least around her parents. The alternative was to speak nothing but Latin.

Luc wandered in with a faraway look on his broad face, his white hair sticking up at the back of his head in an alfalfa sprout. He was dressed in a navy cashmere sweater that had visible moth holes in it, and a dark green scarf that had shed a little tuft onto one of the bristles under his chin. Natalie resisted the urge to pick it off.

Luc either cut himself by shaving too closely or left longish stubble here and there. He was meticulous when it came to the restoration of paintings, but not so fussy when it came to his own personal grooming. He was the sort of man who'd spend ten minutes looking for his glasses when they were perched on top of his head—abstracted in a sort of benign, mad-scientist way.

"Hi, Luc. Who was that Mafioso-looking guy in there?"

"Eh? Ah, hello, Natalie. Nobody important. Just a man with a repair."

A man who makes you laugh like a nervous donkey. But she didn't say it aloud.

"What do you have there?" He squinted at her homely sandwich.

"Two pieces of low-carb toast with duck sauce."

He looked revolted.

"I'm hungry, and the food bandit stole my oatmeal-raisin cookies." She knew her voice sounded plaintive, the closest thing to a whine she'd allow, but honestly . . . did she have to get a safe just for lunch and bolt it to the floor of her office?

"Ah, ze food bandit." He looked furtively at her bread bag. "Why do you not lock the cookies in your desk drawer?"

Wait a minute . . .

"I don't have a desk, remember?" Natalie said, carefully removing the edge from her voice. "You haven't authorized the expenditure."

Luc looked uncomfortable for a moment. "Yes, yes," he said, patting her arm. "Next month, perhaps. When revenues rise."

He'd been saying the same thing every couple of months for the past year, even though revenues had risen enough for him to buy a new Mercedes and garage it in the city. And revenues had risen enough for him to park a rock the size of a robin's egg on the fourth finger of his Russian lingerie-model fiancée's hand. Nat was quite sure he'd find a way to write that off as a business expense, too.

Meanwhile, she was stuck doing restoration work on the top floor at a "desk" that consisted of two white melamine shelves laid over a pair of old sawhorses.

So for Luc to have eyeballed her bread bag so oddly got her ire up. Could Luc be the . . . ? No, surely not. Luc *owned* the place. He could afford to buy great gourmet food. He wouldn't stoop to swiping his employees' snacks, would he?

Natalie told herself she was being silly. And paranoid. After all, Luc took Giraffe—her real name was Giselle, but Nat thought of her as Giraffe—out to a late dinner on the town three to four times a week. She knew this because all the employees had overheard him recently as he complained bitterly about paying $200 for the future Mme. Ricard to eat a stalk of asparagus and three peas, however sumptuously steamed by a five-star chef of Cordon Bleu fame.

Natalie frowned. That, too, was out of character for Luc. He never used to complain. He had always just floated around beatifically on his own foggy planet . . . until Giraffe had galloped into his life—bony butt, cloven hooves, and all.

Nat sipped at her tea and told herself to try to be a nicer person. But it was hard, what with the nasty weather and the duck-sauce sandwich. She tossed the rest of it into the trash, grabbed her mug, and left Luc gazing fixedly into space with the green fuzz ball still stuck under his chin. Really, Giraffe should buy him a new sweater without holes in it instead of eating peas at $50 per . . . but it wasn't Natalie's business, now, was it?

She wandered back toward the staircase and had set her foot on the bottom step when she saw a flash out of the corner of her eye. She turned toward Selia's desk. Her coworker was holding a necklace up to the light—and what a necklace.

She wasn't a jewelry expert by any means, but the piece had to be crafted of at least twenty-two-karat gold, and it was almost more sculpture than necklace. Natalie approached Selia's desk, opened her mouth to speak, and then closed it again.

A solid gold dragon with claws, scales, long tail, and fangs turned its head to breathe fire at a knight in full battle regalia on a rearing horse. Unfortunately for the dragon, the knight's spear penetrated its gaping, toothy maw. Bad day for the dragon.

"St. George," Selia said.

Natalie nodded, every hair on the back of her neck standing at attention. How many times had she heard Nonnie, her grandmother, speak of a necklace like this one? A necklace confiscated by Nazi officers when her great-grandparents fled Russia during World War II. One that they'd never seen again.

What were the odds of it surfacing right here, at Natalie's workplace? Astronomical. But what if . . . ?

How many necklaces like this one could there be?

St. George slaying the dragon was a popular subject for painters and sculptors—Raphael, Uccello, and Donatello had all depicted the legend. But for jewelers, no.

Natalie worked some moisture into her dry mouth. "How old is it?"

Selia drew her sparse, salt-and-pepper brows together and traced the knight's outline with her gloved finger. "Mid–eighteenth century, I'd say. Russian."

A hard pulse kicked up in Natalie's ears. "Why Russian? St. George is the patron saint of England, isn't he?"

Selia removed her glasses and rubbed at her eyes. "St. George has been everyone's patron saint, it seems. Yes, England claims him—and specifically the Scouting movement, which I believe is the origin of our own Boy Scouts here in America. But so do many other sects and countries. The legend is so old that its origins are obscure.

"It may have started with the Greek myth of Perseus, who rescued the maiden Andromeda from a sea monster. But eventually it's come to represent the triumph of Christianity over paganism and even the triumph in general of good over evil." Selia settled her glasses back onto her nose and pushed them as high as they'd go. "Why do I think this piece is Russian? Well, because it's similar to the image on the state emblem of the Russian Empire, which has evolved over many years to become the seal of Moscow."

Natalie nodded and tried to slow her pulse. Was this her family's heirloom necklace? It was an incredible long shot, but if it was, she didn't kid herself that it would be easy to prove that it had been stolen and should rightfully be restored to her grandmother.

The legal issues were torturous. One had to prove the onetime ownership, then the theft, and finally trace the piece through a possible maze of owners since the theft had occurred. Often the process crossed international boundaries, muddying the legal waters even further, because different countries had different precedents and burdens of proof. Then there was the question of whether the current owner had purchased the item with the knowledge that it was "hot."

Natalie knew she should just walk away from Selia's desk and forget she'd ever seen the St. George necklace. But she stood rooted to the spot. "So why is the necklace here? Is it broken?"

"The clasp needs repairs and the whole thing needs to be cleaned," Selia told her.

Nat wanted to hold it in her hands, but Selia's tone directed her to go away. She never had been chatty. So Nat took her tea and went back upstairs, deep in thought.

The only person who could tell her for sure whether that St. George necklace was *the* St. George necklace was Nonnie, who lived in suburban Connecticut. And her chances of getting Nonnie onto a train and into the city were about the same as those of a gnat surviving a swim across New York Harbor.

Still, she had to try. Out of breath by the time she got to her third-floor office, Natalie located her cell phone in the depths of her knockoff Prada messenger bag and hit the speed dial for her grandmother's number.

Three

Reif's was getting crowded, and Natalie's voice could no longer compete with the music, the buzz of thirty other conversations, and the bustle behind the bar.

McDougal leaned into her space, propping his chin on a loosely clasped fist. Natalie blinked at his close proximity, and her cheeks pinkened a bit, but she didn't move away.

The lady appeared to enjoy his company. He figured it wouldn't be long before he could have her horizontal.

As soon as he had the thought, though, something disturbing—like guilt—rapped him on the knuckles.

Leave her alone. You're getting the information you need. It was clearly just a matter of tracking down Granny now.

And what, you're going to mug a little old lady? Even for you, that's low.

Eric took a swig of his Guinness. "So you got your grandmother to come into the city to look at the necklace," he prompted.

Natalie shook her head. "No. She's housebound these days. I'm afraid she's becoming agoraphobic. She won't even go to the grocery store anymore—she pays a kid to deliver stuff. I had to take the necklace to her in Connecticut."

"Why not just a snapshot of it?"

Natalie wrapped both hands around her whiskey glass. "Because Nonnie's now legally blind."

"I'm sorry to hear that." *Fan-frickin'-tastic, McDougal. You're going to mug a* blind *little old lady. Aren't you just the hero?*

"She deals with it pretty well. But anyway, in order to tell anything about the necklace, she had to be able to touch it. She knew the weight and the contours from handling it as a child."

"You're telling me that she identified it by feel alone?"

Natalie nodded. "And then," she said somewhat bitterly, "she started to cry for joy and wouldn't give it back, even when I told her how much trouble I'll be in. I'm going to get fired if I tell my boss. *Fired*. But she says that's insignificant in comparison with having our heritage returned to us."

He raised an eyebrow.

"You have to understand—my grandmother actually prays to St. George. She has a shrine to him in her home. She communicates with . . . ah . . . dead family members through him."

His lips twitched; he couldn't help it.

"Yes, I know how strange that sounds, but it's something to do with the Order of St. George, a centuries-old military organization that my ancestors were a big part of . . . Anyway, this necklace has an almost mystical, religious significance to Nonnie."

Under McDougal's gaze, Natalie swayed on the stool

and put her hand on the bar to steady herself. He should have been gratified—wasn't this exactly what he'd wanted? But instead, he scanned the male faces in Reif's and found too many that looked predatory. Even if he himself did the right thing and walked away from her, the sharks would circle.

Damn it. He'd have to keep her talking until she sobered up. "Surely you can talk some sense into your grandmother? Or failing that, wait until she's asleep and then just take back the necklace."

"I tried that. She hid it! And now she says I have to take her to Russia, and until I show up with the plane tickets she won't open the door to me."

"Russia?"

"The necklace is the key to claiming something. I don't know. I'm really wondering if she's gone bonkers."

"Does your boss know that the necklace is missing?" McDougal already knew the answer to that, since the man had reported the loss to his insurance company, which had promptly hired his company, ARTemis, to hunt down the necklace. Since it had once belonged to a stout, bloodthirsty, German-born empress who'd helped to off her own husband, it was worth a cool two million. That meant a $200,000 commission for him, earmarked for the down payment on a Bertram 540 luxury sportfishing yacht.

Natalie nodded. "He knows."

"Is he a reasonable guy? Is there any way that you can go to him and tell him the story? Maybe *he* can reason with your grandmother?"

"You don't understand." Natalie repeated her habit of moving her now-empty glass in circles on the bar, which prompted the bartender to ask whether she wanted another.

McDougal opened his mouth to say no.

Natalie said, "Yes, please."

The bartender brought her another Jameson's on the rocks.

Hoo boy. "What's there to understand?" Eric asked. "Tell Grandma that if she doesn't fork over the necklace, your boss will go to the cops, you'll be charged with grand larceny, and she'll be charged with receiving stolen property."

Natalie leaned forward to pick up the glass and unwittingly flashed him some very inviting cleavage.

He was only human. He looked and enjoyed.

"What you don't get," she said slowly, "is that I don't think my boss *can* go to the cops. He's scared out of his mind. The people who brought him the necklace—well, I have a feeling that they're not such nice people. And I think they might not have come by the necklace honestly."

She took a large gulp of whiskey. "I can't take the risk of them hurting Nonnie."

Oh, Christ. What had this girl gotten herself into? McDougal found himself feeling sorry for her, of all things. He rubbed a hand over his face.

"Listen, Natalie. If these people are that dangerous, then the only way to protect her—and yourself—is to get that necklace back so you can wash your hands of it. And then you may want to look for another job anyway. Because if your boss is doing business with smugglers or thieves, I can pretty much guarantee you that things are going to end badly for him . . . and you don't want to be around for the particulars."

She met his gaze seriously, even as she swayed again on the stool. He put his hand on her arm to steady her.

"I know," she said a little woozily. She upended her glass.

Then she said, "I'm scared."

Every art recovery agent who worked for ARTemis, Inc., had excellent instincts and situational antennae, so to speak. Now that he had more information, McDougal's were on high alert, but he didn't want to add to her anxiety.

She tossed back the rest of the whiskey in her glass and tried to catch the bartender's eye.

"Natalie," McDougal said. "No offense, sweetheart, but I think you've had enough."

She opened her mouth to deny it but was evidently too honest. She frowned.

"Why don't I get you a cab?" He stood up, removed his wallet from his back pocket, and slid some bills across the surface of the bar. Then he put his arm around her and helped her off the stool.

She was petite, with a lithe, firm little body underneath all the black. Once again, his gaze went to her cleavage as she reached for her bag and removed her coat from a hook under the bar. This time he glimpsed the curve of one breast pushing against a lacy black bra. *Mmmmmmm.*

No.

Why not? He'd done this hundreds of times. Nothing wrong with helping a tipsy woman out of her clothes and showing her a good time . . .

But there was an innocence about Natalie that gave him pause, that tugged at his conscience. She wasn't the hardened thief he'd expected, or even an opportunist like him who'd seen a way to make a quick buck. She'd just wanted to show the necklace to her grandmother.

She was truly what she'd claimed to be: an accidental thief. McDougal had never met one before. As he escorted her to the door, knowing glances followed them, glances that said, "Score!" Normally this would have amused him. Tonight it annoyed him.

The frigid air smacked him in the face like an angry mother hours after curfew. Natalie shivered. He unzipped his jacket and folded her inside it, holding her against him while he searched the length of the street for an on-duty cab.

"You're so . . . sweet," Natalie said, craning her neck to look up at him.

Sweet? McDougal let out a bark of laughter. "No, that I'm not."

"Actions s-s-schpeak louder than words." Natalie had now gone from swaying to slurring.

"They schpeak, do they?" he teased her.

"You haven't even asked if you can come home with me," she pointed out, ignoring him.

"No, I haven't," he said, again faintly surprised.

She frowned. She turned around inside his jacket so that she faced him and tilted her head back. "Do you want to?"

"Er," said McDougal, looking helplessly down at her and trying to ignore the softness of her body snugged up against him. In an effort not to respond, he tried to think of the homeliest woman he'd ever seen . . . his mother's friend Miss Eunice, who looked exactly like a grouper.

But he couldn't ignore the fact that it wasn't Miss Eunice who was pressed against his—

"Are you gay?" Natalie blurted, just as that part of him sprang to attention.

Hell, no, I'm not gay. I'm just planning to rob your sweet little granny. "What do you think, sweetheart?"

"Wow." She grinned impishly. "I think I'm glad you're not gay."

To his bemusement, her hand began a journey up his thigh and then took a sharp turn toward the center. "Do *not* touch that," Eric said through gritted teeth. "Or you won't make it home safely."

Her hand stilled but remained just to the left of his hip bone. "Um. Well. That was kind of the point."

A loopy little giggle followed. Natalie Rosen was the cheapest drunk he'd ever encountered; that was for sure.

The top of her head came barely to his shoulder. He stared down at her, and she up at him. In the bright light of a streetlamp, he saw that her eyes weren't dark brown at all, but closer to navy. The color of deep, deep water.

"I haven't even kissed you yet," he said, feeling mildly outraged. Why? Because he was supposed to be the wolf, not the sheep?

"You don't strike me as the kind of guy who waits for permission."

"I'm not."

They stood there like that, with her wanting to touch him and his cock straining to be touched. It was ironic. It was damn close to painful. And yet he wanted to draw out the moment, savor it for some reason. Clearly he was insane.

She lifted her eyebrows in an unspoken question.

"Oh, hell," McDougal said. "Look, you're drunk. I don't want to take advantage of you." He could hear, in his mind, every guy he'd gone to college with—or hung out with since—roar with laughter. Laugh until they either fell over or pissed themselves. He was not known for having a conscience.

"I know perfectly well that I'm drunk," Natalie said. "Do you think I'd do this sober?"

"Um. Well. That's kind of the point." He smiled down at her and tapped her small freckled nose once, then twice, with his index finger.

Natalie blinked. "Wow," she said unsteadily. "Ch-chivalry is not dead. 'S been run over a few times; it's diseased and dirty; 's hooked on Boone's Farm and m-meth . . . but holy cow, iss still st-stumbling along in rags, raising 's ugly head just when you least expect it—or want it."

She looked so disenchanted that McDougal threw back his head and laughed so hard that he almost coughed up a lung.

Natalie just stepped out of his jacket and wrapped her arms around herself in the cold. Her air of disgust made him laugh all over again. And then he spied a cab with its light on a couple of blocks away. He put his hand in the air to hail it.

"Can I have your number?" he asked as the yellow car pulled over next to them.

She pursed her lips and tapped her foot a couple of times as he opened the door. Finally she said, "No. 'S now or never." And then she put her arms around his neck, stood on tiptoe, and kissed him.

Four

Natalie's mouth was sweet and still whiskey wet and thoroughly unexpected when it touched McDougal's. At the contact he felt a shock of electric pleasure that went straight to his now doubly enthused groin.

McDougal had done his share of kissing. Event planners, lady stockbrokers, lawyers, business owners, teachers, actresses, models, professional dancers . . . even a French would-be murderess with a bad chain-smoking habit.

In his not very humble opinion, kissing was usually overrated, something to get out of the way before he got to the good stuff.

Kissing Natalie profoundly changed his mind.

"Christ," he said as she bit his lower lip and turned him to cold steel. He pushed her into the cab and crawled in after her, damn near falling into her lap.

"Address?" queried the bored-looking cabbie.

Natalie started to speak, but Eric placed a finger across her lips. "Not smart to tell a stranger you met in a bar where you live."

"But—"

"The Waldorf-Astoria, please," he said to the cabbie. "On Park, between Forty-ninth and Fiftieth."

"—you're obviously a decent man."

He marveled at her naïveté. "You absolutely do not know that. I may be a very *in*decent man."

She giggled.

"You shouldn't trust me as far as you can throw me," he said in stern tones.

"I kn-know, but I do."

"You definitely shouldn't go to a hotel room with me."

"Mm-hmm." She lay her head against his shoulder, and something akin to fear rippled through him. He didn't deserve her trust; he was in fact the last man on earth she should trust. She was his *mark*, for chrissakes.

He should be ecstatic, even though she was no longer of much use to him. He had all the information he needed—she'd spilled it with abandon. All he had to do now was maybe get Granny's last name . . . A simple call to Miguel and the ARTemis Nerd Corps back in Miami would take care of the rest.

"I don' even know what you do, Eric," she said, interrupting his thoughts.

No, you damned sure don't—and we're going to keep it that way. He tilted her chin up. "You're illustrating my point, sweetheart. This is a question you should have asked about two hours ago, and definitely before leaving with me."

"Got it. Thanks. So wha' do you do?"

"I'm a . . . security consultant." Close enough, since he clearly demonstrated the holes in people's security when he repossessed stolen art objects.

"Ohhh. No wonder you're so full of lectures."

"Yeah. No wonder."

"You're not married, are you?"

He smacked his forehead. "Again, why did you not ask me this two hours ago?"

"Dunno. You weren't wearing a wedding ring, so I figured—"

"Oldest trick in the book, Natalie. Surely you know that. You can't be that na—"

She dug her index finger into his ribs. "Are you dodging the question?"

"No, I am not dodging the question. I'm not married." *What woman in her right mind would have me? I'm genetically incapable of faithfulness, travel constantly, am often in danger, and sleep with a large, smelly dog named Shaq.*

"Good." They traveled in silence for a couple of blocks. Then Natalie eyed him covertly and said, "Why not?"

McDougal expelled a long breath. "Well, the main reason is that I haven't asked anyone to share in the joys of my paper plates, dirty socks, and rude quirks."

"Do you have a lot of those?"

"Plates, socks, or rude quirks? Actually the answer is yes to all three."

"What's your very rudest quirk?"

"That, I won't share. Not on a first date anyway."

She laughed. "You don't want to scare me off?"

Actually, I do. "I take my laptop into the bathroom and read the news," McDougal said.

She scoffed and waved her hand dismissively. "Oh, that. My dad takes the paper in there."

"Fine. I often drink milk out of the carton."

"Really? Me, too."

"I sleep with a huge dog, and he has chronic gas."

"Okay, *that's* off-putting."

Another three blocks of silence went by.

"Who takes care of your dog when you're away?"

McDougal's eyes narrowed. "At the moment? People who owe me big-time. My friends Gwen and Quinn, and they'd better be taking Shaq to the park and the dog beach regularly."

"Why do they owe you?"

"Long story," he said. Gee, it was so nice when your coworkers thought you were capable of murder and mayhem. They'd be puckering up to his backside for a good while before he got over that one . . .

The cabbie pulled up to the Waldorf, ending the game of twenty questions. McDougal handed the guy the requisite amount of cash and then slid out, towing Natalie with him.

The moody, gray clouds had cleared off, and countless stars twinkled up there in the deep navy sky.

She pulled her coat around her more tightly and stared up at them. "It's cold . . . but it's a magical night, isn't it?"

He nodded. Here he was with a beautiful girl that he wanted—and yet didn't want—in almost equal measures.

Magical? Yeah, okay. Magical as in cursed.

His room at the Waldorf-Astoria was luxurious but not in an over-the-top, Trump sort of way. McDougal liked the hotel because it was historic and top-notch, with unfailingly polite staff. He noted that its grandeur had little effect on his tipsy guest, who didn't seem overly impressed by the scale and elegance of the lobby or anything else.

He poured her off the elevator and through the door of his room. Natalie looked around and then shrugged off her coat and unwound her woolen scarf, exposing the smooth, milky skin of her throat. Why did it make him feel as if his canine teeth were lengthening?

Her neck was vulnerable, just like the rest of her. McDougal stood there wondering whether he should order a bottle of champagne—his usual choice in matters of seduction—or a pot of coffee to sober her up.

He wasn't used to indecision and he didn't like it. Indecision didn't suit him. Cursing under his breath, he dialed for room service and ordered a bottle of Veuve Cliquot.

Then he walked over to her and brushed the pad of his thumb down that long, white throat of hers.

She shivered and stepped closer.

He bent his head and touched her lips again with his, feeling the same jolt of electricity he had before. Eric deepened the kiss, sliding erotically into her mouth with his tongue and exploring what she had to offer. Dark, warm, inviting . . . sexy as hell.

Natalie kissed him back, tentatively at first, and then more boldly, with passion. She made a throaty little noise as his tongue danced with hers, and he instantly hardened. He slid his hands through that glossy dark hair of hers, down each erotic vertebra of her spine, and over her firm little ass. He pulled her against him, lifting her off her feet, and she made that faint, primal noise again.

He wanted inside her, now. Wanted to slide that long black skirt up to her waist and push apart her thighs and plunge into hot, wet oblivion.

But he set her back on her feet and held her away from him, searching her face. "Natalie. You sure about this?"

She didn't answer right away. She seemed breathless, her face flushed and her hair in disarray. She swayed on her feet.

"Natalie?"

She nodded. "I'm sure. I just want to forget . . . everything. For a little while."

He wasn't at all sure that she was sure. But he also wasn't going to argue with a drunk girl. Long experience with inebriated women had taught him that was useless. "Okay," he said. "I'm just going to go take a quick shower. Make yourself comfortable."

She sat down on the bed and kicked off her shoes. She shimmied out of her black tights, then her skirt, and he had a hard time looking away from her slim, muscular legs, at the apex of which were black lace panties.

With a muffled groan, McDougal disappeared into the bathroom and shut the door firmly on the sight. He turned on the shower but didn't have the discipline or the desire to make it cold. Instead, he shed his own clothes quickly and climbed in.

He soaped up, rinsed, toweled off, and stepped out of the steamy bathroom with the towel knotted at his waist, just in time to answer the door for room service. Eric signed for the champagne. "You can put it over there," he said, turning around.

That was when he realized that Natalie had crawled under the covers and passed out cold.

"Uh. Tell you what. Let's not open that bottle just yet." With a tight smile, he tipped the guy and saw him out. Then he stood, hands on hips, watching Natalie sleep. She'd curled a hand under her cheek, and her dark hair streamed over the pillow. Just the tops of her naked shoulders emerged from the covers. And she was on the side of the bed he always slept on.

Half of him was provoked, half relieved. Finally he just laughed, slid in beside her, and turned off the light. She didn't stir at all, and he listened to her deep, even breathing, trying to banish his lust.

Irony of ironies—he, Eric McDougal, had a naked woman in his bed and nothing to do. He groaned and rolled over onto his stomach.

Was she completely naked? Or did she still have those lacy black panties on?

She'd clearly taken off her bra, since no straps appeared over her delectable shoulders. And he hadn't even gotten to see her breasts.

Were they round or pear-shaped? Dusky nipples or rosy? McDougal groaned into his pillow. Why he was torturing himself, he didn't know. He could have just raised the covers and taken a peek, but that seemed slimy. Ungentlemanly.

And since when have you been a gentleman?

His last girlfriend had walked in on him while he was . . . er . . . entertaining two dancers at the same time. Bad scene. One never to be repeated. Not only did he not give anyone a key now, but he also made no promises and never would again. He was just like his father—it was in his blood, inescapable. McDougal men weren't faithful to their women.

Did it make him a dirtbag? Probably. But that was why he didn't make promises or give out rings. He never wanted to hurt anyone as his mother had been hurt. He never wanted to see that hunted, regretful shame on his own face—he'd seen it too often on his father's. And it just drove Dad to drink again, during which the cycle got repeated.

As McDougal lay there in the dark, Natalie rolled over, and her smooth, warm leg brushed against his hairy one. He caught a whiff of her shampoo and resisted the urge to pull her into his arms.

The woman's passed out, for chrissakes. That's how exciting a date you are, man.

When he looked at it that way, it sure took him down a peg.

Five

Oleg Litsky, née Weimar von Bruegel, had enjoyed a very pleasant three-week visit to Paris with his son and daughter-in-law when he returned to his Moscow home. His paranoia of years past had mostly dissipated, and he had no reason to think that anything might be amiss.

So when he walked into his home office on the ground floor and found his safe wide-open, it was something of a shock. The painting that had hidden the safe from view, a very fine Cézanne landscape, was missing. But worse, the cash, silver, and jewelry from the safe were gone—his late wife's diamonds, several heavy gold bracelets, and a platinum Piaget watch.

Worst of all, the St. George necklace had vanished.

Oleg stood there like an idiot, his mouth working, until the telephone rang and scared the life out of him. He let it ring and ring, the noise adding to the pandemonium in his brain. His chest tightened, his pulse spiked, and he felt light-headed. He hobbled to a favorite wing chair and sank weakly into it while he tried to think, but as soon as the telephone stopped he heard the screams of a traumatized child, over and over. He tried to block her face from his mind but couldn't.

Bile rose in his throat, and his chest now felt too tight to take in air. Maybe he would drop dead right here, right now, and his secrets would die with him.

But slowly his breathing returned to normal, the dizziness faded, and he was left with only the bile. Instead of the child's horror-stricken expression as he shot her father dead, he saw the faces of his own granddaughters, dear little girls who'd inherited his blue eyes.

But in this vision, instead of running to him and taking his hands, laughing and searching his pockets for candies, they stood like statues across the room with blank expressions. And they asked him, "Why?"

Why, indeed.

He'd killed a man who'd simply tried to protect his wife and daughters. Killed him because of his race, his religion, because he was in the way.

He had no other explanation, and that seemed the worst crime of all. He'd been seventeen, eager to show that he was a man, and so he'd engaged in acts that rendered him unfit to live as a cockroach. He'd confused brutality with courage, narcissism with pride, and a Nazi uniform with honor. Had he become a man that day?

Oh, yes. He'd become a weak, evil, greedy opportunist of a man. And he'd celebrated by getting stinking drunk, so drunk that he almost succeeded in forgetting that he'd crowned himself a murderer, a thief, and then a rapist.

These were things that he could never, ever allow his family to know. And if he didn't find the St. George necklace immediately, he may as well kiss his son and his granddaughters good-bye. He would die miserably, alone, and in shame.

Litsky walked on rubbery legs to the telephone and curled the receiver into his shaking, sweaty palm. He knew of only one agency that could recover the St. George necklace quickly, with few questions asked: the U.S.-based ARTemis, Inc.

Six

Avy Hunt didn't feel like the wealthy, successful, daring owner of a thriving art-recovery business. At the moment she felt small, defeated, and infinitely weary after hours of being held and interrogated by security at Venice's Marco Polo Airport.

It was her own fault, which made it worse. She'd gotten onto a flight, then forced her way off of it—and who could blame the officials for thinking she must have planted a bomb?

Over and over again she denied it, explaining in her passable Italian that she'd gotten an urgent message that caused her to abruptly change her travel plans. She'd been searched from head to toe, her documents and personal belongings had been scrutinized, and she'd been grilled on the same questions by four different security people, who tried to catch her in any form of half-truth or lie. Only a well-placed contact at the American embassy who vouched for her personally and professionally had prevented her from spending the night in jail.

She'd been able to board a late flight to London out of Venice, and now she attempted to sleep on one from

London to Moscow. But though she was exhausted and emotionally tapped out, her brain refused to cooperate and shut down.

Why did Liam, her fiancé and a former master thief, want her to meet him in Moscow? What he needed was to get back to the U.S., where thanks to a joint sting operation with the FBI, he had a get-out-of-jail card, free and clear.

But Liam had taken very seriously her refusal to marry him until he'd replaced every item he'd ever stolen—and he'd filched things from all over the world.

What had he taken in Russia? A painting? A reliquary? A ceremonial weapon? Who knew? But the stakes had risen. In Europe, if caught, Liam would go to jail. In Russia, he could simply disappear—and even if the British embassy made inquiries, everyone would assume that he'd just gone back to his old ways of living off the grid under a variety of aliases.

Not for the first time, Avy cursed the day she'd ever met Sir Liam James, when she'd pitted her skill set against his in the recovery of the Sword of Alexander.

He was the love of her life . . . and the bane of her existence. He was her weakness, and she'd always prided herself on having none. She'd been calm, confident, and clearheaded before the handsome, silver-tongued bastard entered her life. And now? She'd become a blithering idiot, a quivering Jell-O of indecision. She was betraying all the principles her U.S. Marshal father had raised her to believe in.

All because Liam had shown her that the world and her values weren't a simple matter of black and white. That even the letter of the law and its intent could be pulled and stretched like taffy. And that several wrongs could indeed, in the end, add up to a right.

But could she really trust Liam? The question tortured her, especially under the circumstances. Her father and his cohorts had almost closed in on them in Venice—whether for "her own good" or for justice or for the huge bounty Liam had on his head. Probably for all three. The bottom line, though, was that her dad wanted her fiancé behind bars and away from her.

Avy had gone up against *her own father* for Liam. She still couldn't quite bend her mind around that—or the fact that she'd won—temporarily anyway. She took no joy in the victory.

What she wanted at the moment was to get well and truly drunk, to let alcohol close in and pickle her brain, soak her conscience and logic—shut them down. But getting drunk would solve absolutely nothing. She'd merely wake with a pounding headache and a chaser of depression.

So she sipped bottled water instead and wondered when Liam would send her further information on where, exactly, in Moscow to meet him. She paged through a pocket Russian dictionary she'd picked up in London, since she didn't speak a word of the language.

The Cyrillic alphabet immediately made her cross-eyed, so she focused instead on the phonetic pronunciation of the strange letters and words.

> What a beautiful day! Ka-*koy* pri-*kras*-nih dyen'!
> Are you here on holiday? Vih zdyes'v *ot*-pusk-ye?
> I'm here on business. Ya zdyyes' pa *biz*-ni-su.

Riiiiiiight. Avy could barely wrap her tongue around the foreign words. But supposedly there was a huge American population in Moscow—she could only hope to run into some of them.

Eventually the constant bass whine of the bird's big engines lulled her into an uneasy sleep. She had the sensation of her eyes rolling back in their sockets and then tumbling over and over as they dropped down the well of unconsciousness. When she stopped falling, she was skating on a frozen lake in the middle of a frosty winter landscape. She wore a heavy parka buttoned to her throat, a long red woolly scarf, and a knit cap with a silly pom-pom dangling from its apex.

She glided along on her skates, feeling the wind in her face and hearing the laughter and shouts of clusters of people around her. She zipped in and out and around them, performing turns and dips that would make an Olympic skater proud.

As she came off a dramatic triple axel, a dark figure in a topcoat and a tall fur hat gripped her hand and pulled her to him. Liam's face laughed down at her and pulled her reluctant lips into a smile of their own. He swept her off her feet and skated across the lake with her, then set her down, grasped her hands, and spun with her so that her body flew outward like a child's. And like a child, she laughed in delight.

Then he let go, and she went hurtling backward until her belly hit the ice. She skidded, her hands still outstretched toward him.

In the next sequence of her dream, they were still on the ice, but Liam had dropped to one knee and extended a velvet ring box toward her, while she shook her head and skated away. But he had some kind of homing device or some strange power over her, because despite her intent to leave, she was pulled back by a magnetic force.

He quizzically lifted one eyebrow and plucked the ring from its velvet bed. He doffed his tall fur hat and sent it spinning over the ice. Then he got to his feet and skated toward her. He took her left hand and slid the ring over the knuckle of the fourth finger.

No sooner had he done so than the ice came ablaze with red and blue lights. Men in SWAT team jackets with sniper rifles swarmed the lake. She held up her hands, palms forward, and stared in anguish at the sparkling rock on her hand.

Liam had disappeared altogether, and she was arrested for receiving stolen property. She tried to explain that she was innocent, but they wouldn't listen to her. They cuffed her and stuffed her into the back of a squad car . . .

Avy awakened with a start as the captain's voice announced their initial descent into Moscow. There were no cuffs on her wrists, and though the ring on her finger had indeed been placed there by Liam, it wasn't a big, flashy diamond. It was elegant, understated, a square-cut emerald set in platinum.

Still, the dream had been from her gut, issuing a warning. She stared at her engagement ring until the flight landed, jolting her back to reality. The flaps on the aircraft came up, and the roar of the braking mechanisms screamed into her consciousness.

When the captain turned off the seat-belt signs and

the plane erupted into passenger bustle—the clack and thud of overhead compartments and groans as travelers heaved out their hand luggage—she sat still as long as she could. But eventually, along with everyone else, she was disgorged from the belly of the winged beast and stepped out into Moscow's Domodedovo Airport.

Liam James idly ran his gaze over his lavishly appointed room at the Metropol hotel in Moscow's city center. Really, the place was a bit over the top, with prices to match, but the luxury soothed him. Built in the Style Moderne of the early twentieth century, it was full of stained glass, mosaics, and fabulous chandeliers.

His own room was located on the VIP floor and furnished with classic dark wood furniture set against beige, silk-flocked wallpaper. Blue silk bedcovers covered top-quality sheets, and blue silk decorative pillows lounged artfully against the bed's headboard. To the right was a spacious seating area with a desk that held a complimentary fruit basket.

Despite his top-notch quarters, Liam was in something of a quandary. In a spot where the lines of politics and history and law and ethics blurred and swirled into a sort of abstract expressionism.

This particular ethical dilemma involved Liam stealing something of a whole different magnitude from anything he'd ever taken before. The situation would need to be handled with elegance, discretion, and great care. It involved crossing international boundaries and thinking on his feet. It also required nerves of steel and a capacity for deception and perhaps disguise.

Worst of all, this little mission of his required a partner that he could trust with his life. A partner like his fiancée, Avy Hunt.

Unfortunately, he'd promised this woman he loved that he'd go arrow straight, while he'd been charged by a worldwide organization to do something a little . . . ah . . . skewed.

A bit crooked.

Oh, bloody hell.

It was, in truth, completely illegal and, on the surface, morally reprehensible—even if the endgame was justice.

How Liam was going to explain all of this to Avy and enlist her aid, he hadn't the foggiest notion. As soon as he opened his mouth, she would come out swinging . . . and Avy angry was not a pretty situation. On one occasion when he'd made her truly angry, she'd left him trussed up naked, like a Thanksgiving turkey, for his butler, Whidby, to find.

Liam winced at the memory, though Whidby had seen more humor in it, damn him.

Liam checked his watch and saw that Avy's flight had landed. For security reasons—Interpol had an alert out for him—he couldn't meet her at the airport.

He texted her from his BlackBerry:

Take bus to Domodedovo metro station. Once there, lose any possible Interpol tail. Take metro to Kropotkinskaya station and meet me at Cathedral of Christ the Redeemer.

Then Liam tossed on his coat and made his way outdoors and to the river, where he strolled around the Kremlin, through Krasnaya Place, and past the statue of Marshal Zhukov. To his left was a spectacular view of the famous Red Square.

He finally ended at Alexander Gardens, very close to the station where Avy would arrive. He found a little café and ordered a lemon vodka, or *limonnaya*, along with a dish of *pelmeni*, meat-stuffed dumplings.

It was a beautiful day, if a frigid one. Liam studied a small pocket guidebook as he ate, memorizing the Cyrillic words and pronunciations for as many metro stops as he could. Unfortunately they might have to hire a human guide for their, ah, more nefarious purposes, since he was a fish out of water in Moscow, and Avy would be, too.

He could just imagine calling the local tourism office. "Hello, how are you? Yes, I'd like to hire an English-speaking man foolish enough to take me to the home of a prominent citizen and help me break into the building. Oh, you have just the gentleman for the job? Lovely, thank you."

No, this was a delicate matter, one that might just require his slippery friend Kelso's connections. Kelso had put him up to this, and Kelso owed him.

Liam tapped the tip of his nose with a sterling-silver pen and frowned. Kelso was responsible for him being thrown into an American jail. And yet . . . Kelso was also responsible for hooking him up with the FBI, which in the end had gotten him *out* of jail. Who owed whom?

Liam wasn't sure, but it didn't matter. He needed to get a message to the bloody man, so the next text he sent was to the horrific Sheila, receptionist and office manager at ARTemis.

Seven

Natalie awoke to the gray light of dawn coming through the sheer curtains at the window. A battalion of Lilliputians with sledgehammers were busy pounding her cerebral cortex into mush, and for a bad moment she couldn't remember where she was.

A gentle snore to her left inspired her to roll over, which sent the sadistic Lilliputians into screaming overdrive. She registered a very buff shoulder, a chest full of reddish gold hair, and a square, stubbled jaw first.

Oh, dear God . . . I didn't. Did I?

One laser blue eye opened, squinted at her, and then closed. "Good morning," said the very hot, Newman-like stranger from Reif's.

I did.

Natalie swallowed, which was difficult because her mouth was dry and pasty and . . . yuck, something had clearly crawled into it and died last night. Something with fur.

"Wow," she said. "I've never done this before. I guess I've racked up some big 'ho points.' "

The stranger rolled to face her, opening both eyes

this time. "Nah. No money changed hands." He grinned at her.

He was so good-looking that even with sleep-tousled hair and sheet marks on his face, he took her breath away. Unbelievable. The one time in her life that she had a one-night stand, with a gorgeous man . . . and she couldn't even remember if the sex was hot or not.

"Um. Your name is Eric, right?"

"Brava, Natalie." There was no condemnation in his eyes, only deep amusement.

She screwed up her courage. "So. Um. Was it good?"

"You were absolutely amazing," he said.

Uh-oh. Did that mean shameless? "Please tell me you used a condom?"

He yawned. "On what, the champagne bottle?"

She stared at him, alarmed. Had he done something perverted to her with a *bottle*? She shuddered.

"Relax, Natalie. Nothing happened. You passed out cold."

Mortification threatened to swallow her whole, and she clutched the sheet to her breasts and sat up, to the rage of those angry Lilliputians still banging inside her head. "I did *not*."

"Yup. You did." Eric sat up, too, and then stretched luxuriously. "Not surprising, considering you had at least five stiff whiskeys in the bar and no dinner."

"I am an idiot," she said gloomily.

"Don't be so hard on yourself. Happens to the best of us. Besides, you were upset about the necklace."

Horror engulfed her. "I *told* you about it?"

"In living color."

"Oh, my God. Are you going to—"

"Report you? No. I'm not going to tell anyone."

"You don't feel a moral obligation to—" She stopped. Eric was laughing.

"Do I look like Dudley Do-Right?" he asked. "Seriously."

She sat there, again transfixed by his looks and some charismatic quality that she couldn't identify. All she knew was that she felt almost magnetically drawn to him. She was furious at herself, not for picking him up but for passing out.

"So unfair," she muttered, unconscious of saying the words aloud.

"What's unfair?"

She flushed. "I don't want to say it because your head won't fit through the door."

He just eyed her quizzically.

"Oh, fine. I think it's unfair that the one time I have a . . . a fall from grace and pick up a gorgeous guy in a bar, I manage to go to sleep before anything interesting happens!"

He burst out laughing.

"No, it really ticks me off."

When he could catch his breath, he winked at her. "The offer's still good this morning." Casually, he pulled the sheet tight over his lap, and she almost fainted at what was outlined.

He raised an eyebrow and shot her a come-hither smile. The man didn't have bedroom eyes; he had bordello eyes.

"But I don't have a toothbrush . . ."

"You can use mine."

Ugh. No, thanks. ". . . and my head's killing me."

"I have ways of distracting you from that, not to mention ibuprofen."

"But I'm *sober* now," she wailed.

"So?"

"Well, but—I can't just—"

"You can't?"

"No."

"I'm very sorry to hear that." Eric pushed the sheet aside and swung his legs out of bed, walking stark naked past a stunned Natalie, who couldn't look away.

Uuuuunnnnnhhhhh!

Long, muscled legs. Smooth, taut, tight, positively drool-worthy buns. There was some kind of dark, square tattoo on his left one, but she couldn't quite make it out.

He had wide shoulders that segued beautifully into a trim waist with six-pack abs. And the other side of him . . .

She could *kill* herself for passing out. She was being deprived of the joys of sluttiness before she could even regret anything.

Eric strode past her with vestiges of a naughty smirk on his face. He gave her another wink and then disappeared into the bathroom.

She slumped down under the covers. She was hungover, she was going to get fired when she went in to work, she'd be lucky if she wasn't arrested, and she couldn't even engage in some nice, sweaty, therapeutic sex with a perfect stranger whom she'd never see again. What was wrong with her?

But with sobriety her social awkwardness had returned, and that definitely ruled out getting wild and naked with this guy Eric. In the cold, whiskeyless light of day she recalled that she hadn't shaved her legs in at least a week, her breasts were small, and her toes were probably gnarled, since her feet hadn't seen a pedicure since August.

Natalie glanced at the clock and saw with relief that it was barely seven. She still had enough time to go home and shower before hustling to work and facing the music.

She slipped out of bed just in time to model her almost nudity for Eric, who came out of the bathroom. He wolf whistled, his gaze roving straight to her breasts. She clapped her hands over them immediately.

"*Tetas ricas*," he said with a predatory grin.

"Excuse me?" Her face burned.

"Hmm? Oh, it's nothing."

"No, translate, please."

"I said you have great breasts, sweetheart."

She snatched her skirt off the floor and clutched it to her body. "You shouldn't have looked."

"Hey, they were right up front and waving at me. What's a poor slob to do?"

"Well, it's not nice to comment."

"I told you last night—I'm not at all a nice guy." He flashed white teeth at her.

"Will you turn your back while I change, please?"

"Fine. Seems a little silly, since you slept with me practically nude, but whatever." He turned and faced the other way. Darn it, she could see only the edge of the tattoo and still couldn't quite make it out.

"I was not nude. I had panties on," Natalie said, scrambling into her skirt and then her bra.

"And I coulda had 'em off you at any time."

Hateful man. She pulled her top over her head and stuffed her arms into the sleeves. The fabric smelled just like the bar. Ugh.

Eric had gone back into the bathroom, and when he emerged he held some ibuprofen tablets and a glass of water. He handed them to her.

"Thank you," she said. Okay, he wasn't hateful. But he was still stark naked, and though she kept trying mightily to keep her gaze above his waist, she wasn't entirely successful. Worse, he seemed to know it, and she was sure it amused him.

"Aren't you going to get dressed?" she asked.

"Why?"

"Don't you have to go to work, or do *some*thing?"

He laced his fingers behind his neck and stretched his shoulders. "Not for a while. You?"

She nodded, sat on the bed, and shoved her feet into the toes of her tights. "Yes. I have a nine-o'clock appointment to get fired."

"Great. Can I take you to breakfast afterward?"

She laughed, despite the day's gloomy prospects. "Why?"

He shrugged. "I think you've got a real cute snore, and I'd like to hear it again sometime."

"I do not snore."

"You do." He walked over to the chair where her messenger bag lay, flap open, and plucked her cell phone out of the front pocket.

"What are you doing?"

He flipped open the phone and pressed some buttons. "Making sure you have my number."

"It's nice to ask first . . ."

He raised his head and aimed a wicked blue stare at her. "I thought we'd established several times that I'm not a nice guy." He finished entering the numbers and then hit the call button. His own phone rang, and he got it out of his pants, which were lying on the floor. "And now I have yours," he said.

"Great." She retrieved her phone and bag and headed for the door. Somehow he was in front of it before she got there, blocking it with his body.

He took her face between his big hands and kissed her lips. She melted and her knees went weak; when he lifted his head, she was dazed.

"Natalie," he said softly. "You're gonna do fine this morning. And whatever happens today, you were great last night. Funny and entertaining and infinitely seductive. I'd like the chance to sleep with you again."

Well.

When he phrased it like that, how could a girl say no?

Eight

Because she was nervous, Natalie was twenty minutes early to work. By the time she'd gotten to the brownstone, she'd almost chewed a hole through her cheek.

Her hands trembled as she put her key into the lock, turned it, and swung the heavy wooden door open. Funny, the alarm didn't beep, even though all the lights were off and the place seemed empty. It was very unlike Luc to forget to set it before he left for the day.

She shut the door behind her, locked it since they wouldn't open for business until nine, and flipped the main light switch for the foyer. She'd taken only a couple of steps forward when she heard the moan.

"Who's there?" she called.

Another faint moan and some weak coughing came from the direction of the kitchen. She was torn between fear and curiosity. Should she bolt out the door or go into the kitchen? She'd almost opted for bolting when she realized that someone could have come in early, as she had, and had a seizure or a heart attack, or had simply slipped and fallen.

Natalie pulled her cell phone from its pocket under

the flap of her bag and dialed 911, just in case. Then, her finger poised over the talk button, she crept forward. "Hello? Who's there?"

Another guttural moan emerged from the kitchen. She rounded the corner and stopped, shocked. Luc, her boss, lay sprawled and bleeding on the old linoleum. His face had been beaten beyond recognition, and blood had dried in horrible rivulets from his nose and a split lip.

"Luc—oh, my God! What happened?" Natalie dropped both phone and bag and ran to him, sliding the last couple of feet on her knees.

He opened his bruised eyes but didn't move. "*B'jour*, Natalie," he said with effort.

"Who did this to you?" Her voice had gone high and reedy with alarm. "Luc, are you all right?"

He managed to make a thumbs-up sign with one hand.

"I'm going to call nine-one-one," she said, crawling back toward the phone she had dropped.

"*Non*," he croaked. He lifted his head. "*No*."

"Luc, you need medical attention! And the police—"

"No police," he reiterated. "*Promise*."

"Why not?" But she knew why not. Deep in the pit of her stomach, she knew. Luc couldn't afford for his business dealings to be investigated. Luc was involved in things that weren't aboveboard. It explained the Mercedes. It explained the huge diamond on Giraffe's hand. It explained his nervous reaction to the man who'd dropped off the necklace for repairs.

He struggled to sit up. "Help . . . me."

She was afraid to touch him, since she didn't know where he'd been beaten. But she slid an arm under his shoulders and heaved mightily to get him to a sitting position. Then, using all of her body weight and every ounce of strength she possessed, she dragged him over to the kitchen cabinets so that he had something to lean against.

"*Mer-merci*, Natalie."

They both sat there, trying to catch their breath. He shouldn't thank her at all, since she had an awful feeling that she was directly responsible for the beating. Oh, God. How to tell him? Where to start?

And Nonnie. Fear coiled in her belly, slithered through her gut. *Please God, I can keep Nonnie safe . . . This is all my fault.*

"Luc, who did this?" she asked again.

He shook his head. "Better . . . that . . . you do not . . . know," he said with difficulty.

She jumped up and searched in a drawer for a tea towel, then wet it at the sink and tried to minister to his poor, battered face. "Does this have to do with the necklace?" she asked, though she didn't really want to.

He winced as she wiped blood away from his swollen, broken nose. Then he nodded.

Fear broke the surface of her emotions and then rushed in like high tide. Tears poured down her cheeks. "Luc . . . oh, God. Listen, I'm the one who borrowed the necklace."

He jerked back from her hands and hit his head against the cabinet door. *"What?"*

"I borrowed it," she sobbed. The words poured out of her in a tumult. "I wanted to show it to my grandmother—and she's blind—so I couldn't take a picture. Our family—we used to have a similar necklace—I meant to return it over the weekend—but she won't let me have it back . . ."

Luc grabbed her wrist. "You *get it from her.* Today, Natalie. *Comprends-tu? Now.* You bring it to me, or my life is worthless, eh?"

She nodded, wiping her wet face with the back of her hand. "I'm so sorry. I thought it would be harmless and I'd have it back in the safe within twenty-four hours."

"Go. No, help me to my car first. I cannot have the other employees see me like this . . ."

Natalie mopped up the floor quickly with paper towels.

They left through the back door, which was unlocked. No doubt the men who'd roughed up Luc had entered and exited that way. He directed her to set the alarm and lock up after them.

He wrapped a scarf around his injured face, and they walked outside to his gray Mercedes coupe.

"Do you want me to drive you to your apartment?" Natalie asked, though she didn't want to be responsible for a $70,000 car. It was the least she could do.

He shook his head. "I want you to get the necklace. Bring it to me at home as soon as you can. And say nothing to anyone, eh? Nobody."

Natalie nodded. "I'm sorry," she said again. "I assume that I'm fired."

Luc didn't reply, but his silence said it all.

Natalie took the subway to Grand Central Terminal, and then the Metro-North rail to the Stamford station, where she changed trains and took the New Haven line to the Springdale platform. Springdale was a cozy little neighborhood in Stamford where not much seemed to have changed since the 1950s. Nonnie had lived there in the midst of its working-class charm for more than thirty years.

Natalie exited the train and walked down Hope Street toward her grandmother's house on Knickerbocker Avenue.

The little Cape Cod was painted slate blue with white shutters and doors and had looked the same for as long as Nat could remember. She climbed the three cement steps to the small enclosed porch and opened the storm door, wiping her feet on an ancient straw mat that needed replacing. As she approached the main door, she noticed that not only were no lights on inside, but no classical music played.

Natalie tried the door, but it was locked. She rang the bell, but Nonnie didn't come to the door. She knocked repeatedly, hysteria rising in her throat. Of course she had a key, but she hadn't planned on coming here today, so it was in her apartment in the city.

Finally she left the porch and went around the side of the little house, toward the rear yard and the garage.

She ran to the back door and banged on it, calling her grandmother's name. It, too, was locked, and no sign of life came from within the kitchen. At least Nonnie wasn't lying beaten on the kitchen floor . . .

Just the thought had her recoiling, and she fought to control her growing panic. Where was Nonnie? She never left the house. She hadn't just gone for a walk around the block or made a run to the bank.

What if the people who'd beaten up Luc had been there? What if Nonnie was stiff, cold, and blue in her bedroom? Dear God. Natalie had to break in and make sure she was all right. She whirled and ran toward the garage, and then stopped in her tracks. The side door to the garage was slightly ajar.

Shaking now, Natalie forced herself toward the building, which held only one car: Nonnie's ancient Buick Regal. No sounds came from within. Nat put her hand on the cold metal doorknob and pulled.

The garage was empty, except for old garden tools and various odds and ends. The car was gone.

The car was gone . . . but Nonnie was legally blind and couldn't have driven it. So who had? One of the neighbors? Or had someone broken in, robbed a helpless old lady, and then stolen her car? Oh, God, what if they'd killed her and put her body in the trunk?

Her hands shaking, Nat grabbed a spade from a hook on the wall and started toward the house again. Her cell phone rang and she almost jumped out of her skin, dropping the spade.

She grabbed the phone and flipped it open, half afraid that this was a ransom call. But instead, Eric McDougal's voice said cheerily, "Breakfast?"

She broke down.

"Natalie," he said urgently. "What's wrong?"

The words poured out of her mouth disjointedly.

"Do not go into the house alone," he instructed her.

"But—"

"Go to a neighbor's house. Call the police—"

"Luc said no police," she sobbed.

"I'm coming out there," he said with grim determination.

"What? But you barely know me . . ."

"I don't care. I'll be there in under an hour. Go to a neighbor's and I'll call you when I'm close. What's the address?"

Bewildered but intensely grateful for the support, she told him. After all, he was a security consultant.

"Where could she be? You don't think they killed her over"—her voice broke—"over the necklace, and then took her body to d-d-dump it?" Natalie sank to her knees on the cold ground and shut her eyes against the possibility.

"No," Eric said in reassuring tones. "They wouldn't have known who took the necklace. Luc didn't, so why would they?"

"They have to know it's an employee. There was no break-in. It was clearly someone who has the combination to the safe at Ricard and Associates."

"Natalie, don't jump to conclusions. And don't go into that house alone. I'll be there as soon as I can, okay?"

She nodded and then realized that he couldn't see her. "Okay," she managed. "Eric? Thank you. I don't care what you say—you really are a very nice guy."

A long pause came from his end of the connection. "Yeah. I'm a prince among men. See you soon. Bye." He hung up.

She rose to her feet, stowed her phone, and left the spade where it was. Unbelievable. The handsome stranger from the bar was riding to her rescue like some kind of knight from a fairy tale. Stuff like that didn't happen anymore—it just didn't.

But her parents were hundreds of miles away in Vermont, she knew few people in the city, and she wasn't going to look a gift knight in the mouth.

Nine

McDougal hung up the phone and let out a string of curses. Granny was MIA. Judging by the beaten-up boss, wolves other than himself were closing in, and Little Red Riding Hood was in tears . . . not to mention quite possibly in danger. What if her boss, in order to save his own skin, told his violent visitors who had the necklace?

McDougal reminded himself that the St. George piece was his priority, but in order to track the necklace, he had to get hot on the trail of Natalie's kooky Nonnie, and what better place to start than her own home?

He headed down to the street and got a cab to take him to a well-known rental-car agency, where he picked up an SUV and was headed out of the city on FDR Drive, taking exit 17 for the Triboro Bridge within twenty minutes. En route, he placed a call to ARTemis in Miami to give an update on his activities.

"Ahtemis, may I help you?" sang Sheila Kofsky in her nasal Brooklyn accent. "Oh, it's *you,* 007. Callin' to tell me your thingy finally turned black and fell off?"

"Sorry to disappoint you, Moneypenny," he said dryly, "but my thingy is hale and hearty."

Sheila was the company's receptionist/office manager and mistress of disguise. She ruled over the wardrobe room with an iron fist, not to mention her inch-long acrylic talons. She had a cloud of improbably blond hair that crowned a face like a white raisin, and she always wore somewhat astonishing outfits. Her signature was her vast collection of reading glasses, which she customized to match her ensembles.

McDougal dropped his voice an octave and assumed a British accent. "So, tell Bond what you're wearing today, my lovely."

"Eat your heart out. You're missing out on my violet spandex dress, olive platform peep-toes and the olive readers with the tiny bunches of grapes attached."

Ye gods. "I'm deeply shaken, if not stirred."

"What d'ya want, you rodent?"

"Moneypenny never called 007 a rodent," he protested.

"Moneypenny was a ditz. I got another line ringing, so what d'ya want?"

"I'm chasing the St. George piece into Connecticut now. The target says it's with her grandmother, but Granny's taken a hike. I'll check in with you later on further developments."

"Fine. Now, get lost."

"Love you, too, you old bag." He hung up and shook his head. Without Sheila, life at ARTemis would run way too smoothly. He wasn't sure why she'd been hired, but clearly Kelso, the silent majority owner of the company, liked having her around. It suited his warped sense of humor, McDougal figured.

Nobody had ever seen Kelso, but he pulled all of their

strings from the ether as it suited him. He played practical jokes, fed information, and occasionally interfered in cases. McDougal had tried like hell to uncover his identity but had failed, just like the other agents. Kelso found their attempts endlessly amusing.

But McDougal found little to smile about in his current situation. He had a hunch that Natalie's boss, Luc Ricard, had been working with black-market smugglers—nasty ones.

The fact that he'd told her not to call the police about his beating only confirmed that instinct. Nothing about the black market surprised McDougal, but it was a vast network with many sets and subsets and spinoffs of subsets.

Who were these particular people who'd had the necklace? Where had they gotten it? Were they Italians? Russians? Japanese? Arabs? Did they have a motive besides money? How far were they willing to go in order to get "their" stolen property back? The fact that they'd already resorted to violence was not a good sign.

Unfortunately the black market for art and antiquities had heated up, partially inspired by the utterly insane prices that objects fetched in today's aboveboard market. When a frankly repulsive Lucien Freud painting brought in $33 million at auction—the most ever paid for a work by a living artist—one could hardly blame criminals for slavering over a piece of the profits pie.

And that price paled in comparison to the $83 million paid by a Japanese conglomerate for van Gogh's *Irises*. Or the *$103 million* shelled out for a Picasso recently.

Hell, there were times when McDougal himself was tempted to put his rather unusual skill set to use in crime, but most of his tendencies toward dishonesty had been thrashed out of him at an early age, between his three brothers, his four sisters, and the priests at St. Joseph's.

It was from his siblings that he'd learned to be fast, silent, and some would say stoic, since his brothers had loved to hold the small-for-his-age Eric down and tickle him—or, worse, fart on him—and his sisters had loved to hold him down and dress him up in girls' clothes. Thank God he'd grown like a weed during puberty.

McDougal, now on the Bruckner, headed north on 95 and exited at Atlantic Street. Then, guided by his GPS, he took a few turns that led him to Leonard Street and the picturesque little neighborhood of Springdale. Soon he was easing the rented SUV to a stop outside an unpretentious little Cape Cod.

Natalie came quickly out the screen porch door, her face drawn, anxious, and pinched with cold. The girl he'd left the bar with had disappeared. Today she wore slim brown corduroys and brown leather boots with an oversize, artsy sweater in a purple, brown, and black abstract pattern.

She'd styled her dark hair in an unruly pile on top of her head. The same black woolen scarf from yesterday kept her neck warm, but she wore no coat. Maybe it was still in the neighbor's house.

Both her embarrassment of this morning and the playful sexuality of the night before had vanished. Natalie was simply tense and miserable.

He swung out of the car and approached her. "Hi."

"Thank you for coming," she said. She made no move to hug or kiss him, but then, he didn't expect her to, especially under the circumstances.

He slipped an arm around her shoulders and gave her a reassuring squeeze. "Don't worry; we'll find her."

"Where can she be?" she fretted. "Her car is gone."

He drew his brows together. "She has a car? Why would a woman who's legally blind have a car?"

"She wouldn't let us sell it. I think she's hung on to it with the idea of giving it to me one day, not that I can afford to garage it. I tried to tell her that."

"Maybe a neighbor took her to the doctor, or out to run an errand?"

Natalie shook her head. "I've checked with three different neighbors, now. Mrs. Kolchek is home, and her daughter is in school. The Ormonds are in southern Spain. And nobody's home at Colonel Blakely's."

"You sure the Kolchek girl is in school?" asked McDougal skeptically.

"Pretty sure. She's a good kid, not the type to play hooky."

"Did her mother see or hear any activity at your grandmother's house?"

Natalie shook her head.

"All right." He scanned the exterior of the house, looking for any signs of a break-in. No screens off. No footprints in the snow where they shouldn't be. "Let's go in. You have a key?"

"Yes, but since I didn't plan to come here today, it's in my apartment in the city."

He nodded, and she followed him up the concrete steps and into the sheltered porch area. "Is there an alarm?" he asked.

"No."

He made a disapproving noise and removed the

Glock nine-millimeter from the holster at the small of his back. He slipped it into his jacket pocket without her noticing. Then he whipped out a small zippered case. Inside were his company-issued lock picks.

Natalie eyed them suspiciously.

"I only have these on me to demonstrate to customers how easy it is to break in," he told her. Within seconds, he had the door unlocked. "Wanna purchase a state-of-the-art security system?"

She didn't look entirely snowed but swallowed and gave him a weak smile. Evidently, fear for her grandmother trumped concern that he might not be entirely aboveboard.

"Why don't you let me go in first," he suggested. Without a word, she stood aside to let him enter. She looked as if she dreaded what they might find inside. "It's gonna be fine," he said. "There's a simple explanation for all of this, okay?"

She swallowed and nodded, tugging at the scarf around her throat as if it were cutting off her air supply.

He entered the house and she followed close behind. His first impression was of old hardwood floors and a lot of faded chintz. Musty fabric, ancient plaster, a touch of mildew behind the Pine-Sol. The smell of years of cooking blended with lemon oil.

A silk flower arrangement gathered dust, as did a circa 1978 TV built inside a faux-wood cabinet with a speaker. On top of the TV was a menorah. Squatting in the corner was an old phonograph that played LPs, for chrissakes. And a shelf displayed vinyl albums, all classical.

"Nonnie!"

No answer.

Natalie tried again. "Nonnie! Can you hear me?"

Evidently not.

The layout of the place was simple, with the kitchen, dining room, and small living area on the ground floor. Dark wood stairs led to the second story. On the wall at the foot of the staircase were five Russian Orthodox icons, four smaller ones arranged around a larger one of St. George and the dragon. McDougal had no idea who the other saints were, but they appeared to like gold and wore lots of eyeliner.

Everything so far was neat and orderly, without so much as a breakfast dish left in the kitchen sink.

Hand on the gun in his pocket, McDougal inclined his head toward a door near the breakfast nook. "What's that? The basement?" There was a small pet door installed near the bottom.

Natalie nodded.

"Your grandmother has a cat?"

"Two." She frowned. "They must be hiding."

The door was bolted, so he left it for later. "Let's go upstairs."

"Nonnie!" she called again. "Kitties! Here, kitty-kitty-kitty . . ."

Nothing but silence greeted them.

McDougal rounded the newel at the bottom of the stairs and went up, the old boards creaking under his feet. At the top was a narrow hallway with two doors on the right and two on the left.

Spare bedroom, empty. Bath, empty. The bedroom on the far right was the master. He nudged the door open with the toe of his Timberland boot, not sure what they'd find.

Nothing. Just a queen-size bed with an antique lace coverlet over a bedspread dotted with cabbage roses. A 1930s dressing table with a round mirror. A highboy, which, curiously enough, supported a statue of—a theme was becoming apparent here—St. George and his buddy, the dragon. Maybe the old lady really did say prayers to it. What a kook.

But kook or not, she was nowhere to be found.

Behind him, Natalie exhaled a shaky breath. "Oh, thank God. I was afraid—"

From the room at the end of the hallway, right next door, came a heavy thud. Natalie jumped at least two feet in the air and shrieked.

He pivoted left, bringing the gun out of his pocket and cocking it reflexively.

"Dear God, what is that?!" Natalie said. He wasn't sure whether she meant the gun or the noise.

Two more thuds, lighter this time, came from the room.

"Who's there?" McDougal called.

Silence.

He reached forward, twisted the knob, and threw the door open. Stacks of books greeted them, and nothing else. Apparently one of the stacks had toppled over. He noticed small droppings on the floor and judged that Granny might have a rat in the house. Maybe they'd frightened it out of its literary endeavors. Natalie shuddered and confirmed that the cats were fat and useless.

A check of the basement yielded nothing but old furniture, boxes, and knickknacks gathering dust.

"Nonnie's not here." Natalie looked half relieved, since they hadn't discovered a body, and half mystified and concerned. "Where can she be?"

"I didn't see a purse anywhere," he reflected. "What about suitcases? Are there any missing?"

He and Natalie went back upstairs to check the master bedroom closet.

"Her old Samsonite is gone," she said. "She's taken a trip." Her voice reflected shock. "But . . . with whom? She can't see! She doesn't leave the house, I tell you. God, Eric, what if those people have her?"

"Deep breath," he said. "Take a deep breath. Then tell me exactly who you mean by 'those people.' The ones who beat up your boss?"

She nodded.

"Who are they?"

"I don't know."

"Come on, Natalie. You must have some idea. What's your boss been up to?"

She hesitated.

"Look, I can't help you if you don't help me."

"Who are you really? I didn't know you carried a gun."

"I told you," Eric said. "I'm a security consultant. I'd be a damn poor one if I couldn't protect myself."

Still, she stared at him suspiciously.

He fished out his wallet, pulled a fake business card from it, and slapped it into her palm. Then he gazed right back with his most open, relaxed expression.

She read it and nodded. Seeming somewhat reassured, she tugged reflexively at her scarf again. "Okay. I think that these guys are Russian. About six months ago, Luc's fiancée introduced him to some people who could supposedly help expand his business. They weren't like his usual clients at all. We deal with curators, wealthy individuals, corporate collectors . . . people who have at least a veneer of polish. These other guys aren't like that at all. They're rough. Rude. A little scary. They make Luc nervous. Lately he seems to be making a lot more money, but he's on edge and not really himself. Something weird is going on."

You got that right, sweetheart. "Why do you think they're Russian?"

"I've seen two different guys bring things to Luc for restoration. Both of them had accents, and they sounded just like Nonnie when she gets angry. She doesn't have much of one, since she came to the U.S. as a child, but it's more pronounced when she's emotional."

McDougal nodded. "Do you know the names of these men?"

"No. When items they bring get logged in, it's always under Ben or Bob Ruski, which is patently false."

You think? "What address is in the log?"

"I'd have to check, but I doubt it's real, either."

"Phone?"

"Maybe a cell, but again, I'd have to look in the log."

"Okay. We'll put that on the back burner for now. In the meantime, who could have taken your grandmother on a trip, and where?"

Natalie gripped her scarf with both hands, twisting the ends. "You don't think the Russian guys have her?"

"I doubt they'd sit around waiting for her to pack a suitcase, Natalie," he said, trying to keep the dryness out of his voice.

"True."

"And where are the cats?"

She lifted her hands, palms up.

"The neighbor's not feeding them?"

She shook her head.

"Didn't you mention to me that your grandmother refused to open the door until you brought her tickets to Russia?"

Natalie's face drained of color. "Oh, my God. That's where she's gone. She said the necklace was the key to something. But who would take her to another country?"

"Someone without a regular job; that's for sure. Which leaves students, housewives, or retirees. Who does she know in those categories? Or could she have paid someone to accompany her?"

Natalie shook her head. "She doesn't really have the funds to do that. Whoever went with her would have to have paid his or her own way."

"That rules out most students—" He stopped at the arrested expression on her face.

"Blakely. It has to be Colonel Blakely," she said. "She'd feel safe with him."

Great, McDougal thought. *This is just great. Looks like I need to acquire some heavy boots and a big fur hat with sexy earflaps that tie under my chin. And unfortunately it's time to ditch sweet, naive Natalie . . .*

Ten

Nonnie wasn't dead. Thank God Nonnie wasn't dead. Just to make sure, Natalie went to her grandmother's refrigerator and found the magnetic card for her veterinarian. She rang the vet immediately.

"Hello, this is Natalie Rosen, Tatyana Ciccoli's granddaughter." Nonnie had married an Italian man, which was how she came to be known as Nonnie, rather than Baba.

"What can I do for you, Ms. Rosen? Are you calling to check on Fitz and Floyd?"

"Yes."

"They're doing just fine. They're in a large cage together, with their beds."

"Oh, thank you. Listen . . . I didn't write down my grandmother's exact travel dates. When are we picking up the cats, again?"

"Two weeks."

"And, let's see, I'm just trying to calculate the bill—she dropped them off yesterday?"

"The day before. That nice older gentleman carried the cage for her."

"Colonel Blakely?"

"Yes, honey. He takes good care of her." The receptionist paused and then added coyly, "Do I hear wedding bells in the future?"

Natalie almost dropped the telephone receiver. "I—uh, I don't think so. He just comes over and reads to her."

"Whatever you say. At any rate, don't you worry about Fitz and Floyd. We even have a little gal who lets them out and plays with them every day."

"Thank you so much. I really appreciate that."

"No trouble, hon. I hope your gran has a nice time in Hawaii. See you soon."

"Hawaii?" Natalie said aloud after hanging up.

Eric raised his eyebrows.

"Hawaii doesn't make sense at all. Why would she go there?"

"Maybe that's just a cover story she concocted in case anyone was on her trail," he suggested. "I'll check the flight manifests."

It was Natalie's turn to raise her eyebrows. "And how exactly are you going to do that?"

"Friend in law enforcement," he said smoothly.

She supposed it was plausible. And he had such an open, honest face, with that direct blue gaze of his.

And yet . . . he carried a gun. She didn't like that. What if *he* was in law enforcement?

She shook off the thought, remembering how he'd laughed when she'd been afraid he'd report her accidental theft. *Do I look like Dudley Do-Right?*

No, he didn't. And then there were those lock picks. He had that wicked edge to him that just didn't spell c-o-p.

Then again, did it spell security consultant?

Natalie, you saw his business card. He's exactly what he claims to be. He works for a company that sells alarms and safes. So let the man use his contacts to help you locate Nonnie before she and the colonel get into real trouble, okay?

She was looking her gift knight in the mouth again, and she was a girl who was going to have serious dragons after her. Big, ugly Russian ones. Very soon.

Luc was a nice guy, if a dishonest one. But she had no illusions that he'd keep quiet the next time those thugs paid him a visit. Considering what they'd done to him, she couldn't blame him.

"Okay, then," she said to Eric. "If your friend in law enforcement really doesn't mind checking the flights, then that would be great." She shivered. "Nonnie's evidently turned the heat way down. Would you like some tea?"

He looked for a moment as though he'd refuse. Then he said, "Sure. Thanks." He pulled out his phone and headed into the living room while she stayed behind to put the kettle on.

"It's McDougal," she heard him say. "Put me through to Miguel, will you?" Then he sighed. "Sheila, don't chap my ass right now, okay?"

Who is Sheila?

"How can I just treat you like the hired help? Here's a lightbulb for you, Sweet Cheeks: You *are* the hired help." He laughed. "Yeah, yeah, yeah. You've got me running scared. Now, give me Miguel, will you? Thanks."

Whoever this Sheila person was, they had a very comfortable, mock-abusive relationship. Natalie supposed that Miguel was the friend who would check the manifests.

"Buenos, Miguel. It's Eric. I'm in Connecticut, freezing my nuts off. How's Maribel? You gonna give her that ring she's angling for?"

McDougal's deeply amused laughter followed the unknown Miguel's response.

"Just be warned, my friend," Eric said in low tones. "Everything changes, or so I hear. I wouldn't know personally."

So he'd never been engaged or married himself. Natalie got two mugs out of Nonnie's cupboard and set them on the old tile-and-grout countertop. Then she went to the pantry for teabags and sugar.

"Yeah. I have a big favor to ask. Can you check outbound flights in the tristate area for a Tatyana Ciccoli and a male companion, name of Blakely?"

"Ted," she called from the kitchen.

"Theodore?" he queried back.

"Yes."

"Okay, Miguel. The destination is going to be somewhere in Russia—"

"Moscow," she called.

"Moscow is the likeliest city. Yes. Would have left yesterday, or maybe the day before." Eric fell silent, obviously holding the line while his buddy did a search.

The kettle began to boil. Nat turned off the burner and poured water into both mugs.

"Yeah, Miguel, I'm here. You got a hit? Today? Great. Both of them? British Airways? Brilliant. Appreciate it."

McDougal, grinning widely, strode into the kitchen.

"Bingo. Granny and the colonel took off for Moscow a few hours ago."

"How would they have gotten visas so fast?"

Eric shrugged. "Pay a hefty rush fee, and they can turn a visa around within a day or two."

Natalie handed him a mug and gestured to the sugar bowl, indicating that he should help himself. Then she took a deep breath. "Okay. I guess this means I need a visa myself. Also a guidebook, a dictionary, and a very expensive plane ticket."

He went very still. "Why?"

"Well, I'm going to Russia, of course."

"What good do you think that will do?"

"Eric, I have to get that necklace back from her! As long as it's in her possession, she's in danger."

"And you have a black belt in what, exactly? Fashion design?"

She raised her chin. "Wow. That was patronizing."

"Look, I didn't mean it that way . . ."

"I have to go, Eric. What else can I do? Get the KGB—or whatever they call it now—involved? I don't think so!"

"Hell, no, but—"

"I made the mistake of starting this," she said quietly. "And now I have to see it to the finish."

He seemed agitated, avoiding her gaze and staring down into his tea.

"You want milk in that?"

He snorted and met her gaze with his unholy, heart-breaking blue one. "Got any whiskey instead?"

Eric splashed a healthy two shots of whiskey into the mug of tea Natalie had handed him. *Well, McD, now you are well and truly screwed, aren't you? You have to chase Granny into the great white frozen hinterlands of Russia, but you can't do that if Natalie's chasing her, too.*

Or could he?

He was pretty good at sneaking around—it went with the job territory.

As he saw it, he had two choices: One, declare himself hopelessly in love with Natalie and force his company upon her for the journey. That seemed distastefully manipulative.

Two, he could kiss her good-bye right now and become the shadow-man, tailing her to Moscow and staying in the background until the time was right for a surgical strike. Even if Granny wore the damned necklace for the entire trip, she had to take it off to sleep and shower.

Since McDougal had cut his teeth repossessing cars, often from bad neighborhoods on the other side of midnight, he should be able to grab something as small as a necklace from someone as unwitting and feeble as an old lady.

Natalie chose that moment to bend down and put the whiskey back into the liquor cabinet. The movement stretched her corduroys tightly across her backside, showcasing a perfect upside-down heart of an ass. Mmmmmmm.

No.

It was time to forget completely about any part of Natalie Rosen's anatomy and figure out an exit strategy.

The little red devil on his shoulder suggested that his exit could be a tender one, a naked one.

His newborn conscience squalled at the idea and threatened to pollute its diaper.

He told the devil to get lost and soothed his conscience before things got soiled.

"Listen," he said to Natalie. "Now that we know where your grandmother is, do you need a ride back to the city?"

Natalie hesitated. "I can take the train."

"Why, when I'm driving in myself? It's no trouble."

"You really are the nicest guy."

Oh, this again. If you only knew. "So, can I drive you?" He glanced at his watch.

"You have to be back by a certain time?"

"By six, if possible. I have a dinner meeting with a client." A lie, but it got them moving and away from all the lace doilies and lemon wax.

"Okay, then, drink up. I'll rinse out the mugs, and then we'll go. Thanks again for coming all the way out here. I feel like an absolute fool."

"You shouldn't. Trust your instincts—they're there for a reason."

"Not in this case," she said wryly.

"You're wrong. Instincts aren't tea leaves, but they are sound. You knew something was off-kilter. And it was—your grandmother's gone."

She nodded.

He handed her his mug, having drained the contents.

"You okay to drive after the whiskey?"

"Please. I'm Scots-Irish. They don't make harder heads than ours, sweetheart."

"Sorry to insult you. I guess it's clear that I come from a softer-headed people."

He grinned at her arid tone. As she turned out the lights and locked the door behind them, he tried not to notice the softness of the pure, unblemished pale skin peeking through the black scarf at him. He ignored the curve of her full, nude lips and the gloss of her dark hair under the winter sun. *Time to say good-bye, McD.*

The ride back to the city passed in companionable silence. Natalie had brought along a canvas bag that contained a tornado of colorful fabric scraps and sewing supplies.

"What's all that?" he asked.

"I make wall hangings and art quilts," she said, pulling a half-finished piece from the bag. She spread it out on her lap, sideways, so that he could see.

It was a charming fabric rendition of a Monet waterlily painting, complete with ornately stitched gold frame. But in Natalie's version of it, there were friendly frogs sitting on a couple of the lily pads—frogs with googly eyes.

McDougal laughed. "That's great. Do you hand-stitch everything?"

"No. If it's smaller and more commercial, then I usually sew by machine. If it's a big, elaborate fine-art piece, then I do the work by hand."

"So you sell them?"

She nodded. "Yes, to some small boutiques and galleries. It supplements my less-than-stellar income at Luc's." A look of resignation crossed her face. "I guess I'd better get busy on these, since I doubt that I'll have a job with him after today. He told me in no uncertain terms to bring the necklace back to him, which I clearly can't do."

"Natalie, your grandmother mentioned that the St. George necklace is the key to something—but what?"

"I don't know. Something to do with a legacy or inheritance, which has supposedly remained in a cathedral in Moscow since the days my great-grandparents lived there."

"In a cathedral? But I thought you said the necklace was taken by Nazis, that your heritage is Jewish."

She made a wry face. "My heritage, like most people's, is mixed. Nonnie's mother was Jewish, though her father was not. Their marriage caused quite the scandal, even though my great-grandmother converted."

"Got it."

"Do you?" Natalie chuckled. "It was always a little odd in our household, Eric. Nonnie makes a great matzo-ball soup, hangs Russian Orthodox icons on the walls, and prays to St. George, okay? There's really no explaining her."

He was starting to understand. "So this family legacy she speaks of . . . it's been in the cathedral for how long, sixty-five years or so?"

She nodded.

His natural skepticism kicked in. "Nothing valuable would have remained undiscovered during World War II, and Stalin destroyed countless buildings and churches."

"I agree. But Nonnie clearly isn't using common sense. She's running on emotion and living in the past."

McDougal sighed. "Do you know *which* cathedral she's headed for?"

"No."

"So . . . what, you're going to visit every cathedral in Moscow in search of her?"

"I guess I'll have to." Natalie stitched away, serene and oblivious of his incredulous stare.

"That's crazy!"

She shrugged. "That's Nonnie."

Eleven

Tatyana Malevich Ciccoli hadn't been on a plane since 1968, and things had changed. Instead of walking outside on the tarmac, she and the colonel shuffled down a long, musty corridor that moved on wheels and featured a sort of hood, similar to one on a baby carriage, that pulled right up to the entrance hatch of the plane.

Tatyana could just make out a blurry rectangle of light ahead. Then Ted took her arm and told her to watch her step as they crossed the metal threshold into the aircraft.

The stewardess, evidently now called a flight attendant, welcomed her aboard. Thin carpet underneath their feet served to muffle the footsteps of the passengers and the bumps and creaks from the belly of the plane, where baggage handlers were at work.

The plane vibrated and the low hiss and roar of the air system filled her ears. Her nose caught a whiff of something metallic mingled with stale air, air "freshener," and the not-quite-clean upholstery of padded seats that had held too many derrieres in transit. Then there were different colognes and detergents and shampoos fracturing the scent of burned coffee, someone's peppermint chewing gum, and the aroma of *pizza*? Yes, pizza. People now carried on food in cardboard and plastic boxes.

Flying had once been a rather elegant affair. One wore a traveling suit, even gloves. One was served a complimentary cocktail and a nice dinner in transit, with a real napkin and silverware. But Ted Blakely had warned her that traveling by plane was different now.

Indeed it was! She'd been asked to remove her shoes and relinquish her handbag and carry-on for screening. The security attendants were brusque and scrutinized her purse for far longer than necessary, which made her nervous because she'd stowed the St. George necklace inside it.

But the colonel had taken care of everything, guided her through the metal detector and made sure she got her belongings back safely. "Here, Tatyana," he'd said in his lovely, deep baritone. "Sit down on this bench so you can put your shoes back on."

She briefly wondered about the state of her toes, which must be visible through her nylon stockings. Then she chided herself for being silly. At her age, why bother being vain? And Natalie had given her a pedicure a few weeks ago.

Tatyana bent forward and worked her feet back into the low-heeled loafers she'd chosen for the trip. Her knee-length boots were in her suitcase, along with a thick cashmere shawl that would help keep the Russian cold at bay when they got there.

A thrum of excitement buzzed low in her belly. She was going back home . . . thousands of miles and cultural eons and more decades than she cared to count. Home, where she hadn't been since the age of five. Home, to fulfill a promise that her parents before her had never been able to keep.

The Soviet Union was no longer. It was now the Commonwealth of Independent States. And those bloody, beastly Nazis had never truly known what they had in the St. George necklace. Not that it would have been any use to them then. But with the newly declared independence of the states whose history and wealth had been swallowed by carnivorous Mother Russia . . .

As Ted Blakely guided her down the narrow center aisle of the plane to their seats, Tatyana thought about how worried Natalie would be when she found that her grandmother had vanished without a trace. But it couldn't be helped. The less Natalie knew about this business, the better—until Tatyana's mission was complete.

"Here, my dear," said Ted, and guided her into a seat by the window. Was it her imagination, or was the space diabolically small? She remembered airline seats as being roomy. Then again, she'd put on one or two pounds since 1968, hadn't she? She'd once had slim, supple hips and a graceful posture, an indefatigable energy and a boundless, infectious optimism.

Now she felt ponderous and tortoiselike, her body inching along under a hardened shell toward an inexorable end. Morbid, perhaps, but there it was. No matter how light her spirit, it was trapped in this old, creaky hide of hers and would be until its release, when it would spin, giddy again, toward the angels.

Ted fastened her seat belt, and she tamped down her irritation at being helpless. This getting old thing truly was for the birds. Her vision had once been sharp and clear, but now all she saw were fuzzy, vague shapes. "Thank you, Ted."

"Of course."

She couldn't even discern his features. She knew he had a narrow oval of a face, not much hair left on top of his head, and a wonderful, articulate voice. He was well educated, with a gentle, wry sense of humor. He was taller and thinner than she, and had developed a passion for her coffee cake.

She'd have liked to have read his face with her hands, but somehow the request always died on her lips. It seemed such an intimate act, to touch his features. She contented herself with the deep timbres of his voice; with the subtle, woodsy scent of his aftershave; with the comfort of his presence as he read the morning's newspaper to her over his cup of coffee and her cup of hot tea.

She made out the shape of the paper now and smelled the ink as he unfolded it and shook it out.

"What political antics do we have today?" he murmured.

She found his hand and squeezed it. "Ted, I cannot thank you enough for coming with me on this trip. For being my eyes."

He let the edge of the paper fall and squeezed her hand in return. "Stop thanking me. We're simply leaving our arthritis and heart palpitations behind and having a grand adventure. Shocking at our age, isn't it?"

She smiled and nodded. "Terribly shocking. What will your son say?"

Ted shrugged. "He can say whatever he likes. I may be out to pasture, but I can still kick up my heels."

"Yes, but globe-trotting with an older woman? Some hussy who unquestionably has designs on his inheritance?"

"It isn't his unless and until I leave it to him," Ted said with asperity. "And besides, Mme. Hussy, you're only six months older than I am."

She made out a blurred movement in the vicinity of his left eye. "Why, Colonel, did you just wink at me?"

"I might've," he hedged.

"Flirt."

"I beg your pardon?"

"Read me the headlines, will you? And let a decrepit old hussy buy you a drink."

"Certainly not. I'll buy. What would you like?"

"So old-fashioned."

"And dreadfully chauvinist. Now, what would you like?"

"Well, Colonel, since we're headed to Russia at this ungodly hour of the morning . . . something with vodka seems appropriate, no?"

"Two Bloody Marys, please," Ted Blakely said to the flight attendant when she came by.

A couple of hours into the flight, Tatyana pulled the St. George necklace out of her pocketbook and held it in her hands, on her lap. She stroked the old gold absently and tried not to think about the last time she'd actually seen it, in the sweaty grasp of the young Nazi officer. She tried not to think about her father, lying with a bullet through his brain on the icy country road near the Romanian border . . .

It was 1941 and the cart had been bumping and jiggling over country roads all night when five-year-old

Tatyana heard the warning shot and the guttural German order to halt.

She had spent a total of sixty-four suffocating hours in the dark, hidden with her parents and her four-year-old sister under rough wooden planks, on top of which sat crates of potatoes, onions, and beets. Air and limited light came through the cracks in the cart where the slats didn't quite meet.

Her bones ached and her teeth rattled and her stomach hurt. The cart smelled of onions and soil, mildew and rot, horse sweat and their own body odor. She'd been dreaming for days now of a lavender-scented hot bath in the deep, iron tub at home. But she was afraid that they'd never go home again.

Her sister, Svetlana, gave a startled cry at the gunshot, and their father clapped a hand over her mouth. They lay frozen in fear while old Boris, the driver of the cart, spoke with the Nazi officers who'd stopped them.

"Identification papers!" they demanded.

Silence ensued as the officers examined them.

"And your destination?"

Boris had begun to explain that he was on his way to market when the soldiers probed roughly at the produce with their muskets.

Tatyana tried not to even breathe as some of the blows struck the bottoms of the crates and echoed off the planks that hid them. She heard a rough noise, a creak and a groan as a crate was lifted, then another.

The soldiers asked Boris, "What is underneath?"

"Nothing. Just some straw."

"Unload the cart," one of the Nazis ordered.

The family clung to one another and prayed silently.

Tatyana was still praying when the officers pried up the planks and stared down at them.

Boris ran. He'd taken three steps when they shot him in the back, once and then twice. She shut her eyes but heard his body collapse to the ground. Poor Boris would never drive anywhere again.

The officers turned back to the family. "Get out!" ordered one of them. There were two, one middle-aged and one very young, with a baby face and angelic blue eyes. He looked like a choirboy. The name on his uniform jacket said von Bruegel.

Svetlana made low, keening noises of pure terror, and tears ran down their mother's cheeks. Tatyana was frozen, half paralyzed. Papa's face was masklike, showing absolutely no emotion. He sat up and climbed from the cart, despite his war injury. He had lost his right arm from the elbow down.

Bracing himself, he extended a hand to Tatyana and then to his wife, who pulled Svetlana along with her. Tatyana felt the trembling of his fingers, and it did not reassure her.

"Who are you?" snapped the cherub-faced young officer.

"Alexei Malevich of Moscow. This is my wife—"

"Juden?"

"No."

"Search them," ordered the older officer. "He's lying."

"Never trust a one-armed man, eh?" The young one seemed to be trying to act older than he was. He winked, shot a contemptuous look at Papa's empty sleeve, and spat on the ground.

They found the cash strapped around her father's waist immediately. They ordered him to take off his jacket and boots. While Papa stood in his stocking feet on the frozen ground, they found the gems sewn into his coat lining and the dagger and pistol concealed in his boots. Still, her father stood stoic.

But a muscle jumped in his jaw as the officers grabbed Mama by the collar of her coat and yanked her roughly out of it. They pulled off her scarf. And then the young one ripped her dress from the collar to her waist, exposing not only her brassiere but her rope of good pearls and their most valuable family heirloom, the St. George necklace.

Tatyana's father lunged forward, but the older officer slammed him in the stomach with his rifle butt, and Papa dropped to his knees, retching.

"I'll take the pearls, Weimar. You can have the gaudy one—my wife would never wear it."

The young officer, Weimar, lifted the long strand of pearls from around Mama's neck and handed it to the older Nazi, while she stood shaking from fear, humiliation, and cold. "Unfasten the other necklace," he ordered.

When she fumbled with the catch, he yanked it from her neck, and it took some doing. The gold links were heavy, as was the sculptural depiction of St. George on horseback, ramming his lance down a recoiling dragon's gaping maw.

Mama cried out, Papa lurched to his feet again to defend her, and the young, angelic-looking blond officer turned, his left hand still clenched around the necklace. He fired the pistol in his right hand, and Tatyana's father fell to the ground, a bloody hole in his forehead.

She didn't even realize that she was screaming until the older officer slapped her face and told her to shut up. He shoved the girls toward another uniformed soldier.

They left Papa there on the road in his socks and shirt-sleeves and took her mother into a nearby barn. Tatyana would never, ever forget the boy's angelic blue eyes.

Now, sixty-five years later, she fiercely blocked out the memory of the concentration camp she and her sister were sent to, where they were separated from their mother; they never saw her again.

But the words her mother spoke to her one night still lingered with her. "St. George will protect you, Tatyana. The necklace once belonged to Catherine the Great, who founded the order of St. George. The necklace will come back to you or your sister one day. And when it does, you take it to Moscow. You take it to the Cathedral of the Assumption and speak only to the archbishop."

"Why, Mama?"

"Only the archbishop will know to return to you the pieces of our family history. Priceless things that we could not take with us, things that you will treasure."

"Why don't you take it to the church?"

Mama's smile was infinitely sad. "I will if I can," she said, and squeezed her daughter's hand. "Now, listen to me carefully. Inside the necklace, in the belly of the horse, is a secret compartment . . ."

"What's inside?"

"Something you may need one day. Now, don't be frightened. Remember, St. George will protect you."

Now Tatyana peered down at the blur of gold in her lap and tightened her hand around the little horseman. She'd been unable to find the compartment her mother spoke of, try as she might—and she had, for hours.

She absently ran her index finger along St. George's spear. She'd traced it all the way down to the dragon's mouth when she heard a click, and slowly the entire dragon slid away from the spear. Something fell out of the horse's hollow body and into her lap.

Ted looked over as she picked up the object. "Where did that come from?"

"Out of the necklace," she said slowly. "It feels like a key of some kind. Is it a key, Ted?"

"Why, yes. May I see it?"

"Well, I certainly can't," she said wryly, and passed it to him.

"This looks like a safety-deposit key of some kind. It has the number eleven at the top, and then some letters." He peered at the engraving in the metal. "It spells out M-o-c-k-b-a."

"Moscow," she said. "So it's a bank-box key?"

"I think so. Did your parents store a key inside the necklace?"

"There was something valuable inside, but I don't know if it was a key." She thought for a moment. "Ted, does the key look like an antique?"

"No. I'd say this is machine cut. Definitely twentieth century."

The young Nazi officer had obviously found whatever her mother had hidden in the necklace and confiscated it. Tatyana's mouth hardened. "It looks as if we have a double mission, then, Colonel."

"Let me guess: You want to hunt down the safety-deposit box that matches the key."

Tatyana turned her head toward him. Dryly, she asked, "How did you guess?"

"Male intuition," he said, his tone equally dry.

Tatyana took a sip of her drink. "You understand, don't you, Ted?"

"Of course. I'm seated next to you on an international flight, am I not? I've asked you to marry me, haven't I?"

She stared at the blurry rectangle of the seat in front of her. "You don't want to tie yourself to a blind old bat like me."

"I do," he insisted.

"Why? Without my vision, I'm nothing but a burden."

"Is that right?" Ted asked, an exasperated edge to his voice.

"Mmmm."

"Well, then, Mrs. Burden, I still think you should marry me—if only so that I have something to complain about in my old age. What do you say?"

Tatyana didn't answer. She held the necklace in her lap and pretended she'd fallen asleep . . . but she couldn't completely suppress the smile that played around her mouth.

Twelve

Oleg Litsky stood in his apartment with his back to the fireplace in a vain attempt to warm himself. He hadn't thought about the little girls at the Romanian border in years, but now—in the absence of the necklace—they haunted him, staring at him through the eyes of his own granddaughters. The younger one, the little auburn-haired doll who hadn't made a noise, reproached him almost more than her sister, the one who'd screamed and screamed until they'd smacked her to shut her up.

For a few weeks after the incident he'd dreamed of that family, haunted by what he'd done. But frankly, there'd been so many after them that they blended with the others into one miserable openmouthed howl of horror at the things of which he'd grown capable. Sometimes he'd acted on orders; other times he'd needed desperately to wipe out the reproach on the victims' faces—and the more viciously he banished them, the better.

Violence was a beast that fed upon itself, and it was never satisfied. Anger and guilt and self-disgust festered into further brutality, until each twisted action and reaction created a monstrous stew that he consumed and then purged, over and over, in an agony of subconscious bulimia.

Litsky straightened and moved away from the hearth. As his mind wandered, the heat at his backside had grown unbearable, though an icy draft still clutched at his neck. He reached for the decanter of amber liquid on a side table in front of him and poured three inches into a tumbler.

Good Scotch and the passing of decades had helped, as did his long masquerade as a respectable, retired businessman. And so had the knowledge that the cursed dragon piece, wrapped in old flannel, was shoved to the very back of his safe, the key to his crimes hidden inside its belly.

But now his explosive secrets were out in the world somewhere, and an accidental brush of the fingers could expose him for what he was. At age seventeen, eighteen, or nineteen who feared death? It seemed such a remote possibility. Who feared the glare of shame? He'd had no concept of it, no real reputation to lose.

Now, at age eighty-two, Litsky feared both. Shame in this world and terror of the next. For surely a man like him was going straight to hell without appeals or apologies.

He couldn't escape the consequences of death, but he could still avoid the scandal of discovery. His hands trembled as he waited for the gentleman named Kelso to return his call to ARTemis.

He rued the day that he'd gotten into bed with that whoreson Pyotr Suzdal, not comprehending how dangerous he was. Litsky had steered the Russian a few pieces for ready cash—a mistake. Clearly Suzdal had decided there was more for the taking . . . and his men had broken in while Litsky was in Paris.

ARTemis *had* to locate the blasted St. George necklace for him before anyone discovered the key inside it. Litsky would pay anything and everything to keep Weimar von Bruegel—and his war crimes—dead and buried.

He raised the glass to his lips and tossed back a good half inch of Scotch, feeling it burn like desperation down his throat and conflagrate in his sour, turbulent gut. *Mein Gott*, why would the cursed telephone not ring?

Litsky lifted the glass to his mouth again and his prayer was answered, startling him so badly that he poured the rest of his drink down his cashmere sweater.

"Hello?" he managed.

On the other end of the line, he could have sworn he heard someone snapping *chewing gum*, of all things. Then a nasal voice said, "Ahtemis heah. Mr. Litsky? Please hold for Mr. Kelso."

Thirteen

Natalie's building was on West Nineteenth, and it seemed to McDougal that they got there far too soon. He put the SUV in park and shot her a smile that was equal parts regret and relief. "Well, I guess this is it."

She smiled back at him and tucked a strand of dark hair behind her ear as she gathered her fabric together. "I really can't thank you enough for driving all the way out there, for the moral support—"

*Im*moral support?

"—and for the ride home again."

"You're very welcome."

She pulled the strap of her bag over her shoulder, then hesitated. "Would you like to come up for coffee?"

Hell, yes. No. Yes.

He almost banged his forehead on the steering wheel. "Thank you, but no. I've got some things I need to do."

Disappointment skated over her expression, but she nodded. "Okay, then. Well, see you around. Or not, since Miami's pretty far away. Call me when you're in town again."

"Will do. You take care of yourself, Natalie." He

leaned over and gave her a quick, hard kiss on those soft, delectable lips.

She got out of the car blushing and almost tripped over her scarf, which she'd unwound during the ride. She shut the door and lifted a hand to wave good-bye.

Take care of herself? She wore naïveté like a perfume. And it wasn't going to keep her warm in Russia.

McDougal watched her until she'd disappeared into the building before he drove away.

As he turned down a side street, a flash of color on the floor of the passenger side caught his eye. When he stopped at a light he leaned down and picked up a small sketchbook. A cursory flip through the pages told him it was full of designs and something that Natalie probably needed back as soon as possible.

With mixed feelings he backtracked to her address and double-parked, hoping against hope that he wouldn't be ticketed or towed before he got back. *Yeah, right.*

He sprinted toward the entrance, noticing that nobody sat behind the reception desk. How was he going to get in?

Then, lucky break, the elevator opened and a couple got out. They glanced at him briefly; he met their eyes as if he had every right to be there, then caught the edge of the door as they exited. No problem.

Now, which floor? A list of residents' last names was posted helpfully next to the elevator, and he saw that Natalie was on six. Up he went.

There were six doors to choose from, but only one had a hand-woven, artistic-looking rag welcome mat outside. Natalie's? As he approached he saw the last name woven into the fabric: Rosen. He didn't need to knock—the door was open.

The apartment was trashed. Natalie stood looking around her in shock, seeming unable to comprehend what had happened to her home. It was a single room with a divided kitchenette. A narrow hallway probably led to the bathroom. In the living space, a small red sofa had been overturned, its upholstery and pillows slashed. The coffee table in front of it had been stomped into sticks and splinters. The TV screen was smashed, as were all the dishes in the kitchen. Food had been ripped out of the fridge and freezer, packages sliced open. Jars and canisters were overturned and emptied onto the old wooden floor.

A daybed against the far wall had once been partially hidden from view by a torn shoji screen, and the bed had suffered the same fate as the sofa. The pillows and mattress spilled stuffing and coils—they'd been completely disemboweled.

A trunk at the end of the bed that Natalie had stored clothing in lay upside down, garments tossed on top of it and strewn around the floor.

Her small bookshelves had been decimated, many of the titles ripped in half. Natalie's ideals were revealed in her choices: Shakespeare, *Le Mort d'Arthur*, *Romeo and Juliet*, *The Three Musketeers*, *Don Quixote*, *Tess of the d'Urbervilles*, *Jane Eyre*, *The Scarlet Pimpernel*, *The Last of the Mohicans*, *To Kill a Mockingbird*, *A Tale of Two Cities*, and several hardcover romance novels.

In a final insult, her nasty visitors had ripped apart a once-gorgeous quilt that hung on the wall in a simple wood frame.

"Natalie?" McDougal said. "Are you okay?"

She jumped, startled, moving her hand from her mouth to her heart. "Oh, my God," she said. "Oh, my God."

"Someone was looking for that necklace," he said grimly. "And they were not happy that they didn't find it." He put an arm around her shoulders and steered her to the corridor. "Let me make sure that they're not still here."

She looked horrified.

He'd left the Glock in the car, damn it. But chances were they'd gone. McDougal strode down the hallway that led to the apartment's minuscule bathroom and threw aside the shower curtain. Nothing.

He took a brief but thorough look around, threw open Natalie's old oak armoire. Nobody in there. He saw no other place where anyone could hide. There were no cabinets big enough, and he seriously doubted he'd find anyone in the refrigerator.

"Okay," he called. "Everything's clear."

She came back into the room, hugging her arms around her body. She stared at the destruction as if she didn't know where to start and where to end. Her eyes filled as she looked at the remnants of the big quilt in the frame.

"I'm so sorry," he said, feeling the uselessness of the words.

"It took me years to finish that," she said. "I'd been working on it since I was a little girl. Ever since I saw Faith Ringgold's quilts in a museum exhibition."

Eric stood silent.

"Why?" she asked nobody in particular. "Why would they do this? Destroy everything I own."

"Looking for a hiding place, I'd say. They want that necklace."

She let go of herself, raised her arms, palms up. Shook her head back and forth. Then, wordlessly, she dropped her hands again.

"Listen, Natalie. You can't stay here."

She knit her brows and turned to look at him.

"They might come back. When they know you're here."

"Oh, God," she whispered.

"Come on. Let's get some of your things together. You can stay the night with me at the Waldorf until we get this sorted out."

"I can't impose on you like that—"

"You're coming back to the Waldorf with me," he said firmly. "No argument. Now, do you want to call the police?"

She hesitated. "No. I've already caused enough problems for Luc."

"Do you want to call someone else? Your parents?"

"No. My parents would just worry."

"All right. Let's get your things together, then."

She kept staring around the room. "I should clean up."

"Not right now." He made a mental note to have Sheila send someone over to do the dirty work and salvage anything that could be salvaged. It was the least he could do.

Since Natalie made no move to pack anything, he grabbed a few things for her. A dress, some tights, underwear, socks, a couple of sweaters and some jeans. Comfortable-looking sneakers. Some toiletries out of the bathroom. He threw them all on top of the fabric scraps and sewing supplies in the quilted bag she'd had with her in the car.

"Okay, sweetheart," he said, putting his arm around her again. "Let's go."

There was a fat ticket on his rental car's windshield, which he'd fully expected. There was also a tow truck turning the corner down the street. Why did he have a feeling that it was headed straight for his vehicle? McDougal bundled Natalie into the passenger side and vaulted into the driver's seat. He fumbled the keys into the ignition. They peeled away with the tow truck less than fifteen yards back. At least *something* in this miserable day had gone right.

Natalie was a little bemused to be back in McDougal's hotel room at the ritzy Waldorf, a place where she couldn't even afford the drinks. And had she really only met Eric last night? It seemed impossible.

Then again, it seemed equally unreal that everything she owned had been overturned, slashed, destroyed. The furniture was replaceable. Her work was not.

A hard pulse of outrage, violation, and panic kicked up under her sternum. Her face flushed and her palms dampened as she thought about rough men invading her space, going through her private things, grunting with enjoyment as they kicked over plants she'd nurtured and ripped apart books she'd loved and shredded wall hangings that she'd created in the name of beauty.

She went into the elegant marble bathroom and stared at her face in the mirror, expecting a drastic change that reflected how she felt. But the same old Natalie gazed back, albeit one with circles under her eyes and a hunted look in them.

She turned on the taps at the sink full blast and

splashed water onto her face until the heat receded, and her emotions with it. She commandeered Eric's Aquafresh toothpaste tube, hoping the minty gel would take the bad taste out of her mouth.

Finally she emerged from the bathroom to find him sprawled shirtless on the bed, looking like the poster child for hedonism.

She just looked—and felt—bedraggled. He must have agreed with that assessment, because he eyed her with clear sympathy. "C'mere, sweetheart," he said, patting the spot next to him.

She went because her mind was empty of any alternatives, and he was sexy and warm and she needed his body heat, his energy, and his arms around her. The arms of a stranger . . . It didn't make sense.

But she went anyway and lay down next to him. He encircled her with his arms, and for the first time that day she felt safe. As if she could breathe normally again. Her world was still off its axis, but at least she could stop hyperventilating.

They lay there like that until she was drowsy, almost asleep. Then he said something odd. "Am I doing this right?"

She rolled to face him. "Doing what right?"

He seemed uncomfortable. "Never mind."

"Doing what right, Eric?"

He fidgeted. "Uh . . . holding you?"

Was that an actual blush seeping around the freckles on his face?

"Because, well, it's not really . . . my thing."

She just blinked at him. "Your thing," she repeated.

He actually squirmed. "You know. Holding women."

Natalie bit her lip at his discomfort. "You're doing fine," she assured him. Then she rolled so that her back was to him again and made a wry face at the wall.

Emotionally handicapped, just like her father. And mother, for that matter—both of them related to books better than people.

Well, at least Eric was honest about it, unlike her last boyfriend. Nels, the liar, had told her that he was in a PhD program for physics—when all he did was work in the university library.

He was the latest in a long string of disappointments—men who didn't remotely live up to her ideals. Still, she refused to give up. Somewhere out there was a hero with her name on his lips. Somewhere. But probably not here.

Yet Eric put his arms around her again, even though his body was stiff behind her.

She waited a minute or two, but he didn't relax. This was sweet but almost comical. "Eric?"

"Hmm?"

"Are you going into rigor mortis?"

He chuckled weakly. "Wow, I really am bad at this."

"No, but it's clear that you're outside your comfort zone."

"What can I say? I'm a better smart-ass than a teddy bear."

Natalie rolled to face him once more. She reached out gently and touched his cheek. Then she shook her head and said gravely, "I don't want to ruin your image of yourself, big guy, but you've got some hidden teddy tendencies."

He assumed an expression of mock horror. "Latent teddy-bearism? No! Impossible."

She nodded. "You'll have to come out of the closet eventually, so you may as well practice."

Eric eyed her quizzically. "I've never had a woman phrase it quite like that. Usually they just call me an asshole and storm out. Or do worse." His expression darkened for a moment. "Like spray paint my Ninja pink."

She drew her brows together. "Ninja? As in warrior?"

"Ninja as in bike. Motorcycle. Pink."

He looked so agonized about the color that she couldn't help laughing.

"It's not funny," he growled.

"Sorry," she said, trying to regain gravitas.

"That woman ruined a three-thousand-dollar custom paint job," he said bitterly.

"Wow. What did you do to make her so angry?"

"Hell if I know." He truly seemed perplexed.

Despite her situation, Nat almost got the giggles again. Macho men were alien to her, since her father was a scholar and her brother was a chess champion. They weren't exactly rough-and-tumble types.

"Did you call the police on this Spray-Paint Sally?"

"Yeah, just like you're calling them about your apartment."

"Did you confront her?"

He shook his head.

"Why not?"

"Partly because I wasn't going to give her the satisfaction of a reaction. Mostly because I was afraid I'd strangle her if I saw her again."

"Didn't she deserve strangling?"

"Yeah. But I'm not a guy who roughs up women." He said this in regretful tones, making her laugh again.

"Eric?"

"Hmm?"

"Worse than your latent teddy-bearism is your white-knight complex."

"Lady, I am no white knight! When will you get that through your pretty head?"

"Oh, maybe when you do strangle a woman who deserves it, or when you stop coming to my aid. Let's see, you've done it three times now . . . once in the bar, once at my grandmother's, and now after my apartment got destroyed."

"Completely accidental," he assured her.

"Doesn't matter."

He was midscoff when she poked him in the chest. "But I'm sorry, Sir Knight," she said, deadpan, "that you have to ride off to battle on a pink steed. It must be a little hard on the old ego."

He simmered for a moment. Then he recovered.

"It ain't my ego that's hard, sweetheart." His eyes danced as he grabbed her hand and drew it toward his crotch.

She rolled her eyes and pulled away.

He grinned wickedly. "If you insist on calling me a knight, then you can call me Sir LottaLance."

Terrible. Natalie groaned and turned her back on him, but she fell asleep smiling.

When she woke, it was to a delicious aroma. Eric had ordered them dinner from room service.

Fourteen

McDougal woke the next morning with one arm completely dead, since it had been under Natalie for hours. The other arm was still wrapped around her sleeping body, as was one of his legs. Jesus, Mary, and Joseph—had he held the girl all night?

Shocking.

Really.

This was fucking weird.

He was not a holder of women. He was *not* a teddy bear. And he was *damn* sure no white knight.

He felt so strongly about this that he eased his useless arm out from under Natalie. She stirred sleepily and snuggled back against him, which was half horrifying and half titillating. There was one part of him in apparent rigor mortis this morning, and that was his cock—which unfortunately wasn't dead. It rested quite comfortably against Natalie's backside.

Okay. So there were hidden benefits to this teddy-bear stuff. He couldn't resist one gentle poke. She was asleep, after all. She'd never know.

"Better save your spear for the dragon, St. George," Natalie said, swatting at his thigh.

Teddy bears. Knights. Now saints, for chrissakes. "Sorry. I didn't mean to do that," Eric muttered.

She rolled over, her breasts moving tantalizingly under her sweater. "No?"

"Okay, so I did." He shot her an unrepentant grin, which his conscience then immediately knocked off his face.

McDougal. You have a job to do, bud. And you shouldn't get your honey where you get your money. The sooner you stash her somewhere safe and cut the connection, the better.

He rolled away from her and swung his legs out of bed, staggering to his feet and toward the bathroom. Surely that wasn't disappointment on her face?

Eric glanced into the mirror and laughed. Clearly not. His hair stuck out in tufts of orange and his eyes were bleary and swollen.

You sexy bastard, Sir LottaLance.

As he went about relieving himself, brushing his teeth, and showering, he made a mental list of what he needed to accomplish today. One, they needed to talk to Natalie's boss and find out exactly whom they were dealing with. Two, he needed to call Sheila and arrange some kind of safe house for Natalie until this ruckus died down. Three, he needed to get his ass on a plane to Moscow.

Piece of cake, right?

He dried off, wrapped the towel around his waist, and emerged from the bathroom. He strode to the window and threw the curtains open wide. "Let there be light," he said.

Natalie blinked through her mass of inky, disheveled hair and shielded her eyes with her hand. "Does there have to be quite so much of it?"

"Yes."

Her small nose wrinkled. "Does there have to be quite so much of it right *this second*?"

"Uh-huh." He began to make some coffee in the small hotel-room machine. "Natalie, we're going to have to go see your boss in order to find out who these creeps are. Clearly they're Russian, but who do they work for? A smuggling ring? Some kind of Mafia don? And you'll need to brace yourself: They've obviously been back to see him, since he's the only one who could have sent them to your address. He may not be in very good shape."

She took a deep breath and folded her arms across her body in an unconscious self-protective gesture. "I know. I'm afraid to go to his apartment. But you're right. We need to know who we're dealing with."

"Will he talk to you?"

"He'd better," she said ominously. "I'm in danger; you're in danger; my grandmother's in danger. He'll talk or I'll go to the police and his business will be ruined."

"He may be more interested in saving his skin than his business. Breakfast?"

"Huh?"

"Do you want to order some breakfast?"

She shook her head. "Just coffee, please." She slid out from under the covers and looked down at her wrinkled clothes with distaste. "I can't believe I slept in all this."

He raised an eyebrow. "I was afraid I'd get slapped if I tried to take it off you."

The idea of Eric removing her clothes sent a quick spiral of heat through her, but she said nothing.

Even so, he seemed to sense it, and his gaze rendered everything she wore transparent. She disappeared into the bathroom and then into the shower, standing naked under the hot jets of water.

She was still stunned that sweet, vague Luc Ricard would be involved with animals like the people who'd trashed her apartment. How? Why?

Natalie shivered as she climbed out of the shower, wrapped her hair in a towel, and folded herself into the bathrobe provided by the hotel. She belted the robe and stepped out of the bathroom. She hoped—she really did—that Luc would give them some answers.

There was no answer at Luc's Manhattan apartment when they called up from the reception area. The doorman denied them access to go and check to see whether he was all right.

"Can you send the super?" Natalie begged. "I have reason to believe that he may be in danger."

After a long, evaluative look at her fresh-scrubbed face, the doorman called the building superintendant and sent him up to check Luc's apartment.

"Everything's in order, ma'am," he reported. "Nobody there."

Within moments, she and Eric found themselves back out on the street, looking at each other.

"That doesn't make sense," he said, frowning. "Didn't he tell you to bring the necklace to him?"

She nodded. "And he's injured. He didn't want anyone to see him that way. Why isn't he in bed?"

"Any other place he could be?"

Natalie thought for a moment. "His mother's? She had a little place in Brooklyn until she died a couple of months ago. I doubt Luc has sold it yet, since her will is probably still tied up in probate, and there's a brother in Paris."

"Do you know where the house is?"

"No. But Drake, our receptionist at work, would have the number and address on file." She pulled out her phone and called the office.

"Luc Ricard Restoration Associates," sang Drake.

"Hi, it's me, Natalie."

"Natalie! Where have you been?"

"You haven't heard? I got fired yesterday."

"What?" he shrieked. "When? How? Why?"

"Look, it's a long story and I'll have to fill you in another time. What I really need right now is to talk to Luc. Do you have his mother's address, by any chance? I think he might be there."

"I don't know if he'd want me to give out that information."

"Please, Drake. I'll say I got it myself, from the database."

"Oh . . . fine. But you have to give me the dirt later."

"I will," she promised. She pulled out a pen and wrote down the address he recited to her. "You're worth your weight in gold," she said. "Thanks."

"Don't I know it? Now, why won't anyone pay me that much?"

She left him wondering and hung up. Then she and McDougal made tracks for the nearest subway station.

Luc had installed his mother in a tidy little brick house in Park Slope. Two resin bulldogs guarded the little sidewalk that led up to her front door, and on the porch sat a sobbing Giselle.

"Oh, my God," said Natalie, rushing up the sidewalk toward her. "Giselle? Are you all right?"

The woman met her with a glance of such pure hatred that it almost knocked her backward. "*You*," she spat. "You have ruined everything! *Everything!*"

"What? Where's Luc?"

"You bitch!" She rose to her feet and drew back her hand to strike Natalie, nonplussed to find her wrist immobilized by Eric's grip.

"Where is Luc?" Natalie asked, more urgently this time.

"Go inside and see for yourself." Giselle's tone dripped with malevolence. "And you"—she turned to Eric, struggling in his grasp—"*you* take your filthy paws off me!"

He released her wrist but shot her a warning glance.

Natalie took a step toward the front door, but dread held her in place.

"Go on," jeered Giselle. "See the way he greets you with open arms."

Okay. So Luc was still very angry with her. She could handle that. She deserved his anger. Natalie forced her legs the last few steps, quickly knocked on the door, and then turned the knob and pushed it open. "Luc? It's Natalie."

She recoiled, didn't even recognize the scream that tore out of her as her own. Yet the sound filled not only her head, but her whole body. It was a denial of what lay before her, the thing that used to be Luc Ricard.

He lay on his back, arms to either side of him. One was

broken, and a piece of white bone had pierced the flesh. His clothing was stained with his own blood, and a puddle of urine had collected under his body after death.

The bones in Luc's face had been crushed. He'd looked bad when she found him at the brownstone, but he was now unrecognizable, both eyes swollen shut, his nose broken, and his mouth a distorted mess, the jaw broken.

His glasses lay on the floor next to him. Someone had stomped them into bits.

At Natalie's scream, McDougal sprinted for the front door. The psycho woman out front actually laughed before she crumpled into a heap on the porch again, sobbing.

Inside the house, the badly beaten corpse of a man in his mid-fifties lay spread-eagled on the floor.

Natalie barreled headlong into McDougal's chest as he stepped in, her face etched with shock and horror. He picked her up bodily and pivoted, going right back outside. An unintelligible keening came from her throat, and he gathered her close. Christ. How much could one woman take in a two-day period?

He swallowed his own bile, set her on her feet, and did his best to comfort her. But his first words were to the other woman, Giselle.

"Nice of you to send Natalie in like that," he said, tamping down fury. "You're a real sweetheart."

She'd stopped crying but still sat on the porch with her knees drawn up to her chin, her arms around them. She wiped at her eyes with the sleeve of her coat. "She deserved it."

"And why is that?"

"Because if she hadn't taken something that didn't belong to her, none of this would have happened." She got up and approached Natalie. "Where is it, you bitch? Where is the necklace?"

Natalie raised her head; she looked utterly destroyed. "I don't have it."

"Who does?" the woman's voice rose.

"My—" Natalie broke off as McDougal gripped her arm and shook his head.

"Tell me!"

"No," Eric said in hard tones. "You tell us: What the hell happened in there? Were you a part of this?"

"He was my fiancé," she said bitterly. "Why would I kill him before we were married? I have nothing to gain. No apartment, no car, no money, and no business!"

Well, how was that for cold? McDougal sucked in a breath.

"You didn't love him at all, did you?" Natalie said.

"Love? You stupid, stupid little girl." Giselle fumbled in the pocket of her coat and drew out a package of Marlboro Lights and some matches. She lit a cigarette with trembling hands.

"Luc was a sweet man," Natalie said hotly. "He deserved better than you. He deserved better than to die like"—she choked on a sob—"that."

Giselle raked a scornful glance over her. "Luc was a malleable old fool, but he was a useful one."

"He was receiving stolen art, wasn't he? Black-market stuff that he could alter slightly . . . or even forge while it was in his care for restoration."

Giselle said nothing, just inhaled and exhaled smoke while her pale eyes glittered above the fog of it.

"Where did the necklace come from, Giselle?"

She shrugged. "Some rich old man, they said."

"Who said?"

"Our associates."

"Associates," Eric muttered. "What a businesslike term for thugs and burglars."

"Where did it come from?" Natalie repeated. "It used to belong to my family, but it's been lost for a long, long time."

Giselle stood up, dropped the cigarette, and stamped it out with the toe of her boot. "You had best return it, or you will end up like him." She gestured behind her, at the house.

"Who did that to Luc? I'm calling the police, and you are a material witness. They'll want to talk to you."

"Too bad. Because you'll find that I don't exist." Giselle turned on her heel and walked down the sidewalk, away from the house. "But you do," she said. "You're easy to find. And so is your family."

"Eric, stop her!"

"What do you want me to do, knock her down?" McDougal put a hand on Natalie's shoulder. "I took photos," he said in a low voice.

"When? How?"

"I have a small device."

"Fine. Whatever. I'm calling the cops. She knows something about who did this to Luc."

Eric took a deep breath. "May I suggest that you call in an anonymous tip?"

She shot him an incredulous glance. "Why?"

"Because you want to go after your grandmother, don't you? And I can assure you that you won't be allowed to leave the country for a while—in case the police want you for further questioning. Someone at your office is bound to tell them that the necklace turned up missing and that you were fired shortly thereafter. It won't look good."

She stood like a statue.

"I'm also quite surprised that none of the neighbors came out when you screamed. My guess is that one of them may have called nine-one-one already, and that we have very little time to get out of here."

She took a few steps down the sidewalk and then turned, her expression anguished. "But Luc . . . poor Luc. How can we leave him like that?" Fresh tears streamed down her face.

"We have to," Eric said, taking her arm. "That's a crime scene, and we cannot tamper with it. Now, come on, Natalie. We've got to go."

Fifteen

Eric hurried Natalie toward the subway but stopped just outside it and used a miraculously functioning pay phone to call 911. He reported a homicide at Luc's mother's address but declined to give his name.

Then they returned to the Upper East Side and the Waldorf, where he gave a shattered, unprotesting Natalie a sleeping pill and tucked her into bed. As he bent down to kiss her forehead, she asked miserably, "Why are you being so nice to me?"

"Shhhh," he said. The truth was that he didn't know. Maybe he just wanted to live up to her naive expectations for a little longer. Her perception of his character was refreshing, to say the least. Did she really think of him as some kind of hero, instead of a scab and a player? Apparently so . . . and he was low enough to enjoy it. *Jesus, Mary, and Joseph, McDougal—what is your problem? That is pathetic.*

Just as he'd properly chided himself, Natalie opened her eyes, sat up, and kissed him full on the lips.

Oh, fuck. He felt the sensation flow through every vein in his body, right down to his toes. His nerves bubbled and popped like champagne. And just like that, he was hard.

"Make love to me, Eric," she whispered.

Okay! But he groaned.

So tempting. So wrong on so many levels. The girl didn't know which way was up right now. She was filled with fear and just wanted comfort sex.

And that's a bad thing? It had never been a bad thing before.

Yes, McD, that's a bad thing. Because in her current state she could get attached to you in a heartbeat, and the last thing she needs is to have her heart broken on top of everything.

"Please, Eric. Make love to me?"

He eyed her helplessly, squeezed her hand, and stood up. "Soon," he said. "When you're sure it's what you really want."

She sighed. "Oh, this again. You're such a gentleman that you're not really even a gentleman."

"Huh?"

"They *oblige* ladies."

"Oh, they do, do they?" He put his hands on his hips and looked down at her, all seductively heavy eyelids and pillowy—that was the only word for it—lips. Her dark hair was tousled and formed a sort of silky gestalt painting against the pale bed linens.

"Yes." She yawned.

"Natalie, I think you have some very old-fashioned and . . . er . . . romantic notions that you're trying to give a modern twist. It's more than a little peculiar."

"Did I read too many fairy tales as a child?"

"Definitely." But he smiled to soften his answer.

"You know what I liked best about them, Eric?"

"What?"

"It wasn't the witches and princesses and knights in shining armor. It was that they all had happy endings."

She looked so wistful as she said the words. Then she looked up at him again. "Do you believe in happy endings, Eric?"

"What kind of question is that?"

"A simple one."

He sighed. "No. I don't much believe in them. Do you?"

"I want to." She closed her eyes. Her breathing slowly became deeper and more even, the sedatives kicking in.

Naive, he thought again. She was funny and intelligent, but so idealistic and naive. Yet it was charming and oddly appealing; he hated to see it spoiled. He didn't want to see cynicism etched into her features and hardening her spectacular navy blue eyes.

Eric turned out the lamp next to the bed so that she could sleep, but her voice stopped him.

"Don't," she said.

He turned the light back on, and it illuminated the fear in her face.

"I know it's silly to be afraid of the dark."

He shook his head. "No, it's not. You've been through a lot in the past couple of days." He reached down and brushed his fingers across her cheek, smoothed some strands of hair out of her eyes.

She caught his hand in her own and pressed her lips to it.

He was strangely, unexpectedly moved, and yet instinctively he tried to pull away. A girl like Natalie, so sheltered and pure, shouldn't kiss the hand of someone like him. He was little better than a burglar or a mercenary.... He was, for all intents and purposes, a repo man.

"Please, Eric," she said, breaking into his thoughts. "Just for tonight, give me a happy ending?" She sat up, and tears shimmered behind her lashes.

He didn't say a word, didn't think he could. But he sat down on the bed next to her and touched his lips to hers. She wrapped her arms around his neck and opened to him, her tongue meeting his in an infinitely sweet offering of an eager passion. Again, he felt almost as if he were sullying her, but she gave him no chance to retreat.

As his hands moved to her breasts and cupped them through her flannel pajama top, he no longer wanted to escape. He swept his mouth along her jaw, made love to her ear, and listened to her soft sighs. He scraped his teeth down her lovely white column of a throat and stroked the hollow of it with his tongue.

He found her nipple through the folds of flannel and bit it gently while she moaned, her hands raking through his hair. The tiny moan was enough to make every inch of him painfully hard, and he tugged at the buttons of her top with hands that shook with pent-up desire.

At last her torso was bare to his hungry gaze, and he groaned at the sight of her perfect, small breasts. Cherry nipples. He licked one, bringing it to a hard peak, and she whimpered. The helpless, feminine sound trembled through her, vibrated under his chin, and brought out the wolf in him. He devoured the whole breast as her breathing became shallow and ragged.

She moved under him restlessly, and he transferred his attentions to her other breast while she dug her fingers into his scalp and moaned again.

McDougal moved farther south, scraping the stubble of his chin over the muscles of Natalie's smooth, white stomach, which she'd clenched in unconscious anticipation. He tugged at the tie of her pajama bottoms with his teeth, but she'd knotted it tightly.

He spread her thighs anyway, caressing her through the flannel and kneading the muscles in her hamstrings, his fingers working ever higher. He slid his hands under the cheeks of her bottom and deliberately played his thumbs against the mound at the apex of her thighs.

She bucked at the contact, and the material there grew damp, but he didn't relent. Finally he replaced his thumbs with his mouth, sucking and biting and licking while she cried out. She was right on the edge when he got the tie to her pajama bottoms undone and yanked them off her.

He pushed her knees apart once again and just looked at the erotic folds of pink. He brought his face close and gazed his fill, though he could sense an impatience or embarrassment on Natalie's part.

"Eric?" she whispered. "Is—is something wrong?"

"Not a damn thing," he said. "I'm a happy, happy man." He bent his head to her and took a bite, sucking at the same time, as if she were a ripe peach.

She gave a low scream and came apart again and again, since he refused to stop. He growled with satisfaction and simply rode out the female storm. She quieted and he gave her a few seconds of relief, but then a single touch of his tongue had her disintegrating into helpless, thrashing pleasure once again.

He did it a third time, and she finally begged him to stop, unable to take anymore. He kissed her belly and propped himself up on an elbow. "Happy ending, sweetheart?"

"Not yet."

"You seemed pretty happy—you got me confused with God a couple of times."

"I want you inside me, Eric."

He grinned. "You insatiable slut, you."

"Hey!" she protested.

"My very favorite kind of woman," he clarified, rolling onto his back and shedding his own clothes. "C'mere, honey. Why don't you climb on and take me for a ride?"

She did. He was rock hard, and she finally allowed herself the pleasure of looking at him, exploring his body shyly. Up close, she could see there were freckles on his shoulders under the tan. Every inch of him was muscle—Eric spent some time in a gym, no doubt about it.

Natalie stroked her hand down his chest, over each ridge of his six-pack abs, all the way down to the curly red-gold hair at his groin. Just under it, his cock stood at attention, long, thick, and satin smooth.

She wrapped her fingers around it and he groaned. She slid her hand down to the base and then back up again to the ridge that circled the head of him, and he shuddered. So he liked that. She felt awkward, not knowing what to do next. What else did he like?

Nels hadn't been kind about her sexual skills, basically implying that she had none.

Eric opened his eyes and seemed to read her like a

book. He gave her a crooked smile. "C'mere, Natalie." He took her hands and pulled her on top of him before sliding them down to her hips. She was so relieved that she almost opened her mouth and thanked him.

He guided her onto him, gently parting her, and she sank down until he filled her completely and they both groaned with the pleasure of it. She knew what to do now—it was pretty basic.

She rose along the length of him and then sank down again, establishing a carousel rhythm right away, sliding up and down the pole. But within a minute or so he took her hands. "Stop, sweetheart."

His blue eyes evaluated her closely, and she began to feel uncomfortable again. "Am I . . . doing something wrong?"

He shook his head. "You seem awfully worried about your performance," he murmured.

She opened her mouth, closed it again, and avoided his gaze.

"See, that's not the way it should be, sweetheart." He moved her hands up to cup her own breasts, rubbing them over her nipples. And he did something with his hips that altered the way they were joined.

He began to move again, very slowly, and this time his cock slid intimately along the front of her cleft in long, slippery, erotic strokes. She sucked in a surprised breath. "Ohhhhh."

"Mmmmmm, that's better." He dropped his hands from hers and moved them down to her bottom. "Touch your nipples for me, Natalie. Yeah, just like that . . . You're so beautiful."

They moved in an achingly slow rhythm for a time,

while her pleasure built and she relaxed completely. Then Eric flattened his hand against her belly and slipped a thumb down between them, unerringly finding just the right spot to touch.

Natalie's thighs began to tremble, and she lost consciousness of everything around them as the world became reduced to just the sensation of Eric stroking in and out of her, Eric's thumb rubbing against that special spot. She gasped as a tension inside her built unbearably and he thrust harder, deeper.

"Come on, honey," he whispered. "Come for me . . ."

A cry ripped from her throat as her body convulsed around him and color exploded behind her eyelids.

Eric drove up into her in two powerful thrusts and finished with a guttural, primal male noise. He pulled her to him and she lay draped over his body, feeling as if someone had let all the air out of her.

"Jesus, Natalie," he said. "You are so hot." His chest moved up and down and she could hear his heart thundering. Her cheek was coated with a thin sheen of his clean perspiration. She felt connected to him, joined, in a way she'd never felt with Nels. Everything with Nels had been mechanical, and he'd rolled over and snored when he was done.

Eric had been attuned to her, had reveled in her sensations and worked intimately to heighten and share them with her. Eric . . . *got* her. On some deeper level than anyone else she'd been with. Was he. . . was he . . . the one? The one she'd waited so long for?

"What's going through that gorgeous head of yours, sweetheart?" he asked.

She expelled a breath and lifted her head from his

chest to look into his eyes. "Strange, but I feel as if I were a virgin before I met you." Now, what man wouldn't want to hear that?

She searched for the right words to elaborate, to keep the connection, but stopped at his horrified expression.

He blinked once, then twice, before releasing an uneasy chuckle. He swung his legs over the side of the bed and got up to dispose of the condom they'd used.

No, no, no, no, no. This wasn't the way he was supposed to respond. She could *feel* the romantic in Eric McDougal. It was there—something that touched her and that she touched back. It was *there*. But somehow she'd said something wrong. She tried again.

"Really," she said to his retreating back. "I've never had sex like that."

A pause ensued. "Me, either," he said in a low voice. And then he shut the bathroom door.

Well. So much for the spiritual, sexual connection. She had clearly been deluding herself.

She stared at the white panels for a few seconds before they started to blur in front of her exhausted eyes. She shook her head. The sleeping pill was finally kicking in.

Natalie rolled onto her side. No. Drugged or not, she hadn't imagined the thing between them, and she refused to deny it, even if he chose to . . .

Before Eric came out of the bathroom, she was asleep.

Sixteen

McDougal wasn't surprised that Natalie had finally fallen into an exhausted state of unconsciousness. She'd curled onto her side, her dark hair trailed down her nude shoulders, and with the sheet pulled up only to her waist, she looked like an artist's model. But she also looked vulnerable and very young.

I feel as if I were a virgin before I met you. Oh, hell, had she really said that?

Yes, she had. Damn it, she *had.*

He'd known better than to give in to his lust. This girl was all about emotion—she was an artist, for chrissakes! And he'd had to go and dip his brush into her paint.

I've never had sex like that . . .

Well, he, McDougal, hadn't, either. There'd been a connection there with her, a sort of "click" that was simultaneously mental and physical, and it bothered the crap out of him.

Wrong woman, McD!

No clicking allowed.

Especially no clicking with *this* one.

Uh-uh.

Bad, *bad* juju.

But . . . shit! There had been a fucking click.

So whatcha gonna do, dumb-ass? Date her? Yeah, right. Even without this whole necklace business, how long would you give yourself, a couple of months, before you'd be cheating? You are a hound. You can't make her happy. She will curse the day she ever met you, McDougal. You should get down on bended knee and apologize for taking what she offered just now.

Men like you make women cry.

He hated that. He really did. McDougal dragged his hands down his face as he stood watching Natalie sleep. The only way to avoid making women cry was not to get involved with them.

He'd make some phone calls and arrangements, and then he'd walk away before he hurt her, if it wasn't too late already.

He started toward the bedside lamp to turn it off but remembered that she'd asked him not to. Still, how did she sleep with the light burning into her eyelids? He required total darkness.

He stepped back into the bathroom to make his calls, taking his laptop with him. He sat on the edge of the tub, using the closed toilet lid as a desk.

Then he uploaded the images of Giselle that he'd snapped with a tiny camera built into his wristwatch. He e-mailed them to Miguel at ARTemis for identification, putting *urgent* in the subject line. If her picture was in any database anywhere, Miguel the magician would find it.

I don't exist, she'd said.

Oh, yes, you do. And we'll track you down.

She'd threatened Natalie's family, which McDougal didn't like at all. It was time to call some reinforcements of his own to guard them, some biker muscle.

He hit a number on speed dial and waited while the phone rang.

"Yeah," a deep, Florida cracker voice growled.

"Harley, it's McDougal."

"Hayadoin', McD?"

"I'm all right, man. Got a favor to ask, though."

"S'that?"

"How would you feel about an all-expenses-paid trip to Vermont?"

"Ver-fuckin'-*mont*?"

"Yes. You and a buddy. A big, mean-looking buddy."

"I dunno. S'cold up there, McD."

"Change of pace, change of scenery."

"An' what're we doin' up there, tippin' cows?"

"Looking out for a couple of professors that I don't want banged up."

"Pro-fessors? Th'ain't gonna try to teach us nothin', are they?"

"No. If you do the job right, they won't even know you're there. But the Russian assholes will spot you."

"Russians?" Harley sounded more enthusiastic all of a sudden. "Cool. Kin we knock 'em around?"

McDougal cleared his throat. "Well. Not too much. And only if they look at you funny." What happened to a couple of Russian thugs was not really his concern. Maybe it would teach them to stop trashing apartments and killing people.

"I gotta feeling that they'll look at us *real* funny."

"Yeah? Me, too. You and I, we are men of rare intuition and insight, Harley. Even wisdom."

"So how much you payin'?"

McDougal named a sum, reflecting ruefully that ARTemis would not be reimbursing him for this particular expense. But what the hell.

"A'ight. That'll cover some beer. When you want us up there?"

"Yesterday. I'll call you back with an address."

"Okay. But I got a question for you, McD. Elk said he stopped by your place with that kick-ass windshield that you ordered, the Double Bubble. You wasn't home, so 'e picked the lock on your garage door an' went to put it inside."

McDougal winced. He knew what was coming next.

"Elk said he raised that door and almost shit 'imself. Said your ZX-14 you bought from us was a real purty shade of pink."

Eric cleared his throat. "Yeah. It's a long story."

"Fuckin' *pink*, dude."

"I pissed off a woman."

The rumble of amusement coming from the phone sounded like a lawn mower.

"It's not funny," McDougal said tightly.

The rumble turned into a bellow. "Right. It ain't funny at all. It's fuckin' hilarious!"

Eric scowled. "I'll call you back with an address." He hung up.

His next call was to Avy Hunt, co-owner of ARTemis. She needed to know what was going on and what type of people they were dealing with. And he needed to check on his dog, Shaq, before he left the country.

He called Avy's cell phone, but she didn't answer. God only knew where she was these days. She'd been traveling in Europe, and Gwen, her best friend, was being very closemouthed with details. Something was off-kilter, but clearly nobody was sharing with the likes of him, the onetime suspected murderer.

Man, did that burn his ass. With a renewed sense of injury that might be petty but was also justified, he dialed Gwen's number next.

"Hello?" she said in her melodic, upper-class Southern tones. "McDougal?"

"Yeah, just taking a break from murder and mayhem to check in on Shaq."

"Oh, McD. How many times do we have to apologize? Shaq's fine. Kind of mopes around, though—he misses you. Quinn walks him on the beach every day."

"Are you brushing his teeth every night?"

"Yes, and what a disgusting process that is. Chicken-flavored toothpaste!"

"You know you're dying to try it. Listen, I'm going to be leaving the country, probably tomorrow, so I wanted to give you a heads-up."

"How's the job going?"

"It's complicated. More so than I thought. I'm headed to Moscow."

"Avy's in Moscow."

"She is?" That was news. "What's she doing there?"

"Being mysterious, as usual. I have a feeling it has to do with Liam. They're up to something . . ."

"Sheila said she caused some kind of international incident at the Venice airport. Got on a flight and then back off—they had to evacuate everyone, screen every inch of the plane. Is she nuts?"

"I don't know what's going on with her. But once she was interrogated by security, officially bitch-slapped, and then released, she boarded another flight for Moscow."

"Strange."

"Yes. I have a bad feeling that Liam may have gotten in trouble with a Fabergé egg or something."

"That wouldn't surprise me, given that he was an active art thief for years. That guy is like smoke. I went after him twice on recovery jobs and never could catch up with him."

"Liam's . . . unique. Anyway, give Ave a call while you're there. Check up on her."

"Since when has Avy needed checking up on?"

"McD, I'm telling you that something's off-kilter with her. She needs us. Confidentially, her dad, the U.S. Marshal, is out to get Liam."

McDougal whistled.

"Exactly. It's a big, ugly can of worms. And for the first time in her life, she's showing signs of stress."

Avy was, hands down, the coolest and most level-headed woman Eric had ever encountered. This didn't sound like her . . . but then, having her very dogged father trying to hunt down and put away her fiancé had to cause a woman more than a headache.

McDougal promised Gwen that he'd call her when he got to Moscow. "So how's the baby?" he asked.

"Babies," Gwen said. "Fine."

"You're having *twins*? Jesus. Congratulations." McDougal tried to bend his mind around the concept of fatherhood and couldn't. "So," he asked cautiously, "how's Quinn feel about that?"

"Overjoyed—and scared spitless, just like me," Gwen said cheerfully. "We're already interviewing nannies."

"I thought he was staying home with the kids."

"He is . . . but he's going to need some help."

"I'll just bet he is. Tell me he's not going to wear an apron."

Gwen laughed. "I think that's pretty unlikely. Don't worry, McD. Quinn will come out of this with his cojones intact."

Eric made a rude noise. "You'll store them with the baby powder and diapers in some piece of furniture covered with little yellow duckies."

"Evolve, McDougal. Try. I know it's hard, but try."

"Never." But he hung up with a grin on his face.

The grin faded when he went out to check on Natalie again. What had possessed him to have sex with her? It was a complication that he simply did not need. A smart man would pack his bags and check out before she woke up.

McDougal had always considered himself a smart man. So it was almost a reflex for him to pull his go bag out of the hotel room closet, take it into the bathroom, and sweep his toiletries into it. A simple thing to throw in the clothing laundered by the Waldorf, then his laptop and some odds and ends that he'd left on the desk.

And of course it was dead easy to open the door quietly in order to make his escape. A relief to let it close behind him as he walked down the corridor to the elevators. But with every step he took away from the room, he felt like a bigger and bigger jerk.

Nice, McD. You can't even stay until the morning? You have to scurry away in the dark like a rat?

But it was cleaner this way. Better. She'd be angry instead of hurt, and forget him faster.

Why did that thought depress him?

Pull your head out of your ass, man. She's a nice girl. Way too nice a girl for you.

He kept putting one foot in front of the other until he got to the elevators. He hit the down button and waited for the doors to open. But when they did, he couldn't get in. He stood there growing more and more irritated with himself.

Indecision. He couldn't abide it. Indecision made a man weak—and stupid. And slow.

Still, he stood there like a giant waffle.

Just plate me and add syrup. Stick a fork in me . . .

Disgusted with himself, McDougal forced his feet into the elevator car and rode it down to the lobby, where he arranged for Natalie to stay a few days on him.

He got into a cab and directed it to LaGuardia, where he'd arrange to get on the first flight to Moscow. Clean break. He'd find Natalie's grandmother and her elderly escort, repossess the necklace, and be home in Miami inside of seventy-two hours, if all went well.

The cab smelled of oranges, burned coffee, and old vinyl. The hot, stale breath of the cranked heater had him lowering the window to let in fresh air, despite the cabbie's dirty look.

Even well after rush hour, the traffic was bumper to bumper, stop and start. Evidently the cabbie wasn't the chatty sort, and McDougal was relieved. The farther they got from the hotel, the blacker his mood became.

He pictured Natalie waking up alone, disoriented and terrified, at three a.m. or so. Realizing that he'd cleared out. Feeling used on top of everything else.

Damn it. He hadn't used her. But what the hell did he do, leave a note—something about a "click"? Yeah, right.

I don't think so.

He saw a naked Natalie on top of him, mesmerized yet again by a slow build of pleasure . . . the surprise dawning on her face as she came again . . . the sweet, dirty shame as she touched herself for him and liked it.

He couldn't do it. He could *not* leave her this way. She was fun; she was nice; she made him laugh. She trusted him and saw something good in him that not many women saw. He wanted to live up to that. Natalie deserved at the least a good-bye kiss and a big bouquet of flowers.

The cabbie had long crossed the Triboro Bridge and turned onto Grand Central Parkway. They were only a mile from LaGuardia when McDougal said, "Turn around. Take me back to the Waldorf, will you?"

The cabbie raised his eyebrows until they touched the edge of his multihued woven cap. He didn't voice his opinion that his passenger was nuts, since his expression spelled it out clearly. But he just shrugged and took the next right, working his way back the way they'd come.

McDougal could have shot himself. *You're in the middle of a high-dollar job, man. This is not the time to grow a conscience or fake being a nice guy. What are you doing?*

But when they pulled up to the hotel once again and the quizzical doorman stepped over to welcome him back, Eric tipped the cabbie double. He nodded at the doorman, went straight into the lobby, and requested his key again, muttering something about a delayed flight.

Once in the elevator, he couldn't even meet his own eyes in the polished reflective surfaces. He got out, walked back to the room, snicked the electronic key through the slot, and snuck back in.

Natalie stirred and rolled over as he eased the zipper of his bag open and pulled a few things out. He disappeared into his bathroom office again with his laptop and phone, feeling completely crazy but somehow . . . better.

Seventeen

Avy emerged from the Kropotskinskaya metro station and blinked in the sunlight. Across the street, the bright golden domes of the Cathedral of Christ the Redeemer gleamed over the bleached white building. The cathedral was truly spectacular. She'd taken two steps toward it when her fiancé strode up to surprise her.

"My darling!" Liam said expansively, holding his arms wide and breathing something lemony and alcoholic into Avy's airspace. "How was your flight?" He seized her and kissed her on the lips before she could answer, lifting her off her feet. "You look exhausted, my love."

She felt the familiar weakening of her knees at his touch and a singing in her blood. However, she hadn't gotten where she was in life by being stupid. Not only had Liam been drinking during the day, which was unusual, but he was nervous.

Liam was flippant, irreverent, incurably elegant, and inordinately handsome. He possessed a winning personality, buckets of charm, and a colossal set of brass balls. But he was never, ever nervous.

When he set her on her feet again and gave her an

affectionate squeeze, she looked up at his aristocratic countenance and narrowed her eyes. "What's up, Liam?"

"Up? My spirits upon seeing you, gorgeous." He seized her carry-on, which was all she ever traveled with, and slung it over his shoulder. Then he grabbed her by the hand and towed her along the road by the river, all the way to the Bolshoy Kamennyy Bridge, under it, and past a guarded gate that he explained was Borovitskaya Tower, the official, presidential entrance to the Kremlin.

The Kremlin itself was a vast and varied complex, not at all what she'd expected. Instead of looking like a Russian version of the Pentagon, it contained all sorts of buildings, from towers to palaces to cathedrals and gardens.

Liam kept up a constant stream of tourism patter, and she almost fell for the distraction. But once they were alone in his sumptuous room at the Metropol, Avy fixed him with a no-nonsense stare. "Liam, why exactly are we here in Moscow?"

"Oh," he said airily, "you know. The usual."

"What are we replacing?"

"Well . . ." His tone downshifted into cautious. "It's not precisely—that is to say, not quite a, ah, um—"

"Liam!" For him to be this stumbling and inarticulate, whatever he was up to was very, very bad.

"Yes, love?"

"Do you remember when you promised that you'd never lie to me?"

He squirmed visibly. "Yes. Which is why, my darling—"

"And do you remember when you promised that you'd go straight, for good?"

"I do indeed, my love. There's just been a tiny wrinkle in my overall plan to be a properly righteous citizen . . . nothing that can't be quickly ironed out. I am, I swear, ninety-nine-point-nine percent straight."

Avy shook her head, her mouth set grimly. "Liam, you're more bent than a paper clip!"

"Not so," he protested. "I'm as straight as the edge of a book . . . It's just that at the moment I have a wee—truly *microscopic*—uh, what you might think of as a rather dog-eared page. Only one!"

Avy kicked off her shoes and lay back flat on the bed, putting her hands over her eyes. Her temples throbbed. "I knew it. You're back to your old tricks."

"No, I swear to you, I'm not. I'm up to someone else's trick. Someone to whom I made a promise."

"Then break it," Avy said shortly.

"I can't do that."

"Then you can consider our *engagement* broken."

Suddenly Liam's big body straddled her own on the bed, and he took hold of her wrists. "Please, Avy. Please just listen to me."

"No!" she said, struggling.

He didn't release her wrists. "Please, I beg you. Just hear me out."

Avy didn't do helpless well. Anger began to crackle through her; instinctive female panic at being held down flared it into a blaze like burning newspaper set under dry kindling. Without warning, she bucked, pulled her knees through his, and slammed both her feet into his chest. The force of it propelled Liam into the wall, and his head into a framed painting that hung there. He went down hard, the picture joining him.

"Bloody hell!" he said, staring up at her.

"Don't you ever, *ever*, hold me down like that again," she told him, panting. "Understand?"

"I'm sorry. I meant nothing by it, Ave—you must know that. All I wanted was for you to listen. I still need you to listen."

Adrenaline wasn't finished pulsing through her, but she got her breathing under control.

"Christ, love, remind me never to meet you in a dark alley," Liam muttered, putting the painting aside and getting to his feet. He flexed his shoulders and winced. "I do believe you've imprinted my spine into the Sheetrock, you vixen."

"Talk," she said without sympathy.

"Oh, you're all ears now? There's female logic for you—"

"Liam, I'm giving you one shot to explain before I walk out of this hotel and out of your life. I will not marry a career criminal. I won't do it, understand?"

"Perfectly." Liam sighed and sank down on the bed. "This is not an ordinary theft, by any means. But you could actually look at it as a recovery, Ave."

"Oh, I could, could I? And why would I do that?"

"Because it involves bringing the . . . er . . . item back for a trial."

Avy folded her arms across her chest. "A trial as in test run?"

"No, no, no—a courtroom trial." He beamed as if that explained everything.

"Go on," Avy ordered.

"It's a long story," Liam said, dropping into a wing chair.

"I have plenty of time to hear it."

"All right, then. You are aware, my love, of international efforts to locate and prosecute Nazi war criminals for their heinous acts during the Second World War, correct?"

"The Nuremburg Trials?"

"Those took place immediately after the war. I'm talking about current efforts."

"Aren't the Nazis all dead by now?"

"Sadly, no. And many of them fled prosecution to live under assumed identities in foreign countries."

"Okay," Avy said. "So what is it that you need to steal, and for whom? Evidence of some kind? Photographs? Tape recordings?"

Liam worried at his upper lip with his teeth and squinted at her. "Something rather larger than that."

"Liam, stop being so mysterious and just tell me already!"

"Avy, my darling, what I'm here to repossess is a man."

She stared at him, unblinking. "That's funny, Liam."

"Really. I must steal a live human being, a former Nazi war criminal whom Russia is refusing to extradite."

"You've got to be fucking kidding me, Liam!"

He shook his impeccably groomed head.

"Let me explain something to you: What you're talking about is not theft. It's called *kidnapping*."

He shrugged. "Terminology, love."

"No, no, no. This is a human being. A person. Not a sculpture or a painting or a diamond."

He winked at her. "Your powers of deductive reasoning are impressive."

"Are you out of your mind?!"

"I'm quite sane, I assure you."

"How—what . . ." Words failed her. How could he just sit there so calmly, hands loosely clasped between his knees? "Okay, Liam. Let's pretend, just for shits and giggles, that you somehow manage to overpower this man and kidnap him. How are you going to get him out of the country?"

"By air," he said as if that were all there was to it.

"By air," she repeated scathingly. "What, you're going to shoot him out of a potato gun and over the border?"

"No, my darling." His voice held infinite patience. "We'll have a small aircraft waiting. It's all arranged."

"Oh, it is, is it?" she asked, her wrath rising.

"Yes, but I need your help."

"I'm not helping you kidnap someone. No way."

"But it's a matter of honor, love."

"Since when do thieves have honor?"

"Aha . . . but I'm no longer a thief. I'm working terribly hard to get my honor out of layaway, you see."

Avy rolled her eyes heavenward. "I think we should just go sightseeing, tour a vodka factory, and go the hell home."

Liam shook his head sadly. "I can't do that. I've been asked to help."

"Asked by whom?" Avy had a bad, squishy feeling in the pit of her stomach.

"People in a position to give me another get-out-of-jail-free card, this time for Eastern Europe, Russia, and several former Soviet territories."

Oh, great. "And how badly do you need that get-out-of-jail-free card?"

Liam shrugged. "That all depends on where you'd like to honeymoon, my love."

Avy drew in as much air as she could, and then let it out in a long-suffering groan.

"Avy, in all seriousness, I do feel honor bound to help prosecute these criminals in any way I can. They tortured, starved, and executed millions of people. This is about justice. This is about doing what's right."

She sat silently, reflecting unwillingly on the truth of his words.

"So you see, don't you, my darling, that this isn't strictly a theft. I've simply made a commitment—as you do every day—to *recover* something for a perfectly legitimate organization."

She dragged her hands down her face and peered at him through her splayed fingers. "Which one?"

"Essentially the World Court."

"And they have enough evidence?"

"They say so."

"Then why won't Russia extradite the man? The Nazis were responsible for the deaths of more than twenty million Russians during World War Two."

"Avy, I don't know. From what I understand, there's no documentation right now that Russia's still attempting to investigate or prosecute Nazi war criminals. But in this case it could simply be a case of bad relations with the U.S."

She sighed, straightened, and looked him directly in the eyes. "What's this man's name?"

"Weimar von Bruegel."

"Okay. And where does he live?"

"In the Zamoskvoreche section of the city, quite close to the Tretyakov Gallery."

She was silent for several moments. Then she said in resigned tones, "All right. When do we go in and get him?"

He shot her a brilliant smile. "I *knew* you'd come 'round to my way of thinking on this."

She just shook her head and again looked heavenward. "Why, God?" she asked. "Why me? Why couldn't someone else have fallen for Liam James?"

He bounded out of his chair, took her into his arms, and pulled her hands away from her face. Then he kissed her soundly. "Nobody else would do for me," he murmured. "Only you, my Ava Brigitte."

She melted against him despite her many apparent misgivings.

He raised his head. "Please note," he said, "that I have released your hands."

"So noted," she said huskily.

"Excellent. Now I have every intention of putting *my* hands up your skirt, love . . . with your permission, of course."

"Then do it already," she said, busily unbuttoning his shirt.

"You won't kick my bollocks into my tonsils?"

"Maybe tomorrow . . ."

"That's my girl," Liam said.

And then they got busy.

Eighteen

Natalie woke unwillingly, and only because someone was gently shaking her shoulder. She opened her eyes, and Eric's face swam into focus. "Wha'?" She closed them again and tried to slip back into inky unconsciousness.

But Eric's voice said, "Wake up. We have a flight to catch."

Flight?

The smell of strong coffee wafted to her nostrils and she struggled to a sitting position, but her eyelids felt as if they were made of iron. Whatever he'd given her to sleep last night hadn't worn off.

Eric put a cup of coffee into her hands and she automatically raised it to her lips and drank, burning her tongue. That finally brought her the rest of the way awake.

He'd already showered and was walking around in nothing but a towel, knotted at his waist. A couple of water droplets still clung to his neck and those powerful shoulders. Sunlight caught the reddish mat of his chest hair and transformed it to burnished copper.

He looked as if he belonged in one of those men's

razor commercials, with a stunning woman stroking his jaw to prove the closeness of his shave. Or perhaps on a great white yacht, selling high-end liquor with his eyes reflecting the hue of the Caribbean in the background.

He didn't look as if he belonged in the same reality as normal, average people like her. What was he doing in the same hotel room?

Well, for one thing, he was packing, throwing his clothes into a handsome, dark leather duffel bag.

Natalie said, "What do you mean, we have a flight?"

"Large tin can with wings that transports people from one country to another." Eric winked at her and gestured to the coffee. "Drink up and then get through the shower. Plane leaves in three hours and we have to be at La Guardia in one. We'll fly overnight to London and from there to Moscow."

Natalie just blinked. Then she said slowly, "You booked us tickets to *Russia*?"

"No, Disneyland." He ran a comb through his wet hair. The dampness turned it a dark auburn color.

"Do me a favor and hold off on the sarcasm until you're making sense."

"Sorry." He shot her a sheepish grin. "Yes, Natalie, I booked us flights to Russia."

She finally absorbed it. "Why?"

"Because . . . because you need to go. I thought it was a matter of some urgency."

"Yes, Eric. I need to go. But why are *you* going? We barely know each other."

He flushed and looked extremely uncomfortable. "I just don't want you to go alone, that's all."

"Eric, that doesn't make sense. You're not responsible for me or the mess I've gotten myself into. And don't you have a job? How can you just take off like this, with no notice to anyone?"

"Natalie," he said, his color rising even more. "I'm a consultant—I told you. I travel constantly. As it happens, my company owes me about five weeks of paid vacation and I was only here in New York to wrap up a long-term project. So I happen to be free."

She stared at him warily. Suspicion fired little warning shots into every corner of her brain. He sounded a little glib. She raised the coffee cup to her lips again and drank. Then she said again, "Why?"

"Natalie, do you speak Russian? Do you know the Cyrillic alphabet to even read street signs?"

She shook her head. "You?"

"I won't claim I'm fluent, but I took a year of Russian in college. I'll be able to get us around."

Nat just looked at him, long and hard, clearly extending her question.

"Look, what are you gonna do if you run into muscle men over there, Natalie?"

"So you're coming with me to protect me?"

"Is that bad?" he countered.

"Eric, what do you care, really? I'm some random girl you picked up at a bar."

He dropped his towel on the floor—deliberately? To distract her?—and stood there naked while she sucked in a breath and then averted her gaze. Then he stepped into a pair of boxers and pulled them up over his hips. He settled his big hands on them and squared his jaw. "I just care, okay? I like you, Natalie. I don't want to see you get hurt."

Was he saying that he had some feelings for her? Maybe their strange proximity and the violence of the last couple of days had created an unusual bond, which they'd sealed by making love. She did feel as if she'd known him much longer than she had.

He raised his reddish gold eyebrows and fixed her with that Newman blue stare, the one that blended challenge with integrity and self-awareness with compassion. It was one that said the world both amused and disgusted him, but what the hell—he'd play the game. "I'm a security consultant, remember?"

Right. She tossed back the rest of the coffee and stared at the bottom of the empty cup so that she wouldn't fall into the potency of that gaze and get hopelessly drunk on it. What woman in her right mind would refuse a few more days with him? Not to mention nights.

"Okay. I think you're crazy, but I won't turn down the company. How much do I owe you for the plane ticket, though?" She swallowed and hoped she had enough money in her bank account. "I'll write you a check."

He waved a hand at her and stuffed his legs into a pair of well-worn khaki pants. "I have frequent-flier miles out the yin-yang, sweetheart. We're first-class all the way."

"Eric, I can't let you do that . . ."

"Tell you what. Let's argue about it in the taxi on the way to LaGuardia, 'kay? Now, get your cute little butt into the shower or we're not going to make it."

She followed orders and tried to put together a passable outfit from what Eric had taken from her apartment, which was a challenge. Brown tights and a black dress. A couple of bras that didn't fit her anymore, since she'd lost weight.

And underwear that was pretty, but desperately uncomfortable. The thought of traveling for, what, sixteen hours or so in a lacy nylon thong made her cringe. But she had no alternative unless she wanted to turn her current pair of panties inside out, which was equally unacceptable.

She chose one of the thongs and a cashmere sweater that had once been her brother's, but had to ditch the bra because the padding dented in the absence of enough breast. Jeans completed the outfit, but then she was forced to put on running shoes since traveling in high-heeled boots was out of the question. The hems of the jeans puddled and dragged on the floor.

When she emerged from the bathroom, Eric cocked his head, evidently amused.

"Listen, slick, you didn't bring me much to work with, okay? Half of what you packed doesn't fit anymore and the other half is mismatched."

"So the bag-lady look is my fault."

"Pretty much."

"Sorry. I'll make it up to you, but right now we've gotta hustle."

She shoved her wet hair behind her ears and mashed yesterday's clothing into her bag on top of all the fabric scraps, the notebook, and other odds and ends. "Any reason that you packed bubble bath but no deodorant? And nail polish but no razor?"

He already had the door open and his duffel over his shoulder. "See, it's like this, sweetheart. I'm a *guy*. We have no clue at all what women take on a trip."

He was all guy. One hundred percent man. Didn't even like a hint of pillow talk, even if the message was "You're the best I've ever had."

She still wondered what he was doing with her, but she had enough mysteries to solve without trying to figure out that one.

Once they got to London, McDougal called ARTemis to see whether Miguel had found anything on Giselle, Luc Ricard's fiancée.

The phone rang and rang, which was unusual. Finally Sheila answered, sounding irritated. "Ahtemis, how may I help you? Oh, McDougal, it's you. What do you want?"

"Just to hear your voice. Miss me?"

Sheila snorted. "Try your pathetic lines on some gal who might b'lieve 'em. I'm busy."

"Put me through to Miguel, will you?"

A long-suffering sigh blew through the phone, and then Eric heard a click. But the voice on the other end of the line was not Miguel's.

"All right, Sid, honey, where were we?" Sheila now sounded like a Brooklyn Betty Boop, all breathless and borderline orgasmic. "I'm wearing nothing but your diamonds and the leather bustier. I'm bending over the sofa now, and I'm so hot and willing and ready for you, baby . . ."

"I'm going to hurl," McDougal said. "What is this, 1-900-GET-SICK?"

"*Shit!*" said Sheila. "Why are you still there, McD? I transferred you!"

"Why are you giving phone sex on our business line? Who's this Sid guy?"

"Nobody," Sheila said hastily.

"Sid *Thresher*?"

"Of *course* not."

Sid Thresher was an aging rock star, the former lead guitarist for the world-famous band Subversion. He'd had an unrequited crush on Gwen for more than a year and still hadn't quite accepted that she was going to marry another man.

"I'll be damned," McDougal said with rising disgust. "What's he paying you to talk dirty to him?"

"Nothing!"

"Does Marty-the-Hubby know about this?"

"No!"

"I'll just bet he doesn't. Maybe I should mention it to him next time I submit an expense report." Marty was also the accountant for ARTemis.

"Listen, McDougal. If you say anything, I will personally kick your—"

"I don't really think you're in a position to make threats, Sheila, do you?"

Silence.

McDougal chuckled gleefully. "What's the information worth to you?"

"Are you blackmailing me?"

"Why not? You've tried to extort money out of all of us. Payback's a bitch, ain't it?"

"Look," she said, desperation in her voice. "How 'bout if I give you phone sex, too?"

McDougal shuddered. "That won't be necessary. But thanks for the offer."

"McD, what do you want? We can come to some kind of agreement, here. Just tell me."

He took a moment to think about it. "Okay. I want you to be courteous. No, more than courteous: *sweet*. Not just to me, but to all of us."

"Sweet." Disbelief, even horror, permeated her voice.

"Yeah."

"I can't. Not in my nature. Ask for something else."

"Sweetness," he affirmed. "And I want you to offer us refreshments when we come into the office."

"Refreshments!" Her voice rose. "*Refreshments!* I suppose next you'll be asking for me to kiss your spoiled butts . . ."

McDougal grinned like a large, satisfied crocodile. Too bad she couldn't see him. "Pucker up, Kofsky. Oh, and by the way, I need one helluva maid service to go to a Manhattan apartment and clean up. The place got trashed during a burglary."

"*Maid service!*" she shouted.

"Yup."

"I suppose you think I should fly up there myself, in a short, ruffly black-and-white uniform and CFM pumps, with a pink feather duster."

He could have done without that visual. "Sure, if you've got the time. And make sure to do the oven and the windows . . ." He grinned as she sputtered, then gave her Natalie's address.

"Who's paying for this?" Sheila wanted to know.

"I am. Now, can I please speak to Miguel?"

A snarl came from Sheila's end of the line.

"Remember, you'd better be nice!"

Silence.

With an evil chuckle, McDougal just waited her out.

He heard her swallow hard. Then she said, "Why, yes, sir. Right away, sir."

Nineteen

Tatyana held tight to Colonel Ted's arm as she drew the Moscow air deep into her old lungs. It was chilly but clean, and tinged with old memories.

She saw her mother and father, decked out for a holiday party. Papa wore his dress uniform and all his medals, while the St. George necklace nestled against her mother's white bosom, framed to perfection by her low-cut green velvet evening gown.

As girls residing in the Arbatskaya district, Tatyana and her sister, Svetlana, had pressed their noses against the glass of their bedroom window until the taillights of the chauffeured Daimler were out of sight and their governess shooed them off to bed.

Tatyana recalled the two of them huddled in the warm, cavernous kitchen drinking chai, or black tea, made with water from the samovar. They'd sipped it slowly as they observed the family cook making borsht, rye bread, blinis, and fish stew.

Tatyana smiled up at the sky and wiped a tear away with the finger of her glove. "What do you see, Ted? Be my eyes and show me the modern Red Square, mmm?"

He cleared his throat. "All right. There's a light sprinkling of snow on the dark brick courtyard. It's not as large an area as I expected, but the buildings are fantastic, like something out of a fairy tale. The historical museum looks like a twin-spired gingerbread castle, made in perfect symmetry by a painstaking pastry chef. It glows reddish brown in the weak sunlight, but all of its towers and cupolas seem dusted with confectioner's sugar."

She was enchanted with the vision he conjured, as well as his gorgeous baritone. "Go on. St. Basil's? Is it the same?"

"St. Basil's Cathedral was created by an entirely different, and probably mad, pastry chef. Instead of gingerbread, it looks as if it were sculpted out of very fine white cake, with swirls of brightly painted candy atop the five towers."

"The onion domes," she murmured. "It's the same . . ."

"They don't look like onions. More like upside-down hot-air balloons, slightly squished. Or dollops of meringue, painted like Easter eggs."

She laughed and clapped her hands. "Lovely description, Ted. What else?"

"The Kremlin Wall runs forever, and inside is a whole complex of buildings—the Kremlin palaces, the state armory, various cathedrals with more onion domes—but gold ones this time. In front of the wall, there's Lenin's mausoleum with the poor man inside, embalmed for viewing. It's a rather plain, modern structure with evergreens standing like sentries around it. There's the monolithic GUM department store, with its great glass roof . . ."

Tatyana listened as he re-created the iconic sights for her, his voice adding a rich poetry to the visual feast. At last his voice tapered off, and they simply stood together, arm in arm. She could feel the tentative sunshine of spring bathing her face, and her hair lifting in the gentle breeze. She sensed that Ted was looking at her and not at the architecture.

"What is it? Do I have lipstick on my teeth?" She carefully applied a soft shade each morning with her finger and a magnifying mirror. Natalie had chosen the color for her.

"No. You look . . . radiant," he said. "Happy." After a moment he added, "Beautiful."

Her breath caught. No one had called her beautiful in decades. "Ted—"

His hand tightened on her arm. "Tatyana, did you mention our trip here to anyone?"

"No. Not even to Natalie, who's probably worried sick. Why?"

"Because we're being watched."

"Watched?" she repeated. "How do you know?"

"My uniform may be dusty after years of retirement, but basic surveillance techniques don't change—even if they've got fancier equipment these days. There are three different men, and they've been on us since we left the hotel. One's in an old Volvo. Two are on foot."

Just like that, Tatyana's pleasure at being back in Moscow dissipated. "Ted, what do we do?"

He covered her hand with his. "Well, for starters, we lose them. Then we change hotels."

* * *

Natalie and Eric checked into the Savoy upon arrival in Moscow. He definitely traveled first-class.

"Do you mind if we share a room?" he asked her.

Natalie looked around the lobby, focusing on the luxe seating, the gorgeous chandeliers, the fresh flower arrangements. She gulped, not even wanting to know what it cost to stay a night here.

He raised his eyebrows and gave her a quizzical look. Belatedly she realized that he was still awaiting an answer from her.

"Of—of course not," she stammered. "But Eric, I can't af—"

"I can get you your own room if you'd like," he said. "I just thought we could have more . . . fun . . . if we stayed together."

He winked at her, and heat bloomed in her cheeks, spread down her neck and then lower.

"Yes," she managed. "I'd like to stay together."

"Great. With all that hesitation, I was beginning to think that I was a terrible lover or something." His eyes danced as her mortification deepened.

The hotel employee behind the registration desk kept his face carefully neutral, for which Natalie was intensely grateful. But she decided on a little revenge.

"Oh, no," she said coolly. "You were fine. Quite competent."

Eric's eyes lit with challenge and he poked his tongue into his cheek as he slapped down his American Express card. "Competent," he repeated. "Well, I'm so glad." His expression promised retribution when they got upstairs.

Uh-oh. But she just smiled sweetly at him as they waited for their registration to be processed.

During the hours on the plane, she had worked almost nonstop on a small art quilt, which spilled over her lap in a colorful waterfall. Airport security had confiscated her good fabric scissors, but she managed to painstakingly cut out shapes with a tiny nail scissors.

Eric asked about the subject matter of the quilt, but she just smiled and shrugged enigmatically. The atmosphere between them felt strained and odd, caught between the sexual intimacy of the day before and the unspoken question: What next?

What was next physically, of course, was Moscow and finding her grandmother. What was next emotionally was on ice.

She noticed small things about Eric. He was invested in seeming casual, with not a care in the world, yet he was tightly wound and unable to relax on the plane. He fidgeted and squirmed; got up to pace the aisle; messed around with his BlackBerry. He'd watch five minutes of a movie before flipping to another selection, then watch five minutes of that before going on to yet another. Then he was back to pacing the aisle.

Natalie observed him while she sewed and wondered about his odd behavior the night before. She'd woken when he'd come into the room . . . and he'd come in with his packed duffel bag. Then he'd artfully *un*packed it, tossing a shirt here and a belt there, a paperback book on the desk. He'd surreptitiously looked over at her while doing it.

The only explanation was that McDougal had planned to disappear on her but then changed his mind. Why?

But the most interesting thing about his actions—the

most important thing—was that he'd come back, and that spoke for his character.

Eric was an enigma; that was for sure. But she didn't ask him about his odd behavior, since they remained in that no-man's land between being acquaintances and being strangers.

She had loved sex with him, especially loved the freedom that he'd encouraged her to take with her own body. Nels would have been horrified and offended if she'd touched herself—he'd have taken it as a reproach, as a sign that he wasn't an adequate lover. He wasn't, but she'd never informed him of the fact.

Done with their paperwork, the clerk handed them back their visas and Eric's credit card along with two room keys. He asked politely if they needed help with their bags, but they declined. Eric, ever the gentleman, took hers. No matter what he claimed, he was a sweet guy.

Their room was beautiful and elegant—done in chocolate browns, taupes, and pale blues—but she'd barely taken a glance around before Eric advanced upon her. "*Competent?*" he growled.

She backed away. "You deserved that. You were trying to embarrass me."

He stalked her into the corner, where she ran out of room to retreat. Her heart began to pound at the look in his eyes, which was pure sex, pure challenge, and raw with something peculiarly male and perverse.

She put her hands up—she wasn't sure why—and he took her wrists prisoner, pressing them to the wall above her head. He invaded her personal space, took possession of her mouth, and kissed her senseless. Then he let her wrists go and slipped his hands up her sweater to touch her bare breasts. A raw surge of power—or was it weakness?—washed through her, leaving her breathless.

He withdrew his hands from her body but pressed his palms against each of the adjoining walls, so that she couldn't escape the corner even if she'd wanted to. "Take off your clothes, Natalie," he said huskily. "Strip for me."

Heat streaked through her. Feeling self-conscious, she kicked off her shoes, toed off her socks, and slowly peeled her jeans down her legs until she wore nothing but the too-large cashmere sweater. She took hold of the hem and pulled it up, but he stopped her, sweeping his warm fingers down her belly, around her waist, down to her bottom.

He lifted her, and she wrapped her legs around his waist, feeling the fabric of his jeans against her most vulnerable spot. Then, with the rasp of a zipper, the fabric was gone and he entered her in one long, smooth, hard stroke that made her thighs tremble.

If she admitted the truth, she'd been ready for him ever since he'd asked her if she minded sharing a room.

He withdrew and then impaled her again, pressing her back against the wall, moving a hand under the sweater to ruck it up and expose her breasts to his mouth. He circled a nipple with his tongue and then suckled it.

But all she could focus on was him stroking inside her, pressing her against the wall, holding her hostage to rising, cresting waves of pleasure.

"You like that, sweetheart?" he asked in a thick voice.

She nodded, then gasped as he pushed into her again.

"Say it. Say my name."

"I like it, Eric . . ."

"You want me?"

"Yes," she moaned. "Eric, I want you. Please."

He drove harder, faster. "Tell me what you like, honey."

"I like your . . ."

"You like my cock in you?"

She did. She nodded, and his eyes darkened.

"Tell me."

But the words wouldn't form on her tongue. "I'm not used to talking dirty. Or talking at all, during sex."

He laughed. "We're not talking dirty, babe. You want me to talk dirty? C'mere, nice girl." He bent his head and whispered words into her ear, filthy words about what he wanted to do to her that made her feel hot, shamed, over the edge—and so alive.

Such a contradiction that she loved the bad boy in him—the wild, no-promises *fucking*, because that was what this was—but she was equally drawn by the need she saw deep in his eyes. It was that need she sensed that got to her, that took her up ever higher.

Eric McDougal was an emotional fraud. He was lonely for connection, ripe for tenderness, longing for trust. But he was such a *man* that he couldn't admit any of that. Eric wanted entry to her in more ways than one . . . but something held him back. What was it?

Physical sensation eventually pushed rational thought aside. She let her head drop back and her legs go wide and sensation take over. Eric's hands held her bottom as if she weighed nothing, and his strength appealed to something primal in her.

He channeled his hidden need into stroking her intimately, and she found it harder and harder to catch a breath. He continued to whisper husky, sexy, sinful words into her ears, chuckling as she blushed fire.

The hot, dirty-sweet shame lapped at her, crested, built to a raging crescendo, and then rushed over her. She disintegrated with an unintelligible cry and felt Eric join her moments later. Then they slid down the wall into a boneless, sated heap.

"Welcome to Moscow, sweetheart," he said.

Twenty

McDougal drank in the sight of Natalie's naked body as she slipped from the bed and headed for the shower. She was fine boned but not thin, with curves in all the right places. Her breasts were beautifully proportioned, and her ass—God, that ass. So fine he wanted to draw it, which was a big laugh because he couldn't scratch out a stick dog to save his life.

But physical attraction wasn't even the half of it.

He didn't know what it was about Natalie that got to him, but she did. That "click" had been there again . . . that damned click. It was driving him crazy that he couldn't put his finger on it, identify it, classify it.

Natalie just seemed to understand him on a very basic level. She observed and tolerated and rolled with him. She was the only person he knew who called him by his first name. Everyone else called him by the more impersonal "McDougal," and usually he liked it that way. But the way her lips moved when she said Eric—*God*, that was sexy.

Then there was the way her breath had hitched and her eyes had gone smoky as he took her against the wall . . . her sense of humor about wearing the terrible clothes he'd picked for her . . . her storybook view of the world . . . her insistence on his decency. He still winced at that.

So wrong that she thought of him as a nice guy.

McDougal sighed and rolled toward the phone, unable to shake his guilt. He ordered an elaborate appetizer tray from room service while Natalie showered.

Then he called Miguel again to see whether he'd come up with anything on Giselle. He was having a hard time tracking down exactly who she was, and she definitely wasn't in the U.S. legally.

This time Miguel the Magician had answers. "Giselle Oblomov. Russian born with a French mother who died when she was young. Giselle ran wild at an early age, got into partying and drugs. Became essentially a mob moll for a particularly nasty branch of the Russian Mafiya. The head of it, one Pyotr Suzdal, got to the top by murdering his predecessor—not an unusual story. There appears to be only one other branch with more power than his, and it's headed up by a Vasily Somov.

"But back to Giselle Oblomov. Her father's affiliated with Suzdal's outfit, too. They're into a lot of stuff: prostitution, nightclubs, gambling, racing. Within the past couple of years, they've developed a ring of art and antiquities smugglers. They rip off jewelers, galleries, and museums with poor security, and also individuals.

"They get the hot items out of the country within hours, if they can. Then they sell them elsewhere, deposit the proceeds into legal businesses, and launder the money. Giselle Oblomov was operating in New York for them and had gotten real cozy with a restorations specialist—"

"Luc Ricard," Eric said. "The insurance company's client."

"Exactly. He not only had rich clientele who could become future marks, but he could alter items so that they wouldn't pop immediately on the international Art Loss Register. He also did a lot of international shipping of items to and from overseas clients, and Giselle apparently used that to her advantage in getting things in and out of the U.S. illegally."

"Clever girl," Eric mused.

"Yes. But get this: Ricard was found murdered just yesterday, and she's wanted for questioning in connection with his death. The cops can't find her, though. They're also looking for an employee of Ricard's who's disappeared, a Natalie Rosen."

"Interesting." McDougal chose not to mention his traveling companion.

"Anyway, if I were you, I'd stay away from this Giselle *chica*. The men in her life seem to turn up dead a lot of the time, and her buddies in the Mafiya aren't nice guys."

"Thanks, Miguel. I don't know how you find this stuff—"

A rich Cuban chuckle came from the other end of the line. "Nobody does. And believe me, we're gonna keep it that way."

"Okay, one last thing—"

"It's always one last thing with you recovery agents," Miguel mock-groused. "*Coño*, you can't find your own assholes without me."

Eric ignored the barb. "I forgot, when I asked you before about the old lady and her traveling companion—can you find out where they're staying? They'd have to have filed proof of a prebooked reservation along with their tourist visas."

"*Sí.* What are the names again?"

"Ciccoli, Tatyana, and Blakely, Theodore."

"I'll call you back in five minutes."

"*Gracias*, Miguel."

"De nada."

Natalie came out of the bathroom in a towel as he hung up, and the sight of her wet and naked reignited his lust. As she bent over her bag to find something to wear, he sidled up behind her and reached a hand under the terry cloth to grab a handful of beautiful booty.

Startled, she jumped a foot into the air and shrieked.

Eric grinned his best naughty-little-boy grin. "Sorry; couldn't resist."

"Pervert," she said with feeling.

They stood there looking at each other with that same awkward gap between them, the space between acquaintanceship and something deeper. Then McDougal tried to bridge it again with sex. He tugged at the towel.

"No," she said, but smiled to soften the word. "I just got clean. Besides, you don't get any more sex until you tell me more about yourself."

"Uh," Eric said, and shifted from foot to foot. "Well. What d'you want to know?"

"More about you, your life, your interests."

Oh, gee, what's to tell? I'm a professionally sincere liar who keeps ten different fake business cards in my wallet at any given time. I'm a thief with a permit: I spend my life hunting down stolen objects for money and occasionally get shot at or beaten up for my trouble. My interests are pretty shallow; they consist of money, motorcycles, big yachts, and women. Any further questions can be directed to my attorney.

But he couldn't say any of that. Eric cleared his throat and rubbed a hand over the back of his neck. "Well, uh. Grew up with three brothers and four sisters in upstate New York. My dad's an engineer; my mom stayed home with us. I worked my way through NYU repossessing cars and driving a snowplow."

Natalie nodded encouragingly. "What did you major in?"

"Business. But I couldn't get one of the courses I wanted sophomore year, and the only thing open was an art history class. Boy, was I pissed. Then I got in there and it was kind of cool. I ended up with a secret minor in it."

"Why secret?"

"Are you kidding me? I couldn't tell any of my buddies that I was minoring in *art history*! Not cool. Not cool at all."

"None of them found out?"

Eric scowled. "Yeah, they found out. That was a bad day for me. That's how I ended up with the Mona Lisa tattooed on my ass."

She choked. *"What?"*

He nodded. "You didn't notice?" His hands went to his fly. "I'll show you."

"Later," she said, her face turning pink. "So how did you get into the security business?"

"Oh, you know, almost by accident." The phone rang, thank God, saving him from having to manufacture any anecdotes about alarm systems or safes.

"Yeah, McD here."

"Okay, I checked. Your couple is staying at the Metropol in the Kitay-gorod district."

"Thanks, Miguel. I owe you one." Eric ended the call. "All right, Natalie—we now have your nonnie's hotel. I'm going to get through the shower and then let's see if we can track her down there."

She nodded. "Miguel is your police friend?"

"My what?" Eric said without thinking.

"Your buddy who's a cop. That's Miguel, right?"

"Right." He cursed himself for slipping up.

"You know he could get into a lot of trouble accessing that kind of information for you."

"He's careful."

She looked at Eric steadily, as if she could sense that he wasn't being straight with her. He met her gaze calmly. Then he started shedding clothing as he headed for the shower, and he knew that she noticed.

"Oh, my God!" she exclaimed, laughing. "That *is* the Mona Lisa on your—"

Eric grinned and waggled his eyebrows. "Uh-huh. Eat your heart out, Louvre: no velvet ropes, no glass, and touching not only permitted but encouraged."

"Your *friends* did that to you? How could you let them?"

"Well, it's like this. They got me so drunk I passed out. Woke up in a tattoo parlor with a guy named Bruno sticking needles in my ass. By that time, he was half done, and it kinda balanced out the headache."

* * *

The appetizers were called *zakuski* and consisted of blinis, salted fish, marinated mushrooms, rye bread, tiny pickles, sour cream, and spiced feta cheese. Eric had also ordered two bowls of borscht and a bottle of Georgian wine.

Natalie eyed the spread and chuckled. "Just like Nonnie used to serve."

"Good," Eric said, "because I don't have a clue how to eat this stuff. What do I do, make a mushroom and pickle sandwich?"

"You can mix some mushrooms with sour cream and spread them on a blini. Or you can spread sour cream on the rye and put fish on top. Or you can eat things however you want to eat them."

Eric poured them each some wine and handed Natalie's glass to her. "Cheers," he said. "To our arrival in Moscow."

Natalie clinked his goblet with her own. "Cheers. Now, why don't you tell me the truth about why you're here."

Eric froze with a blini halfway to his mouth. "What do you mean, the truth? I thought we went over all of this before we left New York. You don't speak Russian or read Cyrillic, and there are thugs breaking into your apartment and killing people around you."

Natalie took a sip of wine, held it on her tongue, and evaluated him, much as she had earlier. "Eric. Come on. There's something you're not telling me."

"What do you want to know?" he countered.

"You're able, just like that, to take off from your job. You organized our visas faster than I can order Chinese takeout. You have a mysterious friend in the 'police department' who feeds you privileged information. Not to be ungrateful for the ticket or your company, but what aren't you telling me? If there's one thing I hate, it's being lied to."

"Look, my job is essentially in outside sales. I work purely on commission. I travel internationally all the time on . . . uh . . . consulting jobs. And I really do have weeks of vacation due me. That's it—I swear."

"Eric, if you work for the FBI or CIA or something, it's okay. You can trust me."

He opened his mouth and then closed it again.

Clearly, she was on to something. Was this his secret? She waited.

He stood up and took his wine over to the window, where he looked out at the city. "It's not a matter of me trusting you, Natalie. Please understand that, okay? Let's just say that you have good instincts. But I am not at liberty to tell you who I work for."

She'd known it. He was some kind of government agent. Some kind of spook. "So that business card you showed me—"

"Is a cover."

"Is your name really Eric McDougal?"

He paused. "Yes."

"But that could change? Or does change occasionally?"

"Yes." He swallowed a large mouthful of wine.

"Do you ever wear . . . disguises?"

"The answer to that question is yes, too."

She took a deep breath. "So is Miguel really a cop?"

"No. And that truly is all I can tell you."

"One more question, please."

"You can ask," he said in noncommittal tones.

"Why are you here? Does it have to do with this Russian smuggling operation?"

He nodded.

"Or does it have to do with me?"

He nodded again.

She threw up a hand and drank some wine. "Well, thanks. Don't elaborate or anything. It might kill you. Or is it me you'd have to kill, if you told me?"

He lifted an eyebrow and his mouth relaxed into that wicked grin of his. "Yeah, slowly. Death by fornication."

"Oh, good. I've traveled halfway across the world with a *wisecracking* international man of mystery."

"Sure beats traveling halfway across the world with a boring, humorless international man of mystery, right?"

"I don't know about that."

"C'mon . . . we wisecrackers are so unappreciated. We're better than animal crackers, Florida crackers, and firecrackers put together."

Natalie groaned. Then she said, "You missed Christmas crackers."

"Did I? Gross negligence! Report it to the federal government."

"Aha. So you *do* work for the government."

"Do I?"

Natalie curled her fingers into fists. "Can I kill you now, or should I wait until you're asleep?"

Eric laughed again and came over to kiss her. "Unfortunately for you, we international men of mystery always sleep with one eye open. Now, if you're done peppering me with questions, can we eat? Then let's go find your grandmother."

Twenty-one

The Savoy wasn't far at all from the Metropol, as both hotels were located in the Red Square/Kitay-gorod area of Moscow, the city center. All Natalie and Eric had to do was walk several blocks down the quiet Ulitsa Rozhdestvenka to the bustling Teatralnyy Proezd and turn left.

The Savoy was elegant, but the Metropol took interior design to a whole new level. It was stupendously lavish, full of mosaics and stained glass, and gilded to within an inch of its life.

Eric enjoyed the awe on Natalie's face.

"Nonnie's staying here?" she said in hushed tones.

"It appears so."

But appearances, it seemed, could be deceiving. In terrible, stilted Russian that made Natalie smile even as the hotel staff nodded encouragingly, Eric asked for Mrs. Ciccoli and Colonel Blakely.

The man behind the registration desk checked his computer, nodded, and then frowned. "I'm sorry," he said in English, "but madam and the colonel have checked out. Only hours ago."

Frustrated, Eric ran a hand over the back of his neck. "Do you know where they've gone? Were they leaving town?"

"I do not know. Though I believe that they were staying in Moscow, because the gentleman carried a guide book to the city."

"Do you have any idea why they changed hotels?"

"Our service and facilities are impeccable," said the staffer, his chin rising.

"Of course, of course." Eric shot him a winning smile. "The Metropol is one of the best hotels in Moscow. Which is why I'm puzzled as to why they would leave. Did they feel they were being followed? Were they trying to avoid someone?"

The staffer averted his eyes from Eric's gaze and looked uncomfortable. Eric realized that he thought the older couple might be trying to avoid *them*. It did make sense, ironically.

They wouldn't get anything more out of the man. "Look," Eric said, sliding the equivalent of a hundred dollars in rubles to him, "if you happen to see them again, will you have them contact us at the Savoy? We'll be there for the next couple of days."

The money disappeared under the guy's palm and he nodded.

"Thank you for your help."

When they got outside, Natalie stuffed her hands into her coat pockets and blew out her breath. "What now? How do we find two elderly tourists in a city of ten million people?"

Eric shook his head. Miguel would shoot him if he asked the poor guy to hack into the databases of every hotel in Moscow. And rightly so. Miguel had his contacts and shortcuts in the States, but Eric doubted that he had many buddies in Russia.

"What kind of place would your grandmother want to stay in? And where, besides this mystery cathedral, would she go? What would she want to see? Does she still have friends here that she'd want to visit?"

"Nonnie's not fancy. She's cultured, but she's not a luxury lover. That's why I was surprised that she'd stay at the Metropol. My guess is that the colonel chose that. Nonnie would be more comfortable in a two- or three-star hotel." Natalie paused, thinking.

"She'd want to see her old neighborhood. She'd want to visit any important sites that have to do with St. George. And there *is* an old friend that she talks to every month or two. He's a retired professor at Moscow State University. She would definitely go to see him. If only I could remember his name."

"Does she call him, or does he call her?" Eric asked.

"He calls—she has a hard time dialing the phone because of her eyesight. And I think he calls on the university's dime. He still has a small office there, for research purposes. They let him keep it in exchange for the occasional lecture."

"If he calls her, I can have Miguel check the phone records and get us the number. From that we may be able to get a name—though the number will be registered to the university itself."

Natalie gave him an enigmatic look. "You know, sometimes it's very convenient to be traveling with an international man of mystery. One with sinister connections."

Eric snorted. "Nothing sinister about Miguel. He's a young Republican with designer pecs and flashy taste in watches, cars, and women. His girlfriend, Maribel? She's the type that makes men walk into telephone poles just trying to get a good look."

"I pictured Miguel as a frizzy-haired, four-eyed nerd in floodwater pants, high-tops, and an old Rush T-shirt."

"Not in Miami. Very fashion conscious, is Miami."

"Oh. Well, they probably would deny me a license to live there, then. Especially right now." She looked ruefully down at her mismatched clothing.

"I promised to take you shopping, didn't I?"

"You don't need to take me shopping."

"Yeah, I do. This street-vagrant chic you got going, it's bad for my image." He ducked, smirking, as she swung at him.

The March day was sunny and clear, the sky turquoise and naked of clouds. The temperature was in the mid-forties, cold but not achingly so.

It was an absolutely gorgeous day to be walking around. Natalie looked beautiful and utterly dorky at the same time, in the running shoes, the too-long jeans she'd rolled at the ankles, and the three-quarter-length coat. He grinned, then pictured her in the coat and the track shoes and nothing else. The grin segued into a deep chuckle, and he impulsively took her hand.

They'd gone three blocks before he realized that (a) they hadn't decided on a destination and (b) he, McDougal, did not hold women's hands. He patted their asses. He nibbled on their necks, among other things. He pleasured them while they flopped around like orgasmic fish in his bed.

But holding hands? That was for old, sappy Beatles songs. He might as well move into a yellow submarine, for chrissakes.

Yet Natalie looked delighted and had woven her fingers into his. It seemed a little rude to pull away now and—what? Give her a friendly punch on the shoulder?

"So where the hell are we going, Natalie?" Eric asked, actively plotting now to disengage his hand. He could point at something. Or sneeze, which required covering his mouth. Or smooth some hair out of her face.

He opted for the last choice, which seemed the gentlest. He pulled his hand away and used three fingers to comb a few strands of her hair back. Then he tucked them behind her ear.

She leaned into the gesture like a cat and tilted her head back so that he fell into those navy eyes of hers. He stumbled over the tiny freckles on her nose and the way her lower lip got puffier right in the center, like a provocative little bolster pillow.

He kissed her, and a passing woman put a hand to her heart and sighed.

Yeah, that's me, lady. Poster child for romance.

But he lost his cynical edge in the sweetness of Natalie's mouth and the surprising tenderness that crept over her expression. He loved that it was for him. But it also scared the piss out of him.

He raised his head and tried to get his bearings again. That was when he saw the photographer, who immediately turned and ducked into the crowd when he realized that he'd been seen.

"Hey!" McDougal shouted. He started after the guy,

crossing the street and leaving Natalie standing on the sidewalk, staring. "Hey!" But the portly little man was fast on his feet. Eric started pushing through the crowd, but the man had disappeared.

He looked back to see Natalie stepping into the street to follow him. Then a motor gunned and an old Volvo veered sharply around the corner. It screeched to a halt, and a burly man with blond hair erupted from the passenger seat to grab Natalie.

As the guy opened the rear door and shoved her inside the vehicle, Eric sprang into action, but he had no hope of reaching her side of the car before it sped away. So instead he focused on the driver, whose attention was on the rearview mirror. He wrenched open the door and grabbed him around the throat with his left arm. In the next instant, he had his perfectly ordinary, stainless-steel pen gripped in his right fist, poised to stab it into the man's jugular.

"Let her go, or you're dead," Eric said. He shouted it again at the second man. "I will kill him." The driver struggled, tried to break the grip at his neck, but McDougal hadn't sweated his guts out with Cato, ARTemis's trainer, for nothing.

The driver tried stepping on the gas, but the car was a standard and it wasn't in gear.

In the meantime, passersby had started to gather and stare. Natalie screamed, kicked, and fought to get free from the other man. A couple of tall, athletic-looking guys exchanged glances and then stepped in to help.

The driver said something that Eric didn't understand, but it must have been the equivalent of "we have to get out of here; let her go." Because the burly man suddenly ejected Natalie, feet first, from the car. She stumbled forward, into one of the athletic guys, who caught her and stopped her from falling to the pavement.

Satisfied that she was safe, Eric released the driver, who spat curses at him while slamming the car into gear. The Volvo shot forward like a four-doored rocket.

Eric stood robotic in the street for a moment, gripping his pen as if it were a spear. Then he ran to Natalie.

"Are you okay? Jesus, Joseph, and Mary, that was close."

The athletic guy had set her on her feet and was asking the same question in Russian.

"I'm fine," she said shakily. But the pulse at her throat throbbed as if someone was in there with a sledgehammer.

The Russian's friend said in English, "You are very lucky that those men didn't have guns."

True. But McDougal didn't want Natalie any more scared than she already was. He shot the guy a meaningful stare and said, "Thank you for helping."

He caught on fast. "Eh," he said to Natalie, chuckling, "you are also lucky that Mikhail did not head-butt you back into car. He is not used to using hands, you see. He is professional soccer player."

Natalie gave him a weak smile. "Thank you so much," she said to Mikhail, who nodded.

"I am Ivan," the English-speaking one said.

Mikhail said something in Russian.

"No, not Ivan the Terrible," Ivan retorted. "He is comedian as well as soccer player. He refers to sixteenth-century Russian czar who killed his own son."

Eric stuck out his hand. "Eric McDougal. And this is

Natalie Rosen. Really, we can't thank you enough. Who do you think those guys were?"

The two Russians exchanged another significant glance. Then Ivan shrugged. "Mob. You may have heard—it is very bad here. You want to call *militsya*? The police?"

"No," Natalie said quickly.

"We can give license plate numbers. You want to go to American embassy?"

Eric shook his head. "We'll be fine. Thank you."

Ivan eyed him shrewdly, then pulled a scrap of paper out of his pocket. "You will allow me to borrow your very, ah, how you say, *dangerous* pen?"

Eric gave it to him, and he wrote down two numbers. Then he gave the paper and the pen back to Eric.

"The first is license plate of car, yes? The second is my telephone. You need witness or help—or good Mongolian barbecue—you call. I have restaurant."

"You're very kind." Natalie took a step forward and kissed him on the cheek.

"Ah, for this, you eat my restaurant for free!" He enthusiastically kissed both *her* cheeks, and she blushed, to McDougal's unaccountable annoyance.

"Okay, enough already," he muttered.

Mikhail grinned at him and spoke Russian to Ivan, who backed off. "We make apologies that you have bad experience in Moscow, eh? Most Russians, we very, how you say? Hospitable, yes?" He blithely ignored the fact that Americans weren't at all popular in his country.

But Eric and Natalie nodded, and they all said their good-byes. He took her hand and held tightly to it as they walked away, with no thoughts whatsoever of trying to disengage. Instead, he wanted with every fiber of his being to protect her from harm.

"What I don't understand," he said, "is why that guy would be taking photos of us one second, and two other guys try to grab you the next second."

"You think they're related incidents?" she asked.

"No, I don't. That's what's bothering me. We're being tracked by two different people or organizations, and I don't like it. I don't like it at all."

Twenty-two

"Kelso wishes to know when the wedding is," Liam said to Avy when he looked up from his iPhone.

"Why is *my* boss e-mailing *you*? Especially when I haven't heard from him in at least a week."

"You know Kelso and I are old chums, my love. And you're frightfully competent at your job, so why should he feel the need to e-mail you?"

Avy twisted her long brown hair into a knot on her head and secured it with a pencil. Then she fixed her fiancé with an implacable stare. "Don't tell me. It's Kelso who's put you up to this whole kidnapping thing."

Liam deliberately focused on the screen of the iPhone and began to whistle. When he looked up, Avy was stepping out of her panties and twirling them around on her index finger. "Liam? Cutie-pie? If you'd like to have sex with me anytime in the next five years, you're going to put down the crackberry and tell me exactly how this whole plot came about and whether or not my boss is behind it." She blew him a kiss. "'Kay?"

Before he could respond, the panties hit him in the mouth.

He stared at her long, tanned, muscular legs. She wore high-heeled black pumps, a black leather miniskirt, and a tailored jacket.

Liam licked his lips and meekly put down the iPhone. "Where would you like me to start?"

Avy sat down in a straight-backed chair that faced him, smiled sweetly, and pulled a classic Sharon Stone maneuver before crossing her legs.

Liam's eyes glazed over. "Right. How about if I start at the beginning, then, my love?"

She nodded.

"A couple of days ago, Kelso got in touch. He told me that ARTemis is working on tracking down a very valuable necklace that used to belong to Catherine the Great. This necklace was stolen from a restoration specialist in Manhattan, and the specialist's insurer had engaged your red-haired colleague to find it."

"McManWhore," Avy said, nodding.

"I beg your pardon?"

"Just a nickname we gave him. He's quite the ladies' man. I'm actually amazed that he's back on the job this soon. He took quite a beating recently."

"Ah. Well, at any rate, ARTemis got a second call, this one from an old gentleman in Moscow who, quite curiously, claims that the same necklace was stolen from his safe. And he, too, would like to engage ARTemis to hunt it down."

"Kelso smelled a rat," said Avy.

"Precisely. The old man's accent held traces of German, even though he professed to be Russian, and so our Kelso toddled off to do a spot of research. He found that there've been rumors swirling around this Oleg Litsky for years, the gist of which are that he's a Nazi war criminal with the blood of hundreds on his hands."

"Knowing Kelso, he tapped into his vast network of international contacts." Avy uncrossed and recrossed her legs, which resulted in great distraction for poor Liam. He quite lost the thread of his narrative.

"Liam!"

"Yes, my love?"

"Focus."

"Oh, but I was, my darling." He smirked evilly.

She glowered at him.

"Right. Kelso has indeed poked around and substantiated the rumors. Which leads us to right here and right now. You and I, my sweet, are about to pay Litsky a formal visit to discuss just what ARTemis can do for him."

"Oh, we are? How professional of us."

"Indeed." He beamed at her. "Though you might wish to put those back on." He pointed at the panties, which lay on the floor.

"You think?"

"I think." Liam nodded. "Unless you aim to give the gentleman a heart attack."

"And just how are we going to get him out of his house, Liam?"

"I thought you'd never ask." Liam's expression changed to one of gravity, even sorrow. "Our poor Mr. Litsky, you see, is eighty-two years old, and at that age, almost any medical emergency can arise. One will, thanks to the syringe in my pocket. Or, come to think of it, maybe you *should* leave your panties here?"

"I don't think so. What if he takes Viagra and gets a boner instead of a heart attack?"

"I should *not* like that," Liam said.

"Funny; me, neither. Let's use the syringe."

"Quite so. You and I will then call an 'ambulance' immediately, and he will leave his home on a stretcher. The ambulance will go not to the hospital, however, but directly to a small airfield."

"So we're going to airlift him out of there?"

Liam's lips twitched, and all sorrow dissipated from his aristocratic features. "Oh, not exactly, my love. Not exactly."

"Tell you what," said Avy. "You can fill me in on the details later, after you assure me that you understand something very clearly."

"And what might that be, my sweet?"

She gritted her teeth. "The next time you make plans involving *me* and *my* company with *my* boss behind *my* back, I will break every bone in *your* high-handed, low-minded, aristocratic body. And then I will turn you over to my U.S. Marshal dad, who has definitely not given up his search for us and could be in Moscow as we speak. Do you read me?"

"Yes, Commander Hunt, I do. Like a very sexy book."

Twenty-three

Moscow State University was a little way outside the city, in an area called Sparrow Hills, or Vorobyovy gory. The university was housed in a massive, thirty-six-story Stalinist-Gothic building that had been completed in 1959.

After several evasive maneuvers to lose the men tailing them, Tatyana and the colonel succeeded and arrived at the university. There they found the history department and knocked on the office door of her old friend Professor Dmitri Prokofiev. A gaunt, stoop-shouldered man with a thin mop of gray hair, he embraced Tatyana warmly and shook hands with Colonel Blakely.

"Tell me, Ted, what the professor looks like after all these years," Tatyana said. "He's thin; I can feel that. And"—she chuckled—"you smell of pickled herring, Dmitri."

He kissed her cheeks. "But yes, my favorite cologne."

"What does he look like?" Ted mused. "Well, it all depends on whether or not he's an old flame."

"Yes," claimed Dmitri.

"No, no," Tatyana said, feeling herself blush like a schoolgirl.

"Well," said the colonel. "This rival of mine, this Dmitri character—you must understand that he has only one tooth left in his mouth, and a rotten one at that."

"Eh?" Dmitri said, clearly startled.

"He's bald as an egg, too . . . and pulls his pants up to his armpits."

The professor burst out laughing. "This is not true, my dear Tatyana!"

"Ted!" She reached out, found the colonel's arm, and lightly smacked it.

"Well, I'm just trying to make sure you don't ditch me for him," Blakely teased her.

"Dmitri, pay no attention to him. *You* tell me what you look like. All right?"

"Yes, yes, much better. I am, of course, six and a half feet tall, with full head of yellow hair, square jaw, many very white teeth. I have the big shoulders, yes? And the wash-machine stomach. All the women in Moscow, they desire me."

"You're filthy liars, both of you!" Tatyana said as the professor guided her to a chair. The two men laughed.

They chatted about the trip, about the changes in Moscow since she'd left, and about current events. Then a lull came in the conversation, and Tatyana said, "I need to show you something, Dmitri. I need your help."

"Of course."

She nodded at Ted, and he pulled the strange key from his pocket. Especially since they were being followed, they hadn't wanted to risk her purse being stolen. The necklace was locked in the hotel's main safe.

Ted handed the key to Dmitri, who found his reading glasses on his desk, put them on, and then bent to examine it. "It appears to be some sort of safety-deposit-box key," he said.

"Yes, but do you have any idea which bank it's from?"

Dmitri peered at it again and pursed his lips, turning it over in his hands. He clucked softly like a Slavic hen, then whistled. He then clucked again as he turned to his computer and pulled up the Internet. He typed something in using Cyrillic letters and waited for a moment. He nodded.

Smiling, Dmitri turned his monitor so that Ted could see it. Ted compared the logo on the screen to the one on the key. "I think you may be right. It looks like part of the SovBank design."

"Is medium to big bank; three locations in Moscow," Dmitri said, tapping the addresses noted on the screen.

"Which location should we go to?"

"Central," said Dmitri decisively. "Will have boxes at central, most likely. Bolshaya Dmitrovka Street." He frowned. "But you will not be allowed access without proper identification, you know this? Even with key."

Ted leaned back and crossed his foot over the opposite knee. "Ah, but this is where years of government bureaucracy come in handy. All we need is a convincing-looking power of attorney."

"Dmitri, do you know of an attorney who could help us?"

The professor looked disapproving. "Tatyana, this is not ethical."

"I understand your reluctance," she said. "But was it ethical of that Nazi officer to shoot my father in front of his wife and children? Was it ethical of the officer to steal our belongings?" Her voice rose. "Was it *ethical*, Dmitri, for my mother to be violated or for her to starve to death in a concentration camp?"

She lapsed into Russian, the words tumbling from her now-trembling mouth. "Don't talk to me about the ethics of this!"

"But, Tatyana, the box may not be that officer's. You understand? He perhaps sold the necklace to someone else."

"I don't care," she said bitterly. "I have to look."

"He is probably living under assumed name. You cannot get blank power of attorney. You see?"

Tears from her impaired old eyes began to pour down her face. "Help me, Dmitri," she begged. "Please. You know it is the right thing to do, even if the methods are wrong."

He stood, went to her, and took her hands. "Is okay, Tatyana. Is more simple than you think, hmm?"

"Is it? What can we do?"

He cast a speaking glance at Ted and rubbed his thumb against his index and middle fingers.

Light dawned across Ted's face. "Of course," he said. "Tatyana, we don't need a forged power of attorney. All we need is cold, hard cash delivered to a susceptible bank employee."

"Everyone," Dmitri said, a trifle embarrassed, "take the bribe in Moscow."

* * *

Natalie clung to Eric's hand, acutely conscious of each step she took on solid ground. There was nothing like being grabbed by a complete stranger and tossed around like a sack of oranges to make one appreciate liberty and autonomy.

What frightened her was how easy it had been for the thug to snatch an adult woman off the street. He'd stolen her as easily as someone else might pocket a package of beef in the grocery store, and God alone knew what he might have done to her.

She felt jittery, as if she'd just inhaled a tank of helium. She knew it was still adrenaline from the incident coursing through her system, but she literally feared that if she let go of Eric's hand, her body might defy gravity and rise up into the clouds like a woman-shaped balloon.

"So you think two different people are after us?" she asked. "Obviously our Russian Mafiya friends are, but who else?"

Eric's expression was taut and grim, his eyes shuttered. He shook his head. "Like I said, I don't know. But what happened back there was way too damned close for comfort. I want you to stay in the hotel from now on."

She tried to pull her hand out of his, but he'd laced their fingers together, and he refused to loosen his grip. If anything, he tightened it. "Stay in the hotel? And not find my grandmother or see anything of Moscow? You've got to be kidding me, Eric."

He stopped and turned to face her. "Do I look like I'm kidding?"

His eyes glittered an icy, sapphire-saturated blue. You could break rocks on that jaw and those cheekbones. The area just around his sensual, mocking mouth had turned white with rage. He looked intimidating, dangerous, and vengeful.

She shivered, and it hit her with full force that she did not know who this man was, not at all. He showed her the face that he wanted her to see. He turned charm on and off like a tap. But what was behind the charm and the sensuous sexual appetite? Did he look like he was kidding? No. No, he most certainly did not.

"Eric," she said carefully, "I'm not going to stay locked in a room for the next few days. That is not on my agenda."

He dropped her hand and took her by the shoulders, his fingers digging painfully into her flesh. "Is it on your agenda to be kidnapped? Is it on your friggin' *agenda* to be killed? Which part of what happened back there do you not understand, Natalie? Huh?"

"You are hurting me," she said in cold, clear tones.

He released her immediately, but his furious face was still inches from hers.

"Why are you angry?" she demanded. "And at *me*? Do you think I put on a sandwich board that said, 'Attention, thugs, please kidnap me!' Well, I didn't. So back off, buddy."

He stood there staring at her for a long moment. Then he scrubbed his hands over his face. "I'm sorry. I'm not angry with you, babe. I'm angry with myself. For leaving you at risk and unprotected like that."

"Eric—"

"When I looked across the street and that guy had

you, I dunno, Natalie. I freaked. For the first time in my life, I was . . . scared. No, scratch that—I was heart-in-my-throat terrified. Beyond all reason."

"It's okay," she said.

"No. No, it's not okay. I need to tell you this. Look, I don't do fear. A guy like me, it's not part of my vocabulary. You page to the F in the McDougal index, kiddo, and you'll see maybe three words: *fast*, *fuck*, and *fun*. But *fear*? No way."

"I get it."

"No, you don't." Eric looked at her and shook his head. "Because *I* don't get it. All I know is it made me mad to be afraid. But none of any of this is your fault. So again, I'm sorry."

He looked so miserable that she stood on tiptoe, reached up, and kissed him. He wrapped his arms around her and held her close, so close that she could barely breathe.

"I would have killed that man," he said, in bemused tones.

"What?"

"The driver. I would have torn open his throat without a second thought." He drank deeply of the cold, clear air as if to cleanse himself. Then he shook his head.

"It was self-defense, Eric. A normal response to being attacked." She'd laid her head on his chest, and his heart beat against her ear.

"No. This wasn't about self-defense, Natalie. I'm not sure exactly what it was about, but it was something primal. Something that came from a deep, dark place that I don't think I want to visit again anytime soon."

Eric took her hand in his once again and held on a little too tight.

But Natalie liked it. "I don't care what you say, Eric McDougal. You just saved my life—and that makes you a hero."

An expression of deep discomfort crossed his face. "Don't call me that."

"I will," Natalie said mulishly. "I *will.*"

Twenty-four

McDougal hated authority almost as much as he hated fear, but it was easier to hate authority because it was always external. Fear came from inside, from some hidden, filthy, primordial place in the bowels. Authority, however, usually came from an open and irritating location: the mouth of a boss.

Unfortunately, he had no choice now but to check in with Avy. He'd drop dead before asking for help on his own account, but today's incident with Natalie had illustrated for him in full color that he had to ask for help in order to protect her. He could risk his own life guilt free, but not hers.

Calling Avy was akin to shrinking his balls in a hot dryer, but it would soothe his own fears for Natalie's safety, so he'd suck it up. In the great scheme of things, Natalie's life was more important than his own pride.

Shocking, but true.

Once they were back at the hotel, McDougal told Natalie that he had to make a private business call and stepped out of the room. He grimaced and cracked his neck before hitting the speed-dial number for his boss.

He didn't dislike Avy, exactly . . . but there was the inevitable head butting between two highly intelligent, rebellious, and competitive personalities.

Not to mention the perplexing fact that Avy was, and always had been, utterly impervious to both his looks and his charm. And, okay, maybe the fact that she'd out-earned him for the past couple of years got under his skin a little bit.

Avy was like another bossy, annoying older sister, and he didn't relish explaining what was going on to her.

"McManWhore," she said, by way of a greeting. "What's up? How's the noggin?"

He had been jumped and knocked unconscious recently by one of their own people, a rogue agent who was now in jail awaiting trial. "My head's as hard as they come, Avy. You know that."

"I'm glad. So to what do I owe the pleasure of this phone call?"

"I'm in Moscow."

Pause. "Are you? Why?"

"Following a strong lead. And you're here, too. Don't bother denying it—Gwen told me."

"Let me guess. Our Gwennie is worried and asked you to check up on me."

"Something like that."

"Well, you can tell her that I'm fine."

"Will do, Ave, but there's something else we need to cover. You know that I'm on the hunt for the St. George necklace, right? The one that used to belong to Catherine the Great."

"Yeah. Why?"

Damn, but he hated doing this. "Look, I'm going to

need some backup. I seem to have the Russian Mafiya on my tail, and they've left at least one dead body in their wake. I'm also worried that they may come after a source of mine."

After an appalled silence, Avy whistled, long and low. "McDougal, we don't need this kind of trouble. You don't need it personally, and ARTemis sure as hell doesn't need it on a corporate level."

"I agree, believe me, but I'm already in it, and up to the neck. They were on the source's trail in the U.S., which was bad enough, but now somehow they've found u—" Christ! He'd almost said *us*. The last thing he wanted to do was let Avy know that he was here with Natalie.

"Now somehow they've found me here in Moscow," he continued. "I had an unpleasant incident this morning, a little matter of being narrowly missed by a car."

"A car almost ran you over? But you don't have the piece yet. That doesn't make any sense," Avy said.

"I didn't know the Mafiya was required to make sense."

"Funny. What else?"

"Okay . . . what else is that not only do I have these Russian thugs after me, but someone entirely different was taking photographs on the street."

"It's 'cause you're such a stud muffin, McDougal."

"No. Trust me, these pictures were not meant for a caviar advertisement. I'm being double-teamed."

"Okay, look. I can give you some insight into the photographer. He may have been hired by an old man here in Moscow who claims the St. George necklace was stolen from *him*."

"What? But the necklace was stolen from a restoration outfit in Manhattan, and the care and custody policy was written through Hiscox. So how would he know that I'm on the trail?"

"You tell me. What have you been up to? Is this source of yours pretty and female? Did you bring her with you to Moscow?"

He didn't say a word.

"Okay, play coy, but do the math, McDougal. Seems likely that the Russians stole the necklace from the old man, funneled it to New York, and then someone else stole it from the restoration outfit."

"And in the meantime, the Russkies had faked a provenance on the insurance paperwork," Eric murmured.

"Yeah. Happens all the time—you know it and I know it. Listen," Avy said brusquely. "I want you off this case."

"Excuse me? No, I—"

"This isn't up for debate, McDougal. Drop the case. We do not need the Russian mob after us. That's a problem that I doubt even Kelso could solve."

"But I'm so close that I can practically reach out and touch the damned necklace. Come on, Avy. Don't overreact, here. You weren't this worried when you knew the Greek mob was after you."

"That's different."

"Oh, yeah? How?"

She muttered something under her breath. "I'm not having you killed for this thing, understand? We may not always see eye to eye, Eric, but I'm still kind of fond of your tattooed ass."

He winced. "How the hell do you know about *that*?"

Avy laughed. "Sheila."

"And how does *she* know?"

"She probably talked to one of your bimbos. Maybe your mysterious 'source.' You'll have to ask her. Anyway. Go tour a vodka factory and then go home and get a different assignment, McDougal. I'll deal with the insurer."

"Damn it, Avy—"

Her voice changed from friendly to frigid in milliseconds. "You want to cuss and argue with me, or you want to hang on to your job?"

"Fine." Disgusted, he ended the call. This was what he got for asking for help and keeping his boss in the loop: thrown off the case. And what galled him even more was that unless he ditched Natalie, his quitting the case wouldn't do any good. He had a bull's-eye on his forehead, and they wouldn't stop until they hit the target.

Avy wasn't stupid. She'd sensed that he'd been carefully editing what he told her. And she was ordering him to distance himself from the Mafiya's real target, even if she didn't know precisely who it was.

A smart man would do exactly as she said. A smart man wouldn't jeopardize his job or his life. But McDougal had been steadily losing brain power since he set out to get Natalie drunk in Reif's. He felt responsible for her.

Walk away now and leave her defenseless against the mob in a foreign city halfway across the world? He couldn't do it. Besides, that necklace was going to finance his deepwater fishing boat.

Drop the case, McDougal. Avy's voice echoed in his ears.

Screw that. He came from a long line of Scots-Irish rebels; he was a born management problem and damn proud of it.

So the first thing he did was to call ARTemis's *other*

management problem, so that she could arrange for him to pick up a gun at a prearranged dead drop.

Sheila was filing her inch-long acrylic nails, admiring her new diamond tennis bracelet from Sid Thresher, and wondering just how she'd explain it to Marty when the phone rang again.

"Ahtemis, how may I help you?" she said, for at least the forty-ninth time that day. God, it was killing her to be polite to the agents—and Avy had actually asked her if she was feeling all right.

Sheila turned her wrist so that the diamonds in the bracelet sparkled under the office's fluorescent lighting. Was the bauble worth it?

Does a bear shit in the woods, Sheila Ann? Of course it's worth it.

Sid's voice rasped in her ear. "Are you wearin' any knickers today, luv?"

"Wouldn't you like to know," she said saucily.

"I would indeed, gorgeous. Give old Siddie a wee hint, now, will ye? The Big Banger, 'e's ready to play, 'e is."

"Fine. I'm wearing pink-and-black lace, crotchless panties."

"Ooooooooohhhhh," Sid moaned. "Crotchless, are they?"

"Uh-huh." Sheila rolled her eyes and then looked at her watch. But it was only a Seiko, and she aspired to a Rolex. So she made her voice a little more husky and whispered, "I wanna lick the Big Banger, baby."

"Do you?" Sid's breathing quickened. "Tell me more. What else would ye like to do, luv?"

"I want to slide it right into my mouth." He moaned again, and she yawned.

"And run my tongue in slow circles over the tip—"

"Aw, Jesus, enough already," McDougal's voice cut in. "That's disgusting."

"*Aaaahhhhh!*" Sheila yelled. "I'll kill you myself, McDougal. I swear I will!"

"Do you know how many places the Big Banger has been? He's done easily thousands of women, and probably men, goats, and chickens—every barnyard animal under the sun."

"I'm gonna choke you with my bare hands—"

"And you have the nerve to ask me if *my* thingy has turned black and fallen off?"

"And then smear you with Alpo—"

"You'd have to gargle with hydrochloric acid to kill all the diseases infesting one inch of the Big Banger . . ."

"—and feed you to my dogs!"

". . . and then you'd need to swallow it, unless you spit with Sid, in which case it's too late for the rest of the planet, thank you very much."

"If you think that I would actually come within ten feet of that man's naked *anything*, you are dumber than a box of rocks, McDougal."

"Then you're just marginally smarter than one, old bag. So what's he paying you to talk dirty to him?"

"Nothing!"

"Sheila, your nose is growing faster than Sid's Big Banger at the sound of your voice."

Suddenly she had a horrifying thought. "Did you tape-record me?"

"Wouldn't you like to know," Eric said, stealing one of her lines.

"Yes, I would, you dirtbag!"

He dropped back into Sid's cockney accent, well-known to the world from overexposure on MTV. "Should I give old Sheila a wee hint, now? Should I? My Sony cassette recorder, it was ready to play . . . Do you wanna lick it?" He dissolved into helpless bellows of laughter.

"Don't think I won't get even, McDougal," she promised.

"For God's sake, woman! At least get yourself a cell phone so you're not using the ARTemis business line."

"So you called for a reason, right? What do you want, jerk?"

"Hey, where's that courtesy I requested?"

"What d'you want, *Mr.* Jerk?"

"I need a standard-issue Glock, left at dead drop seven in Moscow. Okay?"

"Did you really tape-record me?"

"Promise to get me that Glock within twelve hours?"

"Yeah. So did you?"

"No. Who owns a cassette recorder these days? You're dating yourself, Sheila—"

She opened her mouth to hurl an insult at him, but he preempted her.

"—which is only marginally better than dating Sid!" And he ended the connection.

Sheila snarled at the receiver before hurling it back into the cradle. She should have a water gun left at that dead drop, not a Glock.

Twenty-five

Colonel Blakely flipped through the photographs that the portly little man had brought to him at their new hotel, the Sovietsky. "These are the people who asked about us at the Metropol Hotel? You followed them?"

"Yes."

A tall, good-looking man with blue eyes, reddish gold hair, and an air of supreme confidence strolled hand in hand with a pretty, diminutive brunette who had the fashion sense of a ragpicker. She looked vaguely familiar, but he couldn't quite place her. Then it came to him.

He'd seen the girl standing in Tatyana's kitchen. She'd served him tea on a couple of occasions. She was Tatyana's granddaughter! What was she doing in Moscow?

"You recognize?" the photographer asked Ted curiously.

He nodded and reached into his pocket for his wallet. "How much?"

The man named a sum that was predictably outrageous, and Ted paid him. "Thank you."

"Fyodor at Metropol, he say these couple staying at

Savoy, eh?" With a polite and very satisfied smile, the portly man exited the lobby, and Ted went upstairs to talk to Tatyana about this latest odd development in her quest.

"Ted?" she queried as he let himself into the room.

"Yes, it's me." He sat on one of the two twin beds they'd requested, just as she got up.

"Are you ready to go to the bank? I exchanged more money, so I think I have enough for the bribe."

"About that, Tatyana—it's going to be tricky. We have to choose the right person, and it will be pure guesswork."

"I realize this."

The colonel hesitated. "The photographer that the clerk at the Metropol engaged for us—he just brought me some pictures." The call from the lobby had come while she was in the bathroom.

She stilled. "Yes? You have seen who is following us?" Her hands shook a little.

"I believe it's your granddaughter—"

"Natalie? Here?" she asked incredulously.

"—and a boyfriend."

"She doesn't have a boyfriend."

Ted looked down at the photo of the unknown man kissing the girl, and cleared his throat. "I think you may be mistaken about that. Our children and our grandchildren don't always tell us things that they don't wish us to know."

Tatyana got up and then sat down again, clearly agitated and not knowing what to do with herself. "Natalie *can't* have come here! How?"

He shook his head. "It's hard to say."

"She's come for the necklace. She'll want it back, and I cannot give it to her, Ted."

"Perhaps you'd better explain to me exactly how you found the necklace."

Finally, Tatyana told him the whole story, while he sat there, frowning.

"But what about the consequences to her and her career, Tatyana?"

"I know you must think I'm a dreadfully selfish old woman," she said. "But what I'm doing is for her, too. For her heritage. The necklace works in mysterious ways: It didn't turn up after all these years by accident. It has surfaced just as my mother told me it would, so that I can pass it and our family belongings on to the next generation.

"I'm sorry, but I think that's more important than any silly job. Besides, they didn't treat her properly there. She worked in an attic on planks set on top of sawhorses! Can you imagine?"

"But what if they prosecute her? She could go to jail."

Tatyana's mouth set mulishly. "Nonsense. Those people, whoever they are, did not come by the St. George necklace honestly. And by the time we are done here, I will be able to prove it and protect my granddaughter."

"She still took it illegally, and she is the obvious link from her place of employment to you."

"I'm just not going to think about that right now, Ted. How can I? I've waited over half a century to reclaim my heritage, and fear of legal paper pushers is not going to stop me."

"Your granddaughter and her boyfriend are staying at the Savoy. Do you want to see her?"

"Of course I want to see her. I want to show her this great city, the place where her mother's people originated. I'd love to show her all the sights. But I cannot. No, Ted. We must avoid them, at least until we're done at the bank and at the cathedral."

"As you wish."

Her restlessness brought her to her feet again. "Where have I put my pocketbook?"

Ted retrieved it from the dresser and handed it to her, touching her arm and guiding her fingers to the strap.

"Thank you. You're a dear. Now, are you ready to commit further misdeeds at the bank for your Bonnie, my Clyde?"

He sighed and fetched her coat, watching affectionately as she turned her back, put her left arm into the wool sleeve, and then efficiently transferred her purse to that arm so that she could put her right one into the other sleeve. "If this whole scheme backfires, we could be detained and deported in disgrace, without your necklace."

"It's not going to backfire, Ted. You and I look so respectable that we positively creak with decency. And you're good at assessing people."

"I am crazy to become involved in this."

She patted his arm. "Yes, you are. Isn't it marvelous fun?"

"I think I'd rather sit around with my bridge group, exchanging litanies of complaints about gout and arthritis and colostomy bags." But his voice was dry.

"Piffle, Theodore. That is just plain piffle, and you know it. Now, come along . . ."

"You *are* going to marry me after all of this, aren't you?"

"Why do you want to tie yourself to a blind, helpless old woman like me?"

Ted laughed. "You may be blind, my dear, but I'd never describe you as helpless. Not even close."

The central location of SovBank faced the other buildings of Bolshaya Dmitrovka Street like a smugly prosperous merchant, displaying an overabundance of architectural detail.

Arm in arm, Tatyana and the colonel deliberately entered a pastry shop on the opposite side of the street, then exited out the back and circled around to the bank to see whether they were being followed, but that didn't seem to be the case.

Quickly, they walked into the bank using the most unobtrusive entrance. Inside was a small lobby with a group of chairs and a coffee table. Behind a long, wood-paneled counter stood several tellers. Ted dismissed the first two, a sour-looking woman in pearls and an earnest man whose collar seemed to be slowly choking him, as candidates for what they had in mind. The third teller was a young man with longish hair and a bored expression on his face, who kept trying to flirt with the pretty blond girl stationed next to him.

"That's our boy," Ted said under his breath. He put a hand on Tatyana's back. She nodded and they shuffled forward to stand in his line. The woman in front of them finished her deposit, and they moved up to the window.

With a grandmotherly smile, Tatyana greeted him in

Russian, and Ted pushed a fat envelope and the safety-deposit-box key across the counter to him. The young man eyed the key and opened the envelope. He lowered the flap and looked at the colonel, hesitating.

"I think you will find all the paperwork is in order," Nonnie said in Russian, nodding toward the envelope.

"Yes, I can see that," the teller said after a moment. Then he picked up the key. "Come this way. I will show you to your box."

They took an elevator down to the basement level. Here there was a large room lined completely with safety-deposit boxes.

The young man gestured to a room across the hall, empty except for a table and two chairs. "You may take your box in there if you wish to review the contents."

Then he scanned the numbers on the bank boxes until he found the correct one. He inserted the bank's master key first, and then the key Ted had given to him. He opened the steel door and pulled out the box half-way. "You want I take it in there for you?"

"Yes, please."

"When you are done, you lock door and remove your key."

"Thank you."

Ted showed Tatyana to one of the chairs and sat in the other himself. "All right. Are you ready, my dear?"

"My heart is ready to burst out of my body," she admitted.

Ted swallowed and lifted the lid of the box. Inside were several groupings of things: a stack of old identification papers, a box of rings and watches, three rolled canvases, and a leather passport cover. Toward the back was a heavy, solid silver tea service, each piece engraved with the letters A and M.

"Ted?"

"I don't know where to start," he said. Finally he picked up the leather passport cover and opened it. "There's a passport, German, belonging to a Weimar von Bruegel."

"It's him," she whispered. "The devil incarnate."

"What were your mother's initials, Tatyana?"

"Her name was Anika. Anika Malevich."

"Did she have a silver tea service?"

Silent tears streamed down Tatyana's face. "Yes. It was her mother-in-law's before it was handed down to her. My grandmother's name also began with an A. She was Alexandra."

Ted reached for the rolled canvases and unfurled one. "Here's a formal wedding portrait, done in oils."

"I used to stare at that for hours," Tatyana said. "Mama is wearing a white silk gown with a portrait collar and elbow-length white gloves, along with the St. George necklace. Papa looks so handsome and dignified in his morning coat. They were a beautiful couple, and very much in love."

A lump rose in Ted's throat as he unrolled the second canvas. A little girl with auburn curls and large green eyes looked inquisitively out from this picture. She wore a green velvet party dress with a sash tied in a bow around the waist.

"Is my portrait there?" Tatyana asked. "My sister's? I watched Mama cut them from the frames before we fled our house. She wanted to take more, but there was no time."

"Are you wearing a green velvet party dress?"

"No, that was Svetlana. I'm in blue taffeta with white petticoats."

Ted unrolled the final canvas, and there she was, lovely and fresh, laughing merrily at the viewer. She had masses of blond hair tied back from her face with a blue ribbon that matched the shade of her dress exactly. She knelt in a froth of petticoats that emerged like champagne bubbles from under the frock.

He wanted to break down and rail at what had happened to Tatyana's innocence, her simple joie de vivre. What kind of monster could extinguish the light from these childish faces, no matter what their race or religion?

"What else is in the box, Ted? My guess is that he did this to others. He was so young, little more than a child himself, but something evil hid behind those soulful eyes of his. He was a predator."

Ted looked with distaste at the box of rings and watches. "I'm afraid you may be right. There are rings—wedding rings, for the most part. And watches of all kinds." He picked up the stack of identification papers and paged through them. "Papers belonging to entire families, all Jewish. Why would he have kept these things?"

"Maybe he was proud of his head count. Maybe he hoped to be rewarded for it by the *reich*."

"But when it fell? Why wouldn't he have burned them to get rid of the evidence?"

"Perhaps they are trophies," Tatyana said.

Trophies. Revulsion washed over him.

"Somehow, I'm not surprised that he kept the little

paintings of our family. As I said, he was very young. I believe that we were probably his first victims, that my father was his first kill."

They sat silent for a few moments. Then Ted asked, "What do you want to do with these things?"

"You have the camera with you?"

"Yes."

"Then photograph everything." She pressed her hands flat on the table. "Because I will not rest until he is brought to justice."

Twenty-six

The next morning McDougal woke early and told Natalie that he wanted to go to buy an English newspaper. When he emerged from the shower, Natalie had laid out a series of colorful fabric scraps in a pattern across the floor.

She stood in a T-shirt of his with her hands on her hips, eyeing the scraps critically. The T-shirt dwarfed her petite frame, but the sight of her bare legged and probably nude under the plain cotton did things to him that the tightest miniskirt on South Beach failed to accomplish.

He came up behind her, lifted the hem of the shirt, and ran his hands over her smooth, warm skin—the flat abdomen, the gentle swell of her hips, the fuller curvature of her bottom, and the springy curls at the juncture of her thighs.

She leaned against him. "I thought you were going to get a paper," she murmured.

He trailed his fingertips up to her small, perfect breasts and palmed them, rubbing the nipples with his thumbs. He was on the verge of lowering his zipper, pushing her down onto the bed, and sliding into her when his brain registered the pattern of the fabric scraps on the floor.

A long, narrow strip of silver bisected the composition from the top-left corner almost to the lower-right corner. In the center was a rearing horse; below it was a dragon, the strip of silver entering its mouth. Atop the horse was a warrior who could only be the heroic figure of St. George.

Several things pierced his consciousness as sharply as the weapon did the maw of the recoiling dragon:

The image of the necklace.

His true reason for being here.

His inevitable, unavoidable betrayal of Natalie.

With sudden clarity, he despised himself. She didn't deserve to be treated the way he had to treat her. Natalie was one of the few truly good people he'd ever met, raised with the purest of academic ideals. She was content to simply repair and create objects of beauty and demanded very little in return. The malice and greed and sense of entitlement that he saw in others—they simply weren't present in her character. She would never betray someone for material gain—like him.

Eric dropped his hands and stepped back from her, the hem of the T-shirt dropping over her body like a stage curtain on the final act.

She turned to look at him. "Is something wrong?"

He shook his head. "I'm just . . . admiring your work."

"Oh," she said, dismissing it with a wave of her hand. "It's still a mess, really. And I've got to press all the fabric." She walked to the room's closet and stood on tiptoe to reach the iron on the top shelf. She pulled it down, set it on the desk, and plugged it in, turning the dial to medium-high. "I'll do that quickly while you get the newspaper. Then we can map out a plan for the day."

He opened his mouth.

"Because I'm not staying in this hotel room, Eric, and you can't force me to. We're going to find my grandmother before those criminals do." She shivered. "I'm so afraid for her."

He sighed. "We'll argue about it when I get back. In the meantime, at least I know you're safe here." He pulled on his coat and left the hotel, heading southeast in the direction of dead drop seven. He bought a copy of the *Moscow Times* from a small vendor on the next street over and kept walking. Funny, he didn't pick up any sign of a tail today. Maybe the men were late risers.

Moscow stretched in every direction around him, a vast panorama of both ancient and modern buildings. Stalinist-Gothic spires and onion domes and flat-roofed, blocky business centers alike—they all stretched longingly toward the still-weak sun, which graced the city for only four hours a day in the month of March. Miami's sun was a bare bulb to Moscow's candlelit spring.

Eric hailed an official yellow cab and got in. "Gorky Park," he said. "*Skolko eto stoit*?" What does it cost?

The driver mumbled a reasonable fare, and Eric nodded. "Main entrance," he said.

Gorky Park stretched for almost three hundred acres along the Moskva River and had been named for the writer Maxim Gorky. Shaq would have enjoyed a nice brisk hour's walk there, but Eric didn't pay much attention to the park itself once he paid the driver and got out of the cab. While he pretended to scan sections of the *Moscow Times* he'd picked up, he counted trash receptacles along the main path, stopping when he got to the correct one. There he tossed an ad section of the paper toward the can, missing it deliberately. He bent to retrieve the paper and covertly swiped the Glock that had been left under the receptacle. This he shoved into the folded remainder of the paper before he stood up and tossed the ad section into the mouth of the can.

McDougal strolled back to the main entrance and walked a few blocks before hailing another taxi to take him back to the Savoy. All in all, it had been an easy little side trip, and he felt a hundred times better now that he was armed. If he and Natalie ran into any more friendly neighborhood thugs, he'd be better prepared—certainly better than old St. George, with nothing but a spear.

McDougal's mouth curved sardonically. He might be an underhanded, double-crossing jerk of an antihero—and there was no question that Natalie would hate him once he snatched the necklace—but at least he'd do his best to rescue the damsel from distress caused by people *other* than himself.

Nice, buddy. Real nice.

The cab turned down peaceful Ulitsa Rozhdestvenka and pulled up outside the Savoy. Eric paid the driver and got out, turning over in his mind just how he was going to convince Natalie not to leave the hotel. Chain her to the bed? Knock her out with a couple of Benadryl in her chai?

He wasn't looking forward to their upcoming conversation as he got into the elevator and took it up to their floor. He slipped the gun out of the newspaper, double-checked the safety, and tucked it into his waistband before he got to the door.

He was just about to slide his key card into the slot

at the handle when a prickle lifted the hair at the back of his neck.

A muffled noise came from inside the hotel room. The bottom of the otherwise clean door was dirty, and it sported dents and a muddy boot print, as if it had been kicked. Something wasn't right.

He put his ear to the door and heard a scuffle, curse words in Russian, a hard slap, and sobs. "I don't have it!" Natalie's voice said raggedly. "No, please—"

McDougal didn't need to hear more. He exploded through the door, kicking it off the hinges entirely.

Two men. A distraught Natalie between them. She wore the same T-shirt as earlier, but it was ripped down the front, exposing a good deal of her. She also wore an expression of utter terror.

Powered by rage and adrenaline, McDougal knocked down the first thug in a full body slam and smashed him in the temple with the butt of the Glock. Now unconscious, the guy lay on the ground, his mouth still agape in surprise.

McDougal sprang up warily and eyed the second man, who had grabbed Natalie by the throat. Not a good situation.

"One step, I break her neck."

He looked fully capable.

"You hurt her," McDougal said, enunciating each word, "and I will take you apart. I will break you into small pieces."

"Give me the fucking necklace," said the thug to Natalie, ignoring him. "Where is it?"

Tears streamed down her face and she shook her head. "I don't know . . ."

His grip on her neck tightened, and he lifted her off her feet as she whimpered and scrabbled at his arm.

"She doesn't have the necklace!" McDougal thundered.

"Then who does?"

"I do."

"You bluff."

He shook his head.

"Give necklace to me; I let her go."

"Let her go, and then I'll give it to you."

Natalie's eyes were wide and terrified. Eric couldn't let this go on much longer. "Put her the fuck *down*! Feet flat on the floor. *Now!*"

Surprisingly, the man did so.

More silent tears ran down her face, and McDougal revisited that primal protective rage he'd known in the street. It went to his head faster than vodka on an empty stomach.

I'm gonna rip off both of this fucker's legs and shove them so far up his ass that they come out of his mouth.

"Necklace," the guy demanded. Then, to Eric's shock, he screamed and grabbed his crotch as Natalie twisted out from under his arm, throwing herself into a heap across the room and into the corner.

Brave move. *Stupid* move. But McDougal didn't waste time analyzing it. He couldn't risk the noise of a gunshot if they didn't want the OMON, or Russian riot police, to descend on them, so he launched himself at the thug, who'd turned toward Natalie with a snarl.

With the same basic kick that Eric had used to take down the door, he eviscerated one of the thug's knees. The man screamed in pain and went down, but he wasn't done yet by a long shot.

He rolled, toppled McDougal, sat on his legs, palmed his face, and rammed his head into the corner of the room's dresser.

Eric drove the butt of his gun upward, smashing it into the thug's elbow and dislodging his grip on his ringing skull. He pressed his advantage immediately, using forward momentum and that same hard head of his to catch the guy in the armpit and sweep him sideways and off of him.

The thug dove for the Glock, but Eric had no intention of releasing it to him.

They rolled like animals in the tight space, thrashing into furniture and using any means necessary to get the upper hand. This wasn't ring fighting; this was dirty, anything-goes street fighting, in the incongruous setting of the elegant Savoy.

Natalie was just a shaking blur in the corner.

McDougal wrenched away, got in a good solid kick to his attacker's stomach and ribs. A crunch of bone told him he'd broken one. But with a wince, a sharp inhalation, and a curse, the guy just threw himself on top of Eric again.

He felt himself squish like an éclair and was vaguely surprised that no filling squirted out. The man stunk of body odor, cabbage, and dirty wool. He wrapped his hands around Eric's neck, panting, and squeezed. His sour breath reeked of cigarettes and beer.

Shit. Time to get the Glock out of the lunatic's reach. He needed both hands to pry off the maniacally strong fingers shutting off the air to his larynx. Eric sent the gun spinning across the parquet floor, toward the corner where he'd last seen Natalie.

Except she wasn't there anymore. McDougal registered this as the asshole on top of him slammed the back of his head into the floor. Where was Natalie?

A red haze filled his vision as the lack of oxygen began to affect his brain. Air. He needed some fucking air. He could feel himself weakening.

He clawed for the thug's face, hoping to reach his eyes and jam his fingers into the sockets. He was not going to lose this fight. There was more at stake here than his own life—Natalie was in danger and he wasn't under any illusions as to what this guy would do to her.

Eric finally got a finger pried loose from his neck. He bent it back until it snapped and the guy yowled in agony. Inevitably, his grip loosened, since the sweat of pain and exertion didn't do him any favors, either.

McDougal almost had a second finger pried loose to break when Natalie reappeared in his line of vision, wielding, of all things, an iron.

An iron?

He doubted she had the strength to knock out the thug with it. But it might distract him just enough for Eric to get free.

What happened next was a blur.

Natalie bent forward.

McDougal would never forget either the sound or the smell.

Hissing. A scream of agony and disbelief. Human flesh, puckering raw and angry as it seared.

Natalie had pressed a hot iron to the man's back, under his sweater.

Suddenly the fingers around McDougal's neck vanished and the thug screamed curses. He lunged at Natalie, tears of rage and pain streaming down his face.

As Eric lay gasping for a moment on the floor, she held the iron in front of her like the weapon it had become—and even this hardened street scum hesitated.

Not for long, but for long enough.

McDougal vaulted to his feet and used all the power left in his body to knock the thug into the window. There was no Hollywood smash and shower of glass. Instead, the window merely cracked. McDougal grabbed the man by the neck and threw him into it again. This time, the initial crack gave way to the bulk of 240-odd pounds. Thug Boy crashed through the glass and onto the fire escape, where he lay facedown for long enough that McDougal could retrieve his Glock and take aim.

Below, in the street, a couple of passersby had looked up at the noise, then hunched their shoulders and trudged on their way, unwilling to get involved.

In a hoarse voice through what felt like a crushed larynx, McDougal said in Russian, "Who do you work for?"

The man simply moaned.

"Answer me, you son of a bitch!"

Nothing. Eric wanted to kick him off the fire escape and watch him crash to the street below.

Behind him, Natalie sobbed raggedly, still hanging on to the hot iron.

"You want to live?" McDougal rapped out.

A tiny nod of the head.

"Then get the hell up and climb down that fire escape. You stay away from this woman. Do you understand me?"

The man pulled himself up slowly, using the iron bars that surrounded him. "Not . . . me . . . you should worry . . . about."

"Then who?"

The guy shook his head. "You find out soon."

"Tell me or I shoot."

The man turned his head, a ghastly smile on his battered face. He shook his head. "If you want shoot, I be dead when you walk through door."

Eric narrowed his eyes and kept careful aim.

"Too much noise. And you don't have necklace."

"Yeah, so sue me, motherfucker."

He spit a foreign curse at Eric and started down the fire escape. "We do much worse than that."

Twenty-seven

Natalie still held the iron with both hands. Her entire body shook. McDougal threw the Glock into his suitcase and rushed to her. He peeled her fingers gently off the iron and set it on the desk before wrapping his arms around her as if he'd never let go. "Oh, God," he said. "Oh, God. I'm so sorry. I thought you'd be safe here."

Natalie felt catatonic as hotel security stormed the room, about two minutes too late. Uniforms and questions and more uniforms and more questions. Somebody brought her a big terry robe, and Eric wrapped her in it as if she were made of glass. She experienced all of this as if at a great distance. He spoke to her and she saw his mouth moving, but she didn't take in the words.

Catatonic. Weird word, that one . . . Made her think of cats and tonic water, gin and limes. She wondered vaguely what the etymology of *catatonic* was—her mother would know. Probably wouldn't even have to look it up.

Her father would know how to say it in Greek. The word had been on an old vocabulary list they'd made up for her to study. She remembered the words before and after it.

Cataplexy, *catatonic*, *catastrophic*. She couldn't remember what *cataplexy* meant . . .

She'd committed an act of violence today, her first ever. Nat looked down at her hands, still unable to believe that she'd pressed a hot iron to a man's flesh and smelled it burn. Heard him scream.

It didn't really matter that he would have hurt her and had been on the verge of killing Eric. She was horrified at her own actions. Her perception of herself had changed forever. She wanted to be sick, but sheer exhaustion overrode even that basic urge, and while all the uniforms chattered away and fired their questions at Eric, she simply curled into a fetal position on the bed.

A report was filled out. Someone came and taped a tarp over the broken window. Eric picked her up like a baby and moved her into another room while hotel staff followed with their belongings. A bottle of Scotch, an ice bucket, and two glasses magically appeared.

She gazed down at her hands again, seeing the familiar shape of them. They were practical and capable, the skin over them a little dry, the nails short and unpolished. She wore only a simple silver ring on the index finger of her left hand, a gift from a friend.

She used her hands to create art, to restore old treasures. She used them to give, not to punish . . . until today. This afternoon she had grabbed and twisted a man's testicles in self-defense, and seared his flesh in defense of someone else.

With sudden clarity, she understood the cautionary

statement that everyone is capable of violence. She'd always rejected that before. Now she had to accept it.

McDougal finally got rid of all the people surrounding them. He came over, sat on the bed, and said, "You all right?"

She shook her head.

He looked like hell. Mottled bruises rode over his collarbones like an obscene necklace. He was bleeding from a cut to his cheekbone; his shirt was ripped at the collar; his pants were filthy. Adrenaline still pulsed off his body, and his eyes had deepened to an electric shade of blue. His reddish mop stood wildly on end, making him look literally as if his hair were on fire.

He got up and tossed a few ice cubes into each of the two glasses. Then he drowned them in Scotch and handed one of the tumblers to her. "Drink," he ordered.

She didn't need to be told twice. It had been one horrible morning. Natalie sat up and drank deeply, feeling the whiskey burn her throat. She downed half the stuff in a single, needy gulp. Then she closed her eyes, thought about the iron on human flesh again, and finished off the rest.

When she opened her eyes again, she found McDougal watching her, no doubt trying to predict whether she'd start bawling.

She wanted to. It got the pressure out, somehow. The ugly, helpless sounds drained the ugly, helpless feelings. But she found herself dry-eyed and dazed.

Eric took the glass out of her numb fingers and poured her another drink. "Take the second one slower," he advised.

She looked at his own glass, which he'd emptied in record time as well.

"Yeah," he said. "I will, too."

They sat for a moment in silence. Then he said, shaking his head in a kind of wonder, "Do you know how brave you were today?"

She held up a hand and shook her head.

"Yes, you were," he insisted.

The horror rose up in her again. "I burned a man with an iron, Eric. I smelled his skin frying. It was . . ." She shook her head again. "I have no words."

"You did it in self-defense and in my defense, Natalie. You didn't do it for fun, okay?"

Perspiration broke out at her hairline, and her stomach heaved. She sprinted for the bathroom and ingloriously upchucked the whiskey.

She got to her feet to find Eric holding out a damp washcloth with an expression of sympathy. "How long have you been there?" she croaked.

He shrugged.

She took the washcloth, mortified. "You watched me puke?"

His lips twitched. "Yeah. You looked hot."

"You're a sick twist, McDougal. You know that?"

"I do. It's part of my raw animal charm."

She leaned her elbows on the sink vanity and turned on the tap, rinsing the vile taste out of her mouth and then splashing more water onto her face. Then she realized that tears were pouring down her cheeks.

Eric turned off the tap and scooped her into his arms. He walked with her to the bed and sat down with Natalie still curled against his chest. "Shhhhhh, sweetheart. It's gonna be okay. Everything's gonna be okay."

"Nothing's okay. We have to find Nonnie," she sobbed. "I don't want her hurt."

"We'll find her. I promise we'll find her." Eric stroked her hair and her back, his heartbeat strong and steady. He kissed her forehead. She felt cared for, safe, soothed. There was nothing sexual about his tenderness with her as he peeled back the covers on the bed and climbed under them with her still in his arms. He simply held her, his arms tight and secure around her waist, and she eventually slid into a troubled sleep.

McDougal lay wide-awake for two hours with his arms around Natalie, the one underneath her cramped and then eventually numb. He wanted a hot shower, but he wanted to hold her more. He wanted to be there for her. Physically and mentally present. Emotionally present.

He didn't need to ask whether he was doing things right, because this wasn't about him. She had relaxed and found some kind of peace in his embrace, and that was all he cared about.

Except for telling the truth.

McDougal let his fantasy fishing boat sail away, past downtown Miami, under the Rickenbacker Causeway, past Key Biscayne, and toward Elliot Key until it vanished. He had to come clean with this woman in his arms. He wasn't sure what he felt for her, but he did feel. And he couldn't lie to her any longer, even though he came up with great arguments for doing so.

She'd be furious with him, refuse to have anything to do with him, and he couldn't blame her. But she was still in great danger, and he had a responsibility to protect her.

Scratch that. It wasn't an obligation; it was something different, something stronger. It had nothing to do with duty. He couldn't define it. But he *would* keep her safe, and that became much harder if she couldn't stand to be in the same room with him. He would keep her safe, even if it cost him his job, his pride, his silly bachelor dreams. He'd keep her safe if it cost him his life.

He was appalled. McDougal had always been quite comfortable in his selfishness—it fit him like a second skin. Where all of this self-sacrificing garbage had come from, he didn't know. Frankly, he didn't want to give a damn.

But here he was, with his arms around a girl who shouldn't be anything but another pretty little patsy, inhaling the scent of her shampoo and her sleep-warmed skin. She smelled clean and pure, and he wanted to confess everything so that he could smear some of the sludge off his soul.

As if she could sense the struggle going on inside of him, Natalie opened her eyes.

He kissed her shoulder. "How you doing, kiddo?"

"Okay. You?"

"Me, I'm a hundred percent man. I juggle Russian thugs every morning before breakfast."

"Stop," she said. "Don't make light of what you did." She rolled over to face him, and he was able to extract his numb arm.

"It's so odd . . ." she whispered. "All of these terrible things have happened in my life recently, but the best thing in my life has come along at the same time: you."

He stilled. "I'm—I'm just a guy, Natalie."

She tilted her head back and looked up at him. She touched his bruised jaw, the marks around his neck. "Always so self-deprecating, Eric. Always so honest."

He sucked in a breath. "No . . . no, I'm not."

She laid a finger across his lips. "I don't care what you do for the government, okay? That's just your job. I'm talking about you, personally. Your character. It's sterling."

"Natalie, honey, you've known me for less than a week—"

"And it's been an illuminating one. You're kind and intelligent and funny and strong and protective and tender—"

He looked down at her, his eyes troubled. "Don't do this."

"Do what? Fall for you?"

He swallowed and looked away.

"It's too late, you know." She smiled up at him. "I fell in love with you that night in Reif's."

For such a small woman, she sure could wield a wrecking ball. It hit him square in the stomach, and he said absolutely nothing. He couldn't, even though he knew that it hurt her. He was about to hurt her a lot worse.

"It's okay, Eric. I know that guys like you don't end up with girls like me." She kissed his cheek before rolling away and curling up against the pillows at the head of the bed.

"What the hell is that supposed to mean?"

She yawned and tucked a strand of hair behind her ear. She smiled sadly. "Just that I'm not your type."

"Really. And what do you imagine to be my type?"

"Oh . . . curvy, scantily clad party girls. Not too bright, because then you might have to engage instead of maintaining a cool distance."

Heat rose in his cheeks. He slid out of bed and went to pour himself a Scotch. "Party girls—interesting theory. So I like a lot of makeup?"

"No, because you don't want it smeared on your pillows in the morning."

His hand froze in midpour. Then he set the bottle down with more force than necessary. "Do I like my women easy, or do I like a challenge?"

She considered the question for a moment. "Depends on your mood. You like them easy, because there's no guilt involved. But you get bored with that, so alternately, you like a challenge. The only thing that scares you is nice girls. My theory is that you don't like to *like* your dates, Eric."

The burn of the Scotch served only to accelerate the burn of recognition, of shock, of sudden shame. "Excuse me? What kind of thing is that to say?"

She shrugged. "It's that distance thing again. Plus liking a woman probably ruins the sexual tension for you."

He stared at her and shook his head.

"It's related to the guilt," she explained kindly. "What's the matter, Eric? You look like you just swallowed a fish."

He held up a hand, wordlessly asking her to shut up.

"Okay, but let me just say one more thing."

"Do I have a choice?" he muttered.

"Women love your bad-boy attitude and that callous edge of yours—"

"Callous edge," he repeated, nodding. "That's me."

"But they can also smell the guilt on you. And that's how you reel them in and make them truly desperate to own you: that faint chance that your conscience might let them into your heart."

"My conscience," he said, nodding again. "You know what? You are one scary girl. In fact, I think you're a witch."

But unbelievably, she wasn't done. She had to summarize. "It's kind of like putting a Scooby Snack inside one of those rubber toys and watching a dog go crazy trying to get it out."

"Not another word!" McDougal snapped, before tossing back the contents of his glass. "Thank you for the unsolicited psychological analysis, but I have to tell you something, Natalie. When we met that evening in Reif's—"

The phone rang, the volume so loud that he jumped and almost dropped the glass to the floor.

Natalie leaned over and plucked the receiver from the cradle of the phone on the nightstand. "Hello?" Her mouth dropped open. "*Nonnie?* Nonnie, where *are* you?"

Twenty-eight

Avy and Liam were gratified to find that Oleg Litsky lived on the ground floor of his building in Moscow. The fewer the stairs, the fewer the complications.

Not only had Avy put her panties back on, but she'd encased her legs in black stockings and high-heeled boots, which did absolutely nothing to keep her warm but at least didn't look as ridiculous as bare Miami legs in a cold Moscow March.

She'd also donned a dark wig, dark brown contact lenses, and pancake makeup that made her look fifteen years older. She'd affixed a faux mole to her neck that drew attention away from her face, and she deliberately hunched so that her posture was that of an older woman.

Liam wore a dapper mustache and goatee along with spectacles and a three-piece suit. He'd darkened his teeth several shades and adopted a worried, academic look.

"You look like Sigmund Freud as his mother admits to him that she has penis envy," Avy said.

"Thank you, love. You're too kind."

The apartment building was located a few blocks from the Tretyakov Gallery, in the Zamoskvoreche district. The Tretyakov, founded in 1856, housed the largest collection of Russian art in the world.

They'd had a taxi drop them right in front of the gallery itself, and they walked the rest of the way. Liam chuckled as they took in the facade of the gallery. "That frieze, my darling? Designed by Viktor Vasnetsov. Notice anything familiar?"

Avy glanced over at it. St. George and the dragon fought their legendary battle right in the center of the bas relief, and once again, the dragon was having a very bad day. "That poor reptile never wins, does he?"

"How do you know he's a reptile? Reptiles don't have wings. They don't breathe fire, either."

"Liam, I'm not going to argue with you over the biological classification of a mythical creature," Avy said, unable to help laughing.

"Oh, very well. Speaking of breathing fire, did you hear that a drunken electrician actually fell asleep on the premises of the Tretyakov recently? With a lit cigarette in his mouth, no less. He ignited the bloody place. Fortunately, none of the art was damaged . . ."

Avy shook her head. "Vodka for breakfast?"

"It's entirely possible." Liam ruminated for a moment. "You know, it's quite odd, if you think about it: Give an Englishman a potato and he boils it. Give a Russian a potato, and he ingeniously turns it into vodka."

"You should write an anthropological study," Avy suggested, tongue in cheek.

"I believe I shall," he mused. "After all, I'll need something to do in my retirement."

The sky was gray and moody today, sulking behind the clouds, and a light snowfall covered the ground. Despite the fact that she was wearing impossibly high heels, Avy easily outpaced Liam's casual British amble. She kept having to stop and wait impatiently for him to catch up. He merely smiled that sin-grin of his, the flash of wicked teeth that let her know that he was amused at her expense.

"In a hurry, my love?" he asked. "Nervous, perhaps?"

"I'm never nervous," she retorted. "You should know that by now. I'm simply freezing my Florida ass off."

"No, no, my darling. Your lovely tropical arse is still in place, I assure you, and very comely, too."

They had arrived at Litsky's building. "You have the men and the ambulance waiting?" she asked.

"Of course."

"You have the syringe?"

"We're all set, my darling. Really, you must trust me."

"I'm sorry, Liam, if I still have a difficult time trusting a career thief. And I've never repossessed a *person* before!"

"Person, painting—it's very much the same."

"No, Liam, it isn't. Paintings don't kick, scream, or attempt escape. Paintings don't have to be fed, or use facilities. Paintings can't prosecute the people who snatch them."

He heaved a long-suffering sigh. "Yes, dear."

She shot him a dirty look, and he returned her gaze blandly. Then they strolled up the steps and pressed an intercom button along with Litsky's code. He buzzed them in.

Litsky had the demeanor and posture of a general, a weathered gray face like cracked tarmac, and the clear blue eyes of a choirboy. "Welcome," he said with a businesslike smile.

He ushered them into his study, which was lined with leather-bound volumes in German and Russian. His built-in shelves were polished mahogany, as was his desk. A fire burned in a stone fireplace, and a fully stocked bar took up the far corner. Paintings in gilt frames filled various spaces on the walls, but Avy saw nothing that jumped out at her from the Art Loss Register.

"Mr. Litsky, I'm Vera Rockwell of ARTemis, Inc. And this is my associate Trenton Smathers."

Trenton Smathers was among Liam's many aliases, one of the four who had schizophrenically asked Avy's father for her hand in marriage. She shuddered at the memory—her father hadn't found it funny at all.

"Very pleased to make your acquaintance, Ms. Rockwell, Mr. Smathers. Please sit down. Whiskey? Vodka? Cognac?" Litsky offered. His accent was continental but with a definite edge of German.

"No, thank you," said Avy.

"Don't mind if I do," said Liam. "Just a snifter of cognac, if you please."

"But of course, Mr. Smathers." Litsky poured and handed him the drink in a very fine Bavarian crystal glass. He poured himself a potent two fingers of Scotch and joined them. He sat in one of two comfortable-looking wing chairs on either side of the fireplace, while Liam and Avy positioned themselves on a sofa that faced the hearth.

On a side table were several framed photographs,

and one in particular caught Liam's eye. Two lovely little fair-haired girls, aged maybe four and six, played dolls on a deep green lawn. They wore white cotton eyelet dresses and had Litsky's wide, angelic eyes.

"Your granddaughters?" Liam asked.

"Yes." Their host stared at the picture fondly; then his mouth tightened and he averted his gaze.

"They're beautiful. Just precious," said Avy.

"Thank you. And I thank you for meeting with me," Litsky said formally. He raised his glass to them with slightly unsteady fingers and drank deeply.

"It's our pleasure," Avy said, with a professionally warm smile. "What can we do for you, sir?"

"As you no doubt have been informed, I am trying to locate some property which was stolen from me recently, taken from my safe in this very room."

They nodded, adopting expressions of sympathy.

"Some of the items will be untraceable, I fear—cash and some diamond jewelry of no particularly unique design. But there are two items that I must find. One is a Cézanne painting that I purchased in the 1950s and which, frankly, represents my most valuable asset."

"You have the bill of sale, the provenance, and a certificate of authenticity?"

"Yes, I do."

"Forgive me, but may I see them?" Avy asked. He would expect no less.

Litsky nodded and got out of the wing chair. He went to his desk and produced a manila file folder from a drawer, which he handed to her.

Inside was a bill of sale from a reputable Parisian dealer, still in business, and a detailed history of who had owned the piece before Litsky bought it. Avy closed the file as if satisfied and carefully did not look at Liam. She was sure that he had recognized, as she had, that there was no watermark on any of the papers. The dealer in question never released anything with her signature on it unless it was printed on her special, marked paper.

"All right. I believe we can help you with this. What about the other item?"

Litsky looked at the picture of his granddaughters again and raised his glass to his lips, all but draining it. "Yes. The other item is a very unusual necklace. Unfortunately, I do not have a bill of sale or a detailed provenance for the piece, since it was given to me years ago as thanks for a service I rendered during World War Two."

"Oh?" Avy asked.

"Yes." Litsky cleared his throat. "I, ah, helped a family across the border from Russia to Romania. They were Jewish, and fleeing Hitler's forces."

"That was very brave of you, sir. You put yourself at risk by giving them aid."

The old man's face took on a peculiar expression. He waved a dismissive hand and got to his feet again, heading straight for the bar. He poured himself another Scotch and stood gazing down into the amber liquid. Then he remembered his manners and looked at Liam. "Would you like another cognac?"

"Oh, well. I shouldn't, but I will. Here, let me bring you the glass." Gracefully, Liam rose and made his way to the bar, where he set down his snifter. Then in one fluid motion, his hand went into his pocket, came out with the syringe, and plunged it into Litsky's unsuspecting neck. The man opened his mouth to yell, but the drug immediately immobilized him. He made a single croak before his eyes rolled back into his head.

Liam neatly caught the cognac decanter just as it slipped from the old man's grasp. He set it down and then lowered the Nazi's limp form to the oriental rug. Litsky's eyes, before closing, had held shock, belated realization, and impotent fury.

"Oh, dear, oh, dear, the poor fellow's had a stroke," proclaimed Liam. "How shocking. How unfortunate. Nick that file folder and then run out of the building looking distraught, will you, love, while I ring for an ambulance?"

Avy stuffed the file into her soft-sided briefcase.

Liam hit a button on his phone. "It's a go," he murmured. Then he banked the fire in anticipation of their departure.

Within minutes, an official-looking white van with red stripes and a blue light on top screeched up to the main door of the apartment building, and two uniformed men emerged from the back with medical supplies and a stretcher.

Avy played the shocked, concerned visitor to the hilt, babbling and dabbing away tears with a tissue.

The men came inside, exchanged glances with Liam, and then examined Litsky for the benefit of a nosy neighbor who'd followed them in.

"We must get him to the emergency room right away," one of the "medical team" said while another translated the Russian. "Come on—let's load him up."

They promptly transferred Litsky from the floor to the stretcher, swaddled him in white sheets and blankets, and dropped an oxygen mask over his face.

"You should call his son," the neighbor suggested.

"I'll take care of that," Avy reassured him, once she understood. Then she shepherded him out in the wake of the medics and closed the door of the apartment.

The men loaded Litsky, and she and Liam climbed in after them. They started for the airport, relieved that everything had gone so smoothly.

Avy let the air out of her lungs and relaxed. Then one of the medics aimed an unpleasant smile at them. "You want to go airport, you pay double. If no, we drive you to police, eh?"

Twenty-nine

Natalie went weak with relief at the sound of her grandmother's voice, even if at present she was scolding her.

"Natalya, what are you doing, coming after me to Moscow? Who is this man you are with?"

And they both said simultaneously, "You are in danger!"

"Who is the man *you* are with?" Natalie countered. "How could you have just taken off like that, without a word to anyone? Do you know how worried I've been?" Then she added, "How do you know that I'm here? And how do you know about Eric?"

"Pictures!" Nonnie said. "Kissing a red-haired man in the street!"

"How did you get pictures?"

"You have much explaining to do, young lady."

"*I* have much explaining to do? Listen, Nonnie, because of that necklace you took, I've been fired, I'm in trouble with the law, my boss is dead, and the Russian Mafiya has trashed my apartment, almost kidnapped me, and tried to kill me just this morning."

"I am sorry for your trouble, but St. George will protect you," Nonnie said placidly.

Natalie choked. "That offers me so much comfort. You have no idea."

"Do not disrespect me with your sarcasm or St. George with your lack of faith. Eh?"

"Nonnie, please understand, a man almost choked Eric to death this morning!"

"This Eric, he is alive, yes?"

"Yes, but—"

"He was sent to you by St. George," her grandmother said decisively.

"No, Nonnie. I'm sorry, but that's just not true," Natalie said, exasperated. "The ugly reality is that I picked up Eric in a bar."

"You what?"

"And I don't think saints usually frequent bars—"

"No? Natalya, I tell you, I am constantly in amazement that you, at twenty-nine years old, understand all of the mystical workings of God, the saints, the universe. Your brilliance outshines the very stars in the sky . . ."

"Now who's being sarcastic?"

"My dear, do you think this is the first time God has used human weakness and temptation to get his message across? I don't care if you met this Eric in a sewer. He has been sent by St. George. You will see."

Natalie rolled her eyes but said nothing.

"Careful, they'll get stuck that way." Nonnie couldn't possibly have seen her expression! She was just plain eerie sometimes.

"Do you have the necklace?" Nat asked her.

"Of course."

"Why did you bring it here? What are you going to do with it?"

"That's why I called you, but instead of letting me explain, you tell me about dead men and drunk men in bars! This is not how you were raised, Natalya—"

Natalie covered her eyes with her hand.

"—but regardless, you are my granddaughter and you are here, so you should be a part of this exchange. It is your right and your heritage. So. We will meet at the Cathedral of the Assumption, in the Kremlin, at dusk, in front of the iconostasis. You will see the St. George icon there, painted in the twelfth century. I was baptized under it."

"Dusk? But that's in less than an hour—"

"Yes. Hurry, Natalya." And Nonnie hung up.

Eric said, "Where do we need to be?"

"Kremlin. Cathedral of the Assumption."

The Cathedral of the Assumption, with its five gold domes, stood in the east-central section of the Kremlin, dwarfing the Church of the Deposition of the Robe. Whose robe, McDougal didn't know, nor did he particularly care as he and Natalie walked toward the cathedral square.

At last he would meet the little old lady who'd started all the trouble and led him on this merry chase to Moscow. He didn't say much to Natalie, since he was still smarting from her perceptive summation of his dating habits, and now was not the time to confess all and beg forgiveness.

The interior of the cathedral was nothing short of magnificent. Their footsteps echoed loudly in the sacred space, in contrast to the silence of the saints and martyrs who gazed down at them from every imaginable surface.

Just under all five domes were vertical expanses of windows, which welcomed the dwindling light into the cathedral. Giant, colorfully painted pillars stood in the center of the place, framing the visitor's first glance at the awe-inspiring iconostasis, rows upon rows of gilt-framed icons to inspire prayer.

Chandeliers poured fountains of crystal at intervals, creating an atmosphere rather like a holy ballroom. McDougal half expected all of the saints and martyrs to come down and socialize, dance, or perhaps proselytize over cocktails.

The twelfth-century icon of St. George stared sternly out among the others, clutching his spear.

"Our buddy George needs to find a new hairstylist," McDougal said. "And his eyebrows look waxed, like a woman's. You sure he was straight?"

Natalie smacked him lightly in the arm. "Don't be sacrilegious."

"But I do it so well. It's one of my specialties."

The doors opened behind them, and a tall, regal man with a white mustache entered, a small older lady on his arm. She moved slowly and clearly didn't see well, but her face was animated. She drank in the air of the cathedral as if she couldn't get enough, cocked her head as though she were recording every sound.

"Nonnie!" Natalie ran to her and embraced her with obvious affection, despite her frustration with her grandmother's shenanigans.

"Natalya!" The old lady eventually pulled back, found

her cheek, and patted it. She looked secretly delighted. "You're as crazy as I am, aren't you?"

"Probably." Natalie turned to extend her hand to the tall man with the mustache. "It's nice to see you again, Colonel. We've met a couple of times."

"Yes, yes. Good to see you again, young Natalie."

Eric walked up behind her. "Eric McDougal, sir. Mrs. Ciccoli. Pleased to meet you both."

The colonel nodded civilly.

"Is this the boy you've been kissing in the street, Natalya?"

"Um—"

"Yes," McDougal said. "She couldn't resist."

"Aren't you the impudent one?" Nonnie commented. "Give me your hand."

He did, and she took it, tracing her old fingers along his, running them over his palm and even the back of it. She nodded. "Yes. St. George sent you. It's fitting that you should be here today."

McDougal felt an odd energy flow through him at her touch, which discomfited him even more than her words. "It is?"

"Yes."

Natalie seemed to sense his unease. "Nonnie, where is the archbishop you spoke of?"

"He will be here."

Slowly, Tatyana unwrapped her scarf to reveal the magnificent necklace, the miniature saint on his horse nestling against her skin. As if on cue, the chandeliers came on, catching the twenty-two-karat gold and electrifying the scene playing out over her bosom.

The dragon writhed in agony, the horse reared to

crush the beast under its tiny hooves, and the saint kept perfect balance as he ended the conflict. Good conquered evil; all was right with the world.

"St. George," Nonnie said. "Patron saint of England, the Knights of the Garter, the Knights of the Round Table. Hero of Spenser's *Faerie Queene*. Patron saint of the cavalry. Patron saint of the Scouts, both English and Russian. Patron saint of Moscow."

"Old George does wear a few hats, doesn't he?" McDougal commented.

Natalie's grandmother ignored him. "Catherine the Great founded the Order of St. George in 1769 as the highest military honor. She herself was the very first recipient as the grand master of the order, and she commissioned the necklace for the occasion."

"How did it end up in our family?" Natalie asked. "You've never told me."

"Before her death, Catherine gave the necklace to a lady-in-waiting who had been particularly loyal and was said to be as good with a sword as her husband. The lady had foiled an assassination plot against Catherine. That lady was my great-great-great-great-great-grandmother, and she began a tradition of passing the St. George piece down to the eldest surviving daughter of each generation."

Nonnie placed her hand over the little knight. "One day it will pass to you, my dear. But in the meantime, we need it to prove who we are. We need it in order to reclaim the family treasures that my mother and father were forced to leave behind."

"How can it prove who we are? We could have stolen it." Natalie's face fell. "In fact, we *did* steal it, Nonnie. And it's still not right."

Her grandmother looked faintly amused. "It proves who we are, my girl, because nobody else knows that our possessions are here. No one—unless my sister, Svetlana, was ill-advised enough to tell someone before she died.

"And as for having 'stolen' the necklace from your employer? We did no such thing. We took it, which is quite different."

"How?" Natalie challenged her. "The man who shot your father—he took the necklace as well."

Nonnie wagged her finger back and forth. "Von Bruegel? No. He stole it."

"Semantics."

"This has nothing to do with semantics, young lady, and everything to do with precision of language! To *cut* is not the same thing as to *slice*, though they both involve wielding a knife. To *amble* is not the same thing as to *scramble*, though both involve moving forward with one's feet . . ."

"Okay, okay, okay, Nonnie." Natalie buried her face in her hands. "Now I know why my mother became a linguistics professor," she muttered. "*You* are the actual source of my childhood dictionary torment."

Colonel Blakely had stuffed his hands into his pockets and wandered toward the south portal to examine Ivan the Terrible's Monomakh throne. The doors hadn't quite closed; one was cracked open about an inch.

Quickly, the colonel strode back to the group. "I hate to interrupt this fascinating discussion," he said, "but there is a group of men approaching, and I don't think they've come here to worship."

"But this is the Kremlin," Natalie exclaimed. "There are guards—"

"Yeah?" McDougal shot a glance at the one wizened old woman in black sitting on a chair near the south portal.

"Not her, maybe, but outside—"

An explosion ripped through the air, seeming to come from outside the northeast corner of the cathedral.

"A distraction," said Colonel Blakely. "Classic ploy—gets the guards' attention."

The old woman in black ran for the doors and disappeared.

"Move, everyone," McDougal ordered. "Move now, or we're dead." He hustled the group to the left, around the corner, into an alcove that held two tombs. "Down. Get flat on the floor and don't make a sound." He pulled the Glock from his waistband and slid along the wall, back toward the nave of the church.

"Eric, no!" Natalie protested.

He held a finger over his lips and gestured for her to do as he'd said. Then he crept silently away. He heard the creak of the old doors, footsteps, whispers.

"There's no one here," a man said in Russian.

"They're inside, I tell you. The four of them."

"All exits are blocked?"

"Yes."

Not good news. McDougal inched forward until he got at last to the passageway, from where he had a limited vantage point. Three men, not street thugs. Professionals. Armed—and the weapons had silencers. That was both good and bad: good because a silencer played hell with accuracy. Bad for obvious reasons—nobody would come running at the noise when they were fired.

If all the exits were blocked, then he was dealing with

at least six, maybe seven men. McDougal had a healthy ego, but he was under no illusion that he was Batman, Spider-Man, Superman, or any combination thereof. So he backtracked toward the rest of the group.

Yeah, so he couldn't fly, stick to vertical surfaces, or put his fist through cinder blocks . . . but he could draw attention away from Natalie, her grandmother, and the colonel—and run.

After all, McDougal had experience running from furious fathers and bent-out-of-shape boyfriends, not to mention husbands with hatchets. He'd be in his element.

As he slipped back into the alcove, the colonel said quietly, "I can still hold my own in a fight. But there are six of them."

Eric shook his head. "Too risky. And one of us needs to stay with the ladies."

"If they harm anyone in this cathedral," kooky Nonnie said in a stage whisper, "they will be cursed by all the saints and the order of St. George and by the spirit of Catherine the Great herself."

"Um. I'm sure you're right, Mrs. Ciccoli. Meaning no offense, but I don't think they care at this point in time." He paused. "There's only one way to handle this. I can draw them out and away from you, but I'll need to have what they want."

"The necklace," Natalie said.

He nodded. "Exactly."

Nonnie clutched it and shook her head.

"Mrs. Ciccoli," Eric said gently, "this would only be temporary, I promise you. I'm good at . . . getting away from people. Okay? It's"—he looked at Natalie—"part of what I do. We will meet later and I will return the necklace to you, so that you can reclaim your family heirlooms."

She hesitated.

"I swear. Scout's honor," he said, deliberately invoking a group that claimed St. George as its patron saint. None of them needed to know that he'd been unceremoniously kicked out of the Boy Scouts at age thirteen, on account of a girl and a bottle of tequila. "We'll meet up again at the Savoy later tonight."

"Nonnie," Natalie urged, "you can trust this man. He came all the way to Moscow with me. He's prevented two attacks on me."

Mrs. Ciccoli fingered the little St. George around her neck.

"Nonnie, you said yourself that Eric was sent by St. George. Please, take off the necklace and give it to him," Natalie begged. "It's not worth our lives!"

"All right. Help me." She turned her back to Natalie, who fumbled with the clasp. Selia Markovic had done a good job repairing it. Finally Natalie got it open and lifted the heavy piece from her grandmother's chest.

Natalie shoved it at McDougal, her hands shaking. "Be careful, Eric. Please. Come back to me this evening."

He closed his hand around the necklace. Then he nodded and stood up.

"Promise?"

He bent down and kissed her lips. "I promise. Now, stay hidden."

Thirty

Avy changed quickly into a nurse's uniform, and then she and Liam sat in the ambulance with their "repossessed" Nazi and the rest of the enterprising faux medical team. Liam's expression grew thunderous. "Double? You want us to pay double? Sod you pickpockets! You bloody den of thieves, you."

The irony of the situation seemed to escape him entirely, and Avy was hard-pressed not to laugh. "Trenton, just give them the money. We're hardly in a position to argue. We have a plane to catch."

"Just give them the money, she says! Let me tell you, love, finances aren't what they once were, what with this retirement business. I used to be able to nick a bauble or two when times got tough. But I'm just a regular working stiff now—"

"Trenton, you'll never be a regular anything. And besides, my company is going to hire you. You'll work on commission, do what you love, and be paid well."

"You neglected to mention my prospective employment, love."

"I wasn't sure you could go straight. I'm still not. You'll be on probation for a lo-o-o-ong time."

"Double or nothing," the faux medic broke in.

"So pay the man already, darling," said Avy.

Grumbling, Liam pulled out his wallet and forked over more rubles. This worked miracles in terms of getting the ambulance to move, and within thirty minutes or so they arrived at a small private airfield to the west of Moscow's city center.

The driver pulled the ambulance up to what looked like a pile of junk with a propeller stuck on as an afterthought. Two men dressed in coveralls stood leaning against it, looking bored.

"Li—uh, Trenton, what is that?" Avy asked, pointing to the pile of scrap metal.

"That, my love, is an Antonov 72, an old Russian military cargo plane."

"An Antonov 72. Of course."

"She's no beauty, but she's still serviceable."

"Are you sure?"

"Sure as I can be, poppet, without taking her up and testing her out. We'll know in about twenty minutes." He grinned cheerfully, opened the doors of the ambulance, and jumped out.

Avy followed but pulled up short when she heard a deep rumble. It sounded like a cross between McDougal's Kawasaki Ninja and a wood chipper, and it emanated from the interior of the plane.

Liam had gone around the nose to the back, which opened like a hatch, and stood peering inside. He took a step back as the rumble came again, stroked his fake beard, and cast a quick, wary glance at her.

Avy's eyes narrowed as she walked over. The first thing she saw was a very large crate. From the crate wafted a ripe odor that she couldn't quite place. Mangy, earthy, ammonia tinged. Hide crossed with horse barn.

Three more steps brought her face-to-face with the largest cat she'd ever seen. It was at least the size of a Volkswagen and had teeth like a Tyrannosaurus Rex. And it clearly wanted to gnaw on her skull.

Her mouth opened, but no sound came out.

"Genus *panthera*," Liam noted. "Species, *p. tigris*; subspecies, *p. tigris altaica*. Latin aside, my darling, it's a Siberian tiger and it looks quite charmed to make your acquaintance."

"No." She turned on her heel and walked back around the side of the plane. The faux medics were just climbing back into the ambulance after unloading their still-unconscious "patient."

"What do you mean, no?" Liam queried, trotting after her.

"*No.*"

"In this case, I'm afraid that 'no' must mean 'yes,' Avy, darling. I have contracted, as a private pilot, to fly this sweet pussycat from here to a zoo in the U.S., so that he can live a hedonistic life of leisure and produce cubs with a lovely striped lady of similar Siberian distinction."

Avy shook her head. "Too bad."

"But, my darling, you know as well as I do that our friend on the stretcher won't leave the country voluntarily. He's got to be smuggled, and that's utterly impossible to do on a commercial airliner."

"Under no circumstances, Liam, am I going to get

into a flying can with you, a Nazi, and a Siberian friggin' tiger! Have you lost your mind?"

"Perhaps, but it always returns after a pleasant jaunt abroad. Now, do be reasonable, poppet."

"Don't call me poppet," she said through her teeth.

"Right. Stricken from the list of acceptable endearments: poppet. Gone. Vanished. *Finito*."

The ambulance's engine turned over, and Avy spun as it pulled away and picked up speed. "Wait! Stop!" she yelled, running toward it. Neither of the men inside even acknowledged her.

She turned back to Liam, enraged. "You deliberately told them to leave."

He raised an eyebrow. "Not even by ESP, I assure you. Now, come along, love, while I talk to these gentlemen with the clipboards, sign the paperwork, and complete our flight check."

"Hallo there, fine fellows," Liam said to the two men with clipboards. "Let me sign those documents, and then we'll be off, eh?"

They looked at each other, then at him, then back at each other. They shrugged, mystified. Clearly they didn't understand a word of what Liam had said.

Fortunately another man in similar garb emerged from a small office trailer and walked toward the plane. "Er, *sprechen Zie* English?" Liam called.

"Yes, I speak English. Are you the pilot?"

"I am indeed." He glanced at Avy. "And this is my worthy copilot."

"Well, I hope you have accommodations at a decent hotel, because you're not going anywhere with this animal right now."

"I beg your pardon?"

"We have suspicions that the tiger has been poached from its natural habitat."

"Poached? As in stolen or kidnapped? How shocking," Liam exclaimed, furtively looking at the unconscious Nazi on the stretcher. "I'm sure you're mistaken. All the paperwork for this tiger is in order."

"Paperwork can be faked."

"You don't say? But why would anyone go to the trouble of forging paperwork for a Siberian tiger?"

"They're an endangered species, very rare. Only a few hundred of them may exist in the wild at this time, but that doesn't stop certain obsessed hunters from wishing to add them to their collection of kills."

"That's awful," Avy said.

"Yes. This one may have been ordered up by a bored multimillionaire. In any case, you're not leaving here with it until we're absolutely sure."

Liam and Avy exchanged glances, just as a groan came from the stretcher.

"Bloody hell," said Liam.

"Excuse me," said Avy. She walked over to the stretcher, where the Nazi lay fumbling with the oxygen mask, his old blue eyes open and confused. "Leave that alone," she said. "And don't make a noise, or you're going into the crate with the hungry, cranky, six-hundred-pound kitty." She adjusted the stretcher so that he had a clear view of the tiger, and, conversely, the tiger had a clear view of him.

It roared.

The old Nazi shook with fear.

"We know exactly who and what you are, and frankly

it would give us great pleasure for that creature to gnaw on your femur. Understand?"

He nodded.

"Excellent." Avy walked back over to Liam and the official. She folded her arms. "Well, Trenton, it appears that we have three options. One, we can ignore everything these gentlemen have to say, leave them tied up in the trailer office, and take off." She said this drolly, and the official laughed, having no idea that she was serious. She laughed, too. Finally Liam laughed.

"Two," she continued, "we can take off without the tiger, which makes the most sense to me."

"Sorry, love. I gave my word on the tiger."

"To whom? And why?"

"You don't want to know."

Avy glared at him. "Or three, we can have my colleague pick us up—assuming that he's still in Moscow—and we can all have a pajama party with our friend over there."

"What is wrong with him?" the official asked.

"Bad case of schizophrenia. And he's having paranoid delusions." She tapped her temple with her index finger. "So don't worry if he says anything strange."

"Help!" screamed the Nazi. "They're trying to kill me!"

"Oh, dear." Avy raised her hands, palms up, and then lowered them as if to say, "What can you do?" Then she walked back over to the man. "We're not trying to kill you, Oleg. Why would we have brought you here in an ambulance, with medics attending you?"

"It was fake! The ambulance was a fake . . . These people have kidnapped me! Help!"

Liam shook his head sadly. "The poor fellow. He has no idea what he's saying." He turned in Avy's direction. "I fear you're going to have to sedate him again, love."

"Oh, gosh. I hate to do that, but he is a little out of control."

"No!" yelled Litsky, as she pulled a second syringe out of her pocket. "No, no, no—"

Avy injected him in the arm as he was trying to shield his neck. Then he fell silent again.

The official looked on dubiously but seemed reassured at the special care she took in tucking Litsky under the blankets again and the gentle way she took his pulse.

"All right, I suppose we should call your colleague," Liam said. "We'll have to wait until tomorrow to take off. In the meantime, what *are* you going to do with this tiger, my good man? Feed it a bowl of borscht? Toss it a dog or two?"

"Trenton! That's horrible," Avy said.

"Only joking, love. I promise."

The tiger chose this moment to roar again.

The official gulped. He said something in Russian to the other two men in coveralls. "They will stay with the animal overnight."

"How cozy," Liam remarked. "Well, then," he said to Avy. "Ring up McDougal on your mobile, won't you? I don't know about you, but I'm a mite peckish and could do with some dinner."

McDougal needed to distract the three men inside the cathedral so that he could make it to the south portal, the door they'd entered by and the one most likely to not have another man with a gun outside it.

His eyes went to one of the elaborate chandeliers, and he made his decision. The Glock wasn't the most accurate weapon, especially when he screwed *his* silencer onto it, but he'd hit at least one of the crystals. It was better than putting a bullet through a sacred icon.

He attached the silencer, said a brief apology to God for firing a gun in a church, and then discharged his weapon into the mass of crystal. He took advantage of the men's surprise to take cover behind one of the huge columns. A hail of bullets hit his previous location.

McDougal waited a few beats, then fired again and ran for the next column. But the men had split up, and one was circling in his direction to cut off the access to the south portal. Eric was an incredibly lapsed Catholic, but that didn't mean he wanted to kill a man in a church. So he aimed at the guy's feet, wincing as the Russian screamed and went down.

McDougal sprinted for the Monomakh throne and took cover once again. When the ensuing shots stopped, he yelled, "I have what you want! The necklace." He held it out so that it was visible.

"Give it to us," one of the men said in rough English, "or we will find your friends and execute them."

"They're not my friends, you idiots. They're my marks. I couldn't care less what you do to them." *Please, Natalie, don't hear this.* "I've been hunting this damned thing since before it left New York. And now I have it. So if you want it, you'll stop shooting at me and go back to your boss. Tell him that I want my standard ten percent commission, plus another ten percent for my trouble." He waited to see whether they'd take him seriously. *C'mon, c'mon . . . go for it and get off my back.*

The Russian told him to do something anatomically impossible.

Damn. But McDougal chose to ignore that. "You tell your boss to get that money to a dead drop of my choice. Once I have it, I'll leave the necklace at another dead drop. Got it?"

"No dead drops. Let's make a different deal: You drop dead. We kill you and take the necklace now."

Well, aren't you the wordsmith? Ha-ha. "Not interested. No upside for yours truly."

Eric took down the man trying to creep up on him with a single shot to the left thigh. Then he made a mighty dive for the south doors, skidding on his belly. He threw himself out and rolled down the steps, just as more men burst through the main doors of the cathedral.

Darkness had blessedly fallen outside, giving him more cover than he would have had by day. Across the square stood the Ivan the Great Bell Tower, and he tore over to it, rounding it and dodging into the trees to his immediate right.

The men pursued him, but he'd gotten a crucial ten-yard lead, and now he widened that. McDougal silently went up the tree closest to the bell tower and made a risky jump from a limb to a middle balustrade, landing awkwardly. Pain shot through his ankle, but he ignored it as he flattened himself so that he couldn't be seen from the ground. Floodlights lit the building for tourists, but they also cast deep shadows that were convenient for a man in his predicament.

When the Russians rounded the corner, there was no sign of him at all. His lungs were close to bursting with adrenaline, and his breathing would have been ragged if he'd let it be. Instead he pushed his face into his forearm and forced himself to take in air quietly, from his nose only.

The men walked around below him, peering into the trees and debating whether he'd run for the Kremlin wall and simply gone over it. One of them did suggest that he'd gone into the bell tower, but another pointed out that it was locked at night. They went off to double-check that, while McDougal lay pressed against the cold stone, hidden by the architecture of the balustrade.

Then, unbelievably, his cell phone rang. He almost smashed it in his haste to mute the thing, and hung up on the caller. It was Avy. With the phone safely on vibrate, he held his breath and listened carefully to see whether anyone on the ground had heard it. Nothing stirred, thank God.

She called back.

"Avy," he hissed, "I can't talk right now!"

"Good," she said. "Neither can I. But I need you to get hold of a car and come pick up me, Liam, and an unconscious guy out at the Bykovo Airport."

"Not going to happen for a couple of hours," he said.

"Listen, McDougal. You're here on the company dime, and this is a serious situation. I really need your help."

"Yeah? Well, as soon as I get away from the people who are *shooting* at me, I'll be glad to play taxi. Until then, I'm a little tied up."

"People are shooting at you?"

"Isn't that what I just said?"

"Why?"

"I really don't have time to go into it."

"You need backup?"

"No. I'm fine."

"Whatever you say. Explain when you pick us up. Can you bring me enough cash for a hefty bribe? And by the way, do you know what tigers eat?"

"Come again?"

"Tiger. Fierce orange and black creature with really big teeth."

"I *did* hear you right."

"What do they eat?"

"Deer. Bears."

"Well, dang. I'm fresh out of bear meat this evening. So when you come, can you bring the Russian equivalent of Meow Mix or something? And I mean a *lot* of it."

Thirty-one

Natalie, Nonnie, and the colonel stayed bellies down on the cold cathedral floor for a solid hour of silence before they dared to move. For most of that time, Natalie reassured herself that what Eric had shouted to the men in the cathedral was a cover story.

They're not my friends, you idiots. They're my marks. I couldn't care less what you do to them. I've been hunting this damned thing since before it left New York . . .

No, it wasn't possible. She could sense Eric's decency, his sincerity. But . . .

Okay, he'd admitted that he was here with her partially because of something to do with the Russians who were after them. He'd hinted at government work. So maybe he was trying to bust an international smuggling ring. That made sense.

She forced herself to take three deep breaths, exhaling slowly.

It made total sense. Didn't it?

Yes, it did.

Her grandmother began to shiver uncontrollably, and Nat took off her coat and slipped it over Nonnie's shoulders. Then she got to her feet, slipped off her boots, and tiptoed out of the alcove in her stocking feet. She went down the corridor and stopped at the arch that led back out to the main nave of the cathedral.

The chandeliers were still lit, casting a warm glow over the deep, rich, multihued murals, and a solitary woman knelt in prayer toward the front of the nave.

There were no signs of gunmen.

Natalie padded back to the alcove. "I think we can leave now." The colonel helped her shivering grandmother up from the floor. "Are you all right?"

"Just a bit creaky," Colonel Blakely assured her.

"Nonnie?"

"Holding together, my dear."

"I think we should all go back to the Savoy to wait for Eric," Natalie said. "Please God, let nothing have happened to him."

"St. George—," Nonnie began.

"Yes, I know. St. George will protect him," Natalie finished for her. "Forgive me if I'm still anxious about his welfare."

"I don't like guns," Nonnie announced.

"That makes two of us." Natalie kissed her grandmother's cheek and took her hand. The colonel had her arm on the other side. "Come on, let's go."

Ted frowned and said slowly, "You don't think that Eric fellow was telling the truth back there?"

"Of *course* not," said Natalie. "He was bluffing. Scary how good he is at it, too. But I trust him. Don't worry."

They found that the temperature had dropped a good fifteen degrees as they exited the church and walked the few blocks back to the Savoy. Natalie's whole body broke out in gooseflesh, and she had to clench her teeth to prevent them from chattering. The colonel tried to give her his coat, but she refused it. At his age, he needed it more than she did.

Their appearance garnered a discreetly raised eyebrow from the registration clerk, but he made no comment until she asked whether Eric had come in yet.

"Mr. McDougal? No, we haven't seen him yet this evening. There is a message for him, however."

"For him or from him?"

"For him."

"I'll take it up," Natalie said. She took the folded message from the clerk. "Thank you. I'll make sure he gets it."

The three of them went upstairs to the room, and Natalie left the message on the nightstand, under the telephone. She was tempted to peek at it, but it wasn't for her, so she left it alone.

They all needed a drink and a hot meal, so Natalie fixed Nonnie's hair and straightened her clothes. The colonel borrowed a comb. Natalie threw on a different sweater and said a silent thank-you that her blind grandmother couldn't see the sloppy way she was dressed, thanks to Eric's odd choices from her wardrobe.

Then they went down to have a somewhat strained, exhausted dinner in the Savoy's elegant, white-tablecloth restaurant.

Where was Eric? Natalie could barely contain her rising worry throughout the appetizer and soup courses. Was he unconscious or bleeding to death somewhere? Had the thugs outright killed him and disposed of his body in the Moskva River? Should she call the American embassy and beg for help to find him?

By the time the main course arrived, a lovely chicken dish with a Georgian walnut sauce, she couldn't eat more than a bite. Instead she downed more wine in an attempt to soothe her nerves.

Eric McDougal had entered her life less than a week ago, and she refused to believe that he could exit so quickly. Still, her fear mounted with every passing minute.

Colonel Blakely picked up the dinner tab, over her protests, and with a shrewd glance at her face suggested that he take Nonnie back to their hotel. She was fatigued.

"Do you feel safe here alone, after the incident in your room?" he asked Natalie.

"Yes. They've doubled, if not tripled security since then. Hotel management have fallen over themselves to make us comfortable and have even comped part of our stay."

"All right. Let us know when Eric returns, will you? I'm going to take advantage of your grandmother's fatigue and keep asking her to marry me until she says yes."

Nonnie flapped a hand at him. "Stop it, Ted. I'm *blind*."

"And clearly I'm deaf . . . We'll make a wonderful pair."

Natalie shook her head at them. "Just say yes, Nonnie. I couldn't pick a nicer man for you myself." She bundled them into a cab.

Then, left to herself, she wandered into the Savoy's Hermitage Bar and ordered a third glass of wine, telling herself it would be the last.

The minutes ticked by like passing eons. Halfway through her drink, she couldn't take it anymore. She got up and left, riding the elevator back up to the room.

The silence and tastefulness of the furnishings were meant to be relaxing, but instead they screamed at her. The walls closed in, suffocating her in a welter of polished wood, cream brocade, and pastel paintings.

Natalie glanced at the phone, willing it to ring. The message she'd brought up earlier still sat on the nightstand. She wondered whether it might contain any clue about where Eric could be and when he'd return. It was doubtful, but possible.

She tugged the paper out from under the phone and unfolded it, feeling guilty.

McDougal, it read.

> *Trying to find you. If you are still chasing the St. George piece, then we need to talk. There are complications. And be careful! ARTemis can't afford to lose you. Call me,*
>
> *Avy*

Natalie read the message, reeling, and then read it again. ARTemis? The St. George piece?

ARTemis, she knew, was a company that tracked down and recovered stolen art. The "St. George piece" could only refer to the necklace.

She covered her mouth with a shaking hand. "No . . . ," she whispered. "No, no, no."

Eric didn't work for the government?

She tried to process this as her legs began to tremble and refused to support her. She sat down hard on the bed and stared at the note. Her stomach pitched, hurling bile up her throat, but her heart was there already and blocked it.

She was going to choke on her own heart.

She couldn't get any air.

Still, she tried to deny the evidence in front of her. Working for ARTemis could be his cover, right?

But that didn't explain the direct reference to the necklace. It didn't come close to explaining it.

She finally got some air down into her lungs; she didn't know how. But slowly the truth seeped through the blinders over her eyes.

Eric wasn't some secret agent. How could she have been so stupid? So blind?

It's not a matter of me trusting you, Natalie, he'd said. *Please understand that, okay? Let's just say that you have good instincts. But I am not at liberty to tell you who I work for.*

He'd picked her up in Reif's deliberately, and she'd gotten tipsy and made it easy for him. Her face flamed as she remembered begging him to make love to her, to give her a happy ending. He'd never been attracted to her in the slightest. She'd been part of a job to him.

A *job*.

No wonder he'd "dropped everything" to drive to her grandmother's house in Connecticut! No wonder he'd conveniently been there when she'd found her apartment trashed. He'd probably done that himself, the bastard . . .

He'd told her he was a security expert, for God's sake. And he was—he knew exactly how to get around security.

How convenient that he had the urge and the vacation time to accompany her to Moscow! Of *course* he'd paid her way—it was the least he could do, while he was using her to get to her grandmother and the necklace.

Mortification beat a mocking tattoo in her bloodstream and pulsed fiercely at her neck.

Natalie, Natalie. You pathetic, impulsive, naive little product of ivory-tower professors. Believer in honor and chivalry and fairy-tale romance—all the ideals of world literature.

She'd believed in Eric McDougal. Been dazzled by him. She'd trusted him. Worse, she'd declared her heart to him.

I fell in love with you that night in Reif's.

And he'd tried to shut her up, but she clearly wouldn't know a clue if it stabbed her with a spear.

Guys like you don't end up with girls like me.

Oh, Natalie. Ya *think*?

He must have had a hard time containing his laughter.

Natalie cringed, even as her anger and sense of violation swelled to volcanic proportions. She'd been in agony for hours now, worried whether Eric was injured or dead. Waiting for him to come back to her.

And she had given him the St. George necklace with her own hands! *Nonnie, you can trust this man . . .*

Sounds emerged from her throat that she didn't recognize. Little rusty gasps of appalled amusement at her own expense. She should be crying, but she was far, far too enraged.

She'd done intimate, uninhibited things with Eric sexually because she'd trusted him so completely. He'd been so generous and tender—when all the while he'd been planning to use, betray, and steal from her.

He was, for all intents and purposes, a thief. And he'd not only stolen the St. George necklace; he'd stolen her heart and all her faith in humankind.

McDougal waited an hour and a half before moving. He lay on his back, looking up at the stars over Moscow. Inside his jacket pocket his fingers toyed with the St. George necklace. Ten percent of $2 million was a nice chunk of change, enough to put a down payment on that Bertram 540 he wanted so badly that he could taste it.

Easy enough to smuggle the piece back into the U.S. and walk it into the executive offices at Hiscox. The necklace would go back to the thugs who'd insured it, even if he dropped a hint to Hiscox about the fraudulent provenance. The insurer would void the policy but couldn't, under the law, keep the necklace. And Natalie?

Hell. Natalie could still be prosecuted and go to jail, even with Luc Ricard dead and his business presumably defunct. But Natalie was a grown woman and should have considered the consequences of her actions before she "borrowed" the necklace.

"Natalie," he groaned aloud. What to do? He liked her. He cared for her. He hated deceiving her. But it was part of his job—which was to recover the necklace.

Nobody was in the right here. They were all thieves: the Nazi who'd stolen the St. George piece to begin with; the Russian thugs who'd stolen it from the Nazi; Natalie, who'd stolen it from her place of employment; her grandmother, who'd stolen it from Natalie; and now he himself, who'd repossessed it from Nonnie with a lie, by promising to give it back. Who was in the right here? Who among them hadn't broken the law? And to whom did the necklace really belong?

To Nonnie, of course, if he were to throw all legalities out the window. But Eric worked for ARTemis, which had been contracted by an insurance company, which had written a policy in good faith.

Eric broke the law in small ways on a regular basis, simply to do his job. He was a B-and-E specialist, a trained con artist. But his loyalty? No matter what his conscience or his heart told him, his loyalty had to be to ARTemis.

Curiously enough, loyalty was important to him. It was, in fact, sacrosanct. And that was the very reason he never promised it to a woman—he refused to swear a loyalty that he couldn't maintain.

His thoughts returned to Natalie as he fingered the contours of the necklace in his pocket. He'd be a fool to give it back to the old lady. A fool.

What purpose would it serve? The family treasures she spoke of gaining in return for it had to be long gone. The items would never have survived the war or the greed of their caretakers over the years. Even priests succumbed to temptation.

If he gave back the necklace, it would be for nothing but redemption in Natalie's eyes. And even that hope was tenuous at best. Once she found out how he'd deceived her, she'd never forgive him. She'd never trust him again.

How to explain? There was no explaining. How to make it up to her? He couldn't.

So if she was going to hate him anyway, why not give her a damned good reason?

The bottom line was that she and her grandmother

were safer without the necklace in their possession. If he kept the necklace, they'd be protected. Unharmed.

Wasn't that worth something? Didn't saving their lives make him less of a shit?

Oh, McD, buddy. You are good. You can justify anything in that evil mind of yours, can't you?

He did his best to shut down his brain and its labyrinth of twisted logic and deal with his current situation.

Focus, you bonehead. But he couldn't.

He had to find a way to completely neutralize the Russians so that Natalie and her grandmother would be safe. And so, as a last resort, he sent a text message to Kelso himself.

Russian Mafiya boss: Pyotr Suzdal. Need to neutralize. Dirt?

If anyone could find out that kind of info, Kelso could. Miguel was phenomenal at digging up information. But Kelso was the master of interpersonal relationships—who knew whom and how and why on a global scale. McDougal hoped he could help.

In the meantime, Eric had to get down from this building and go rent or steal a car in order to pick up his crazy boss, who was, inexplicably, at an airport with an unconscious man and a tiger.

Where in the hell did you get food for a tiger? Suddenly Eric remembered the two men who had stepped forward to help him and Natalie when she'd been stuffed into the car—one of them had been a soccer player, Mikhail. The other, Ivan, had owned a restaurant.

Eric fumbled his wallet out of his back pocket and dug out the scrap of paper Ivan had given him. He dialed the telephone number and asked to speak to Ivan.

"I'm ready to take advantage of your hospitality," he said, after identifying himself. "Can you do a very large take-out order?"

McDougal had a taxi drop him off a couple of blocks from Ivan's restaurant. Cars lined both sides of the street, and he chose a nondescript beige Renault that had seen better days. He wasn't stealing it, only borrowing it.

His mouth twisted wryly as he fished out his ARTemis-issued set of lock picks, easily opened the door, and had the car running within seconds. He eased out of the tight parking spot and into the street. Within ten minutes he'd pulled in back of Ivan's restaurant and switched license plates with another car.

Called simply Ivan's, it was a casual, cheerful little place with scarred wooden tables, mismatched chairs, and a two-sided stone fireplace that kept the patrons toasty on cold nights.

McDougal asked to use the facilities and was directed around a corner and down a cramped hallway. It was a nasty, dark little room furnished with a crapper that had to date to 1950-something and a sink that also shrieked with age at the turn of its rusty taps.

He glanced around quickly for someplace to stash the damned necklace burning a hole in his pocket. If the thugs jumped him before he could get back to the Savoy, it was better that he not have it on him.

There wasn't much to work with. He wasn't going to plunge the St. George piece into the gray water in the mop bucket. He didn't have any duct tape to fasten it under the commode. It wouldn't be smart to just drop it in the toilet tank.

His eyes went to the dusty window treatment, which surprisingly enough had once been a pretty, floral, padded cornice board. Limp matching curtains still hung under it.

He stepped over to it and peered underneath. Then he dug a small pocketknife out of his trousers, reached up with it, and made an incision. Dust and some crumbly foam rubber fell into his eyes and made him sneeze, but he created a pocket that he could slip the necklace into. Then he tugged the fabric back down and tucked under the edges. Beautiful.

He went to the pocked, pitted mirror over the sink and brushed the particles and dust out of his hair. He washed them down the drain and then cleaned his hands. Now it was time to claim his barbecue.

"You have party?" Ivan asked, handing over three big paper bags of packaged meat, bread, and salads.

McDougal nodded.

"Where is pretty girl? You break up? Give me chance?" Ivan grinned.

"She's spoken for, buddy. All mine. Sorry."

"You are not sorry."

"Well, no," Eric admitted, grinning back at him. "So how much do I owe you?"

Ivan shrugged and named a sum that was ridiculously low.

Eric gave him double the amount. He sniffed the bags. "Mmmmm."

"You will like," Ivan promised.

"I'm sure I will." The question was, would the tiger?

Thirty-two

McDougal's eyes itched as he drove toward Bykovo Airport. The ripped-off Renault reeked of some cheap floral perfume mingled with stale cigarette smoke and mildew. This combination fought with the tangy, smoky aroma of the barbecue and created a strange miasma of vapors that made him sneeze. He'd rolled down the windows to take deep breaths of the freezing air when his cursed cell phone rang yet again. He sighed and rolled up the windows again as he answered it.

"McDougal!" screamed Sheila out of the clear blue night.

"What?" he said, holding the phone away from his ear. "I didn't do it. It was a guy dressed up like me."

"Listen, you have to tell Marty that I'm not screwing around on him!"

"Excuse me?"

"Tell him, McDougal, please! He noticed the diamond bracelet. I lied about it and said it was CZs, but he's not completely stupid—who knew?—and now he's threatening to divorce me."

If not for the very real anguish in her voice, this would

have been comical. "So why didn't you tell him you just bought it?"

"Are you smoking crack, McDougal? Marty is an *accountant.* Me buying a diamond bracelet for myself is much, much worse than selling my body in the town square. That's grounds for *death*, not divorce."

"O-kay. So tell him it was only phone sex."

"I did! He doesn't believe me. But you're a witness. Remember? When I thought you were Sid? The bit about the crotchless panties?"

McDougal shuddered. "Sheila, babe, I'm *so* not getting between you and your husband. That comes under the heading of *extremely personal*."

"Just talk to him, I'm begging you. Here he is."

"What? No, hell, no, I am *not*—"

"McDougal?" Marty growled.

The tic at the poor little man's left eye was probably going nuts, making his nerdy little glasses vibrate. He sounded so mad that his straight, limp comb-over strands had gone corkscrew.

"Hi, Marty," McDougal said, then took a deep breath. "How ya doin'?"

"How do you think I'm doing?" Marty yelled. "My wife's wearing a diamond bracelet that I didn't give her, and she's started up some kind of prostitution thing. Worse, she isn't paying taxes on her illegal earnings!"

"I'm not a whore," Sheila yowled in the background. "I told you, it's only *phone sex*. And I only did it for the jewelry, because you're so damn cheap!"

McDougal winced and pretended he hadn't heard her. "Okay, okay, calm down, Marty. Look, I admit the tax thing is bad."

"Calm down? Are you kidding me? We may have to pay penalties. And *interest*." He voiced this last word in a squeaky, appalled whisper.

"Did I tell you he was cheap, McDougal?" shouted Sheila, who'd evidently grabbed the phone. "Did I?"

"Lesson in man psychology: You are not making this any better. Quit calling him cheap."

"I'll quit calling him cheap when he quits calling me easy."

If the shoe fits . . . "Put Marty back on the phone, will you?"

"Fine." Stomping and rustling ensued.

"Yeah?" Marty barked.

"Look, man. I want you to listen to me. Your wife loves you. She really does. And you've got to understand, Sid Thresher is a deranged sexaholic who flirts with anything that moves. I'm sure he started it first."

"Hmm," said Marty.

"And Sheila, you know she's got a smart mouth . . . She replied in kind. And Sid sends women gifts—inappropriate or not, he does—and I'm sure that's how this all started. You know he sent Gwen a bunch of diamonds, too, don't you? And I can guarantee *she* never slept with him."

"How can you be sure of that?"

"I'm sure because Gwen never slept with me, either, and it wasn't for lack of invitation or opportunity." McDougal coughed, feeling his face flush in the darkness.

"So you really think this is some harmless game?"

"Yeah, man, I do."

"Sheila says you overheard her one time. That she never said anything very dirty."

"Er . . . no." He dragged his hand down his face, steering with his knee for a moment. "Nothing, um, X-rated or anything."

"You swear?"

McDougal sighed inwardly. Oh, who gave a damn? He was already going to hell. No escaping it. "I swear."

"If you're lying to me, I will be happy to put a bug in the ear of the IRS, and you can enjoy an audit."

"Marty, Marty, Marty. Why would I lie to you, Mart-Man?"

"Okay. But how am I going to pay taxes on that bracelet . . . ?"

McDougal thought fast and came up with a way to save Sheila's marriage and yet torture her at the same time. He was good that way. "Easy, man. Easy. You just have Sheila clean a few houses on the side until she saves up the money."

Marty ruminated. "Yeah, maybe that would work . . ."

"Piece of cake. You keep your wife. She keeps her bracelet. Both of you live happily ever after."

"Okay. Okay, I could see that. Thanks, McDougal. Thanks for helping us through this."

"No problem. Listen, you give that naughty girl Sheila a kiss for me, 'kay?" In the face of the ensuing silence he clarified, "On the *cheek*."

McDougal's GPS unit guided him the rest of the way to Bykovo Airport, which was small enough that he found Avy and her group easily, despite her disguise. The stretcher supporting the unconscious man piqued his curiosity, though. Who was he?

Beside Avy, who was dressed as a middle-aged nurse,

was a tall man who looked a little like Sigmund Freud. This had to be the notorious Liam James, also in disguise.

And they were also hanging out with a tiger? What in the hell was going on?

As McDougal pulled up and shut off the car's engine, Avy walked over to greet him, taking note of his bruised face and neck. "Wow. You look like hell."

"Stop it with the compliments already," he said. "You've looked better yourself, Nurse Ratched."

Her lips twitched and she fingered the large, faux mole she'd added to her neck. "Why are people shooting at you, McD?"

"Well, it's like this, Ave: Once you piss off the Russian Mafiya, they want to kill you. I'm a target now."

"How did you let that happen? They should never have been *aware* of you."

"How did you become a target for the Greeks, Avy? For chrissakes, it's not like I registered with these people! I didn't sign my name on their 'Please Kill Me' list."

"You got involved with the mark," Avy said flatly. "You're banging the restoration artist, aren't you? And they're after her."

McDougal clenched his jaw. Then he glanced at Liam deliberately, looked him up and down, before turning his gaze back on Avy. Without saying a word, he'd pointed out that she, too, had gotten involved with her onetime mark.

He opened a rear door of the car and grabbed the take-out bags. When he turned around, a dark red flush had climbed her cheeks.

"Avy," he said, "you may be my boss, but you have no say in how I live my personal life. Understand?"

"You're right, McDougal—as long as your personal life stays personal, and doesn't spill over into your professional one."

Again, he glanced at Liam, wasting no subtlety.

Avy ignored this, but the color in her cheeks didn't fade. "Is she here in Moscow? The mark? Are you babysitting her?"

"I'm not babysitting anyone. But yes, she's here."

Avy didn't look pleased, but for once she refrained from comment. His point had hit home. "We need to talk about this necklace you're chasing."

"Why? You threw me off the case, remember?"

She shot him a glance that said she wasn't born yesterday. "There's evidently a big question about who the legitimate owner of the St. George piece really is."

"I can tell you that, and it's not the Russian thugs who consigned it to the care of Luc Ricard Restoration. It's Tatyana Ciccoli, aka Natalie Rosen's grandmother. You know Natalie as 'the mark,' " he added by way of explanation.

"Oh, yeah? That man on the stretcher claims to be the owner."

"And just who is that guy? Why do you have him here?"

Avy fidgeted. "He's . . . a recovery."

McDougal stared at her. "What do you mean? Since when have we gotten into bounty hunting? And he doesn't look like he's recovering. He looks like shit."

"Ha-ha. He's a Nazi war criminal. We're 'recovering' him for the World Court. But here's the thing: He's the old man I told you about. The second person who tried to hire us to track down the St. George necklace."

"Holy . . ." McD stared at her, then turned to look at the Nazi. "Natalie told me that her great-grandfather was murdered in front of his children over that necklace. What's this man's name?"

"Weimar von Bruegel. He's been living as Oleg Litsky in Moscow since about 1949."

"Von Bruegel," he repeated. "How old is he?"

"Eighty-two."

"Jesus, it's him. Natalie's grandmother is going to have something to say to this guy; I can promise you that."

"You're getting ahead of yourself, McD. We have a major problem: We took on the necklace recovery job for Ricard's insurance company—"

"Why is that a problem? The policy won't cover stolen goods. It's fraudulent and will be declared null and void."

"It's a problem," she said, "because we won't get paid. Two hundred thousand dollars is a lot of money, and we've run up serious expenses here."

He shook his head. "I don't care," he said flatly. "The necklace is going to the old lady. It's the right thing to do. You can dock my expenses out of my next checks."

"McDougal, are you asking me or are you telling me this?" she questioned him in steely tones.

He straightened and looked her right in the eye. "I'm telling you, Ave. I'm telling you. You may be the boss, but there is no debate on this one. If you try to pull rank and force me to give that necklace to Hiscox, then you'll have my resignation as soon as the words are out of your mouth."

Avy gave him a long, evaluative stare through her ugly

makeup. Then she nodded, and the corners of her mouth turned up unexpectedly. "You're all right, McDougal."

He squinted at her. "Yeah?" he said sarcastically. "Good to know that, Ave. Because, being the shy and insecure type, I wasn't sure."

She grinned. "You're all right," she repeated. "And you're also in love with the mark."

He snorted, loudly. Then he said, "She has a name: Natalie. And I'm not in love with her."

"Mmm. I'd bet about two hundred thousand dollars on it," she murmured.

McDougal changed the subject abruptly. "Where's the damn tiger? *This* I have got to see."

Thirty-three

The tiger didn't like Mongolian barbecue, but everyone else did, and the officials liked the cash bribes Avy supplied for dessert so that she, Liam, the Nazi, and the tiger could all take off into the starry night sky.

Liam cheerfully lashed the Nazi's cot into place next to the big, cranky kitty, displaying not an ounce of pity for the man, even when his eyes rolled in his head and he fainted from sheer terror. The big cat twitched its tail and seemed to find Nazi-in-the-raw much more interesting than smoked meat.

McDougal saw them off, shaking his head. Then he exited the airport himself, eager to get back to Natalie. He topped off the Renault's tank and returned the car to the same street from which he'd borrowed it.

Then he took the subway to the Kremlin and made his way back to the Savoy, watching carefully for any sign that he was being followed. There was none. He seemed to have lost the Russians for the time being.

Wearily, he entered the room that he shared with Natalie, hoping that she'd been able to get to sleep. But all the lights blazed and her suitcase stood next to the door, packed and zipped.

"Natalie?"

A tornado in a sweater, she rounded the corner from the bathroom and pummeled him with her fists.

McDougal staggered back under the force of her rage as she caught him under the jaw and then right in the solar plexus.

"You bastard!" she said with loathing.

He caught her wrists before she could hit him again. "Natalie, it's not what you think."

She struggled in his grasp, her small white hands still clenched into fists. "It's exactly what I think, you creep."

He tried to keep his hold on her gentle. He didn't want to bruise her or cause her pain. "No. No, it isn't. Please let me explain—"

"Take your hands off me!"

He was afraid that if he did, he'd never be allowed to touch her again. A nameless emotion tightened his chest, rose painfully to his throat, and threatened to strangle him. For a moment he was unable to speak.

"Let. Me. Go." Her tone was low and deadly.

I can't let you go. You're under my skin; you're inside my head. You see me, truly see me—you understand who I am. God help me, but you're the one. The one I never thought I'd find.

"Please," he said again, drawing her closer in spite of her clear efforts to get away. Her face was six inches from his. If he bent his head, he could kiss her. Maybe his lips could communicate physically what they seemed unable to say verbally.

She seemed to read his mind.

She turned her face away.

He'd never in his life had to say "please" to a woman. They said it to him. They lay down for him. They forgave him instantly.

But Natalie?

Natalie's eyes were no longer navy. They'd gone black with betrayal and contempt. Her lids had become armor, the lashes around them tiny swords to keep him at bay.

Her lips formed tight, straight lines. Even her skin, usually rosy with invitation, had gone pale and blank as a wiped slate.

"Please," he said a third time. "Let me explain."

She tore herself from his hands, her normally sleek hair wild around her face. "There's nothing to explain, Eric. I saw the message from your colleague. You work for ARTemis."

Skewered by her gaze, he could only nod.

"You deliberately targeted me and got me drunk in Reif's to pump me for information on the necklace."

He bowed his head. He would have given anything to deny the fact.

"Admit it!" she shouted.

"Yes," he said, his voice hoarse and strange to his own ears as he damned himself. "I met you on purpose."

"You've used me from the moment we met—"

"It's not that simple, Nat. I didn't count on—"

"You are *despicable*."

"—liking you so much. Caring for you."

"Stop it, you smooth, *sickening* liar. I have been a job to you, and nothing else."

"No—"

"A *job*!" she shouted.

"*No*," he said forcefully. "That's not true."

"What do you know about the truth, McDougal? You're a born manipulator; you lie for a living; you steal for a living. And you seduce for a living!"

He raised his eyebrows. "Did I seduce you, that first night?"

Her face flushed pink in mortification.

"As I recall, I did not."

"You got me drunk," she pointed out.

"Did I? I forced that whiskey down your throat?"

Her color deepened to brick. "You—"

"I took advantage of you later? Tore off your clothes and had my way with you?"

"Why do you have to humiliate me on top of everything else you've done, Eric? Is this fun for you?"

He shook his head. "I'm not trying to humil—"

"I was a slut! Okay? Is that what you want me to say? The nice girl hit the whiskey and her inner slut emerged to dance around your pole. Well, you know what? I'm glad. I've never done anything like that in my entire life, and maybe it was about time."

"That makes two of us. Because I've never done what I did that night, either."

"What?" She turned a still furious but puzzled gaze on him.

"I've never—not once in my life, Natalie—turned down what you offered that night. I'm the king—no, the emperor—of the one-night stand."

"Congratulations," she said in a withering tone.

"Damn it, will you listen to what I'm trying to say? It didn't feel right with you. I couldn't do it—even if you hadn't passed out cold on me. You were different."

Her expression was skeptical, to say the least.

"When I made love to you—"

"Made love?" she scoffed. "You *screwed* me—in every sense of the word—for a *commission*, Eric! Do you know what that makes you? You're a gigolo. A male *whore*."

He winced. McManWhore. "No," he said firmly. "When I made love to you, it had nothing to do with the job. You have to believe me."

Again, that scathing glance. "I thought you were some kind of white knight," she said, shaking her head. "The way you came riding to my rescue. I couldn't figure out why you'd buy me a first-class ticket to Moscow. I was dumber than a brick! You knew I'd lead you right to the necklace."

McDougal couldn't deny this. He was guilty as charged in terms of initial intent. "Natalie, it started out that way. But I couldn't go through with it."

"Really? Then where's the St. George necklace?"

He eyed her helplessly. "I don't have it on me right now."

"Of course you don't," she said. Scorn dripped from her voice. "My grandmother will die of heartbreak, I'll go to jail, and you'll cash your commission check without a trace of conscience."

He shook his head. "I put the necklace in a safe place in case the Russians came after me again. But I swear—"

"Don't bother, McDougal. The lies never end for you, do they?"

"Nat, I'm not lying," he said quietly. "I will bring you and your grandmother the necklace."

She narrowed her eyes. "Why would you do that?"

It was certainly a valid question. Why? And as McDougal stood there, desperately hoping that he could salvage his relationship with her, he understood at last that Avy was right, damn it. "Because . . ."

He'd never said the words to a woman other than his mother. He'd never wanted to betray their meaning, like his father.

"Why would you do that?" Natalie repeated.

McDougal swallowed hard. "Because . . . I love you."

Clearly incredulous, she started to laugh. It was the worst sound he'd ever heard.

"You aren't even able to stop lying, are you?"

"I love you, Nat."

"You don't love anyone but yourself, Eric." She stalked to the door and yanked up her suitcase.

"Where are you going?"

"Why would that be any of your business?" she asked brutally.

"Natalie, don't put yourself at risk because you're angry with me. Those men are still out there."

"How do I even know that those attacks weren't staged? It's mighty convenient that you've come to save me every time I've been threatened. Did you hire those men? Were those exercises just to win my trust?"

Appalling thought. "That's crazy, Nat!"

"Answer the question. Was it you who trashed my apartment in New York? Before you so gallantly rode to my rescue in Connecticut?"

"No! How can you think that?"

"Easily, Eric. Your lies have blown open the door to any possibility."

"I could never—Nat, *I love you*," he said again.

"I don't believe you. You've left me with nothing to believe in." She looked down and pressed her lips together hard, as if to stifle a sob.

"My grandmother," she said, "is still convinced that you're a modern knight, that you've been sent to us by St. George himself." She laughed again, bitterly. "Poor, deluded woman. And now I get to go and inform her that far from being a knight, you're a serpent—the dragon.

"I should have known better. Women who sit around waiting for princes and knights to rescue them are utter fools. We have to be our own knights. We have to wear our own armor, ride our own horses, fight our own battles."

Natalie turned her back on him and opened the door, then stopped. "My kingdom for a spear right now, Eric. I'd ram it down your lying throat."

Thirty-four

McDougal came after her. Why, she didn't know. She could hear the soft rub of his denim-clad legs as he walked. Why did he bother? What could he say? He couldn't defend his actions—they were inexcusable.

And his sudden declaration of love? Pure manipulation. Like everything else about him, the tender words were too damned convenient, meant to con her and defuse her anger.

"Natalie, if you're going to stay with your grandmother, you'd better realize that you'll put her in danger," he said.

She stopped.

"The Russians are following you."

Were they? She squared her shoulders. "Are they really, or did you hire them, Eric?"

"Nat, I swear by all that's holy that the Russians are for real. Please don't expose yourself. No matter how good the security is here at the Savoy, once you leave the premises you are a target. You have a bull's-eye on your back, same as I do—and no way to defend yourself."

"No, Eric. They know that you have the necklace now. Why would they care about me?"

"They may use you to get to me. Natalie, these people don't screw around. I don't want to have your fingers delivered to me in a box, okay?"

She put down her suitcase, then turned and faced him, willing herself not to be suckered again by that honest, direct blue gaze. Arming herself against his professional sincerity. Steeling herself against the attraction she still stupidly felt for him. Even now, her silly, idealistic feminine side wanted to believe in the fairy tale. She wanted to slap that part of her into next year. "If you're so worried about me, then give me your gun."

"Give you my gun?" He stared at her, incredulous. "You don't know the butt from the barrel. Have you ever even fired a weapon?"

She raised her chin. "So teach me. It's the very least you can do."

He spread his hands wide. "I'd be happy to teach you, if it were broad daylight and we could locate a firing range. But it's close to three o'clock in the morning and we can't exactly line up cans of caviar on the windowsill to practice on."

"Fine. Then teach me the basics with the safety on."

"No. It's a bad idea, Natalie."

"Then what options do I have?" she burst out.

"You can stay with me and let me protect you until this business with the necklace is resolved."

Scorn suffused her entire body. "I'd rather die."

"Yeah? You think long and hard about that, sweetheart, because you could. Go back to the room, Natalie.

Please go back to the room until I can figure out a way to neutralize these people."

"And how exactly do you plan to do that?"

He shook his head. "I don't know. But I will."

"After all this, I'm supposed to believe you'll be my hero?"

He sighed. "You can believe whatever you want. You're right: I've been a deceitful son of a bitch. I can regret that, but I can't change it. All I can do is try to make up for it."

She leaned forward and poked him in the chest. "What I'm trying to figure out, Eric McDougal, is why you're still here. You've got the necklace—so what's stopping you from flying home to the U.S. and claiming your commission?"

He eyed her steadily, without flinching. "You," he said.

Oh, how she wanted that to be true! The rush of scorn faded, and she was left with a dull ache. She ached for him to be real, for him not to be the most skilled liar she'd ever met.

Wake up, Natalie, you dumb cluck. Think. What are his real motivations? As she stood there resisting her hormones, resisting his sheer physical appeal, it hit her.

It's because he wants even more. He wants to come with us to claim our family treasures—and take off with them, too. The bastard's still here because of simple greed.

She marveled at his coldness.

The problem was that she did need his protection. He was right about that. But she was so done with being used. She stood there considering her options. Could she beat him at his own game?

Distasteful to descend to his level. Not her style. She wasn't a fan of guile and manipulation . . . but she wanted the St. George necklace back. And, if she were honest, some small measure of revenge for what he'd put her through.

She stood there, caught between attraction and repulsion, the need to get away and the necessity of staying by his side.

"Natalie?"

Keep your friends close, but your enemies closer. So went the old saying. Could she? Was she capable of staying in the same room with him, sleeping in the same bed, tolerating the lies that flew out of his corrupt mouth?

She'd force herself. She'd do it for Nonnie, to get the necklace back. And she'd do it for herself, because Eric McDougal deserved a comeuppance. She'd do it to get back her self-respect.

"Natalie, please . . ."

God, he was good! He must take sincerity pills every morning. Eric looked as if he were about to drop to his knees and beg her to stay.

"I don't know, Eric," she said, shaking her head. "I'd be stupid to believe you. How do I know you're for real?" She produced a wistful expression, mined the genuine emotions she'd tried to banish.

He started toward her, took her hands in his own strong, warm ones. Her body reacted with a surge of longing, and she ruthlessly used it, hating herself for curdling what had been a good and pure and innocent love.

"You can't know I'm for real," he said gently, and

kissed her on the lips. "You have to take it on faith. Please, give me another chance."

Faith? You shattered my faith. She kept her face angled up toward his, her eyes closed so that he couldn't discern her deep, well-founded cynicism.

He kissed her again, deeply this time, and her whole body responded, pleasure seeping through every pore. But she separated her mind from it, kept it fenced off.

He wasn't stupid. He noticed. But the beauty of the deception was that she had every reason to hold back, and he had every reason to understand why.

Eric picked her up, one hand under her knees and one under her back. He held her tightly to his body as he walked back down the hallway with her and nudged open the door to their room, which he'd left wedged open with the security bar. With infinite tenderness, he laid her on the bed.

Unexpectedly, her eyes welled with tears and her cynicism formed a hard, unyielding lump in her throat. The ache returned, a desperate, yearning ache. *Weak! You're weak, Natalie. Stop it.*

"Sweetheart," he murmured, smoothing back her hair.

"I want this to be real," she said, brokenly. "Oh, God, I want this to be real."

"It is real." And Eric went out into the hall and brought her suitcase back into the room.

Appalled at herself, Natalie let him make love to her. He took off his shirt, unbuckled his belt, and threw them on the floor. She couldn't tear her eyes from the hard muscle of his shoulders and arms, the ripped expanse of his chest, and the golden hair that lightly sprinkled it.

He kissed her, his tongue seducing hers, searching for a mate. Eric smelled so deceptively clean, so honest—like lemon soap and leather and hard male.

She wanted to believe that he wanted her, that she wasn't just a convenient body in a convenient bed, and he made that easy. He pushed up her sweater and her bra, worshipping her breasts with that hot, clever mouth of his and tracing around her nipples with his tongue. Her tiny moans seemed to excite him, even as they disgusted her.

She had no self-control, no self-respect when it came to this man. She wanted him without reservation, wanted him thick and hard and pulsing between her thighs. She wanted to lose her mind with him . . . before she lost him deliberately, and for good.

He pulled the sweater over her head and tossed it, with the bra following suit. Then his hands went to her waist, dipping inside her jeans and brushing her skin before he unbuttoned them, unzipped them, and tugged them down her legs like a caress.

She was almost completely bare to his gaze now, her panties the only shield. They were yellow with tiny pink strawberries on them, and the corners of his mouth turned up at the sight.

"Mmm, strawberries," he said. Then he pulled them off, slowly, as if unwrapping a package.

He pushed her knees apart and slid his hands under her bottom. He blew gently where she was most sensitive, and a shiver overtook her. "What do you want, baby?"

What do you think I want? She stirred restlessly.

"Should I lick this little strawberry, here?" His mouth came within a hairsbreadth of her core—she could actually feel his stubble on her inner thighs—but still, he didn't touch her.

Anticipation made her thighs tremble, and another shiver stirred all her nerve endings. His breath, hot and hungry, caressed her again.

She raised up shamelessly for him, hating herself as she did so.

"That's one ripe strawberry, isn't it?"

He was close, so close to touching her, the tease. He chuckled, and the short puffs of breath on her made her almost insane with wanting him.

"I'll bet it's sweet, so sweet . . ."

Oh, God!

"Juicy."

She could come just listening to him, to that husky, dirty innuendo. To the gentle suggestion of her thighs being held apart against her will—though she knew it was only a suggestion. He'd let her go at any moment. The problem was that she didn't want him to.

"What do you want, baby? Tell me." Just a whisper of his lips against her and she was as taut as a bow, teetering on the brink of madness.

She let out an involuntary moan, and he blew on her again, then shucked out of his pants. Then one slow, long lick and she fell crazily into the abyss of pleasure.

He slid inside her as she came, and the sensation of being impaled and stroked internally set off a whole new chain of reactions. Completely out of control of her own body, she jerked, spasmed, shivered, convulsed. She cried out.

Within moments his body, too, went rigid and then pulsed with relief. He groaned softly, lifted himself up onto his elbows, and stared down at her. "I love you, Natalie."

How easy it would be to believe him. She traced his jaw with a finger and searched his face for answers that she wouldn't find.

"I . . . love you, too, Eric." *You stupid, stupid girl.* If only she weren't telling the truth.

Thirty-five

McDougal was up well before dawn the next morning, since he'd never shut his eyes. Natalie was fast asleep. He looked over at her, so sweet and graceful even in unconsciousness.

I . . . love you, too, Eric.

She loved him.

He rubbed at his eyes, trying to take it in. Did she? Could she really have forgiven him that easily?

She'd gone from punching him to making love with him in the space of what, thirty minutes? It seemed too quick a transition for her, but then, she was a woman and he didn't pretend to truly understand them.

He could charm them, seduce them, persuade them . . . but comprehend them? Not a chance. Mysterious, mercurial creatures, every last one.

McDougal dressed in the dark and then let himself out of the room without a sound other than the snick of the door as it shut. His first order of business was to get back to Ivan's restaurant and retrieve the necklace without anyone knowing he'd been there or anyone tailing him back to the hotel.

He exited the hotel through a rear service door and turned up the collar of his coat as the chilly March air circled the bare skin of his neck. It was still pitch-black outside and would be for some time.

There were no sounds other than the hum of compressors, the sway of branches in a determined breeze, and the barely audible pats of his rubber-soled shoes on concrete. He walked a couple of blocks west and borrowed another car, a newer-model Saab this time that smelled of cigarettes and men's hair product.

Again, he parked a couple of streets away from Ivan's restaurant and slipped through the shadows until he reached the building.

A little finagling with his trusty lock picks had him inside the back door within a few moments. He shut it behind him and stood still, just listening, for a moment.

He heard a rhythmic noise that sounded like a yak in labor. What the hell? Someone was snoring. In the damned kitchen. At—he checked his watch—4:49 a.m.

And in order to get to the bathroom, he had to walk right by the kitchen, in full view, with nowhere to hide. Beautiful.

McDougal thought about it. Clearly the occupant of the kitchen was asleep, but how deeply? Would the creak of a floorboard wake him? Or was he comatose from booze?

Eric gambled on the latter. Why else would anyone sleep in a kitchen instead of in the comfort of his own bed at home?

He cracked his neck to relieve tension and then stepped forward in the dark. Only a small creak gave him away, and the snoring continued undisturbed. He crept forward a few more steps and then eased around the corner to the narrow hallway he remembered from the evening before. The bathroom door was only twelve feet away.

Eric resumed his progress, inching past the open door to the kitchen, where the dark shape of a man slumped in an uncomfortable-looking chair, his head leaning back against the wall and his arms dangling to either side.

McDougal got out of sight quickly, tiptoeing past the far jamb. He'd just lifted his foot and set it down again when something dark and solid wound through his ankles and a hideously loud meow echoed up to the rafters. *Shit!*

The snoring segued into a sort of pig snort and then stopped.

"Dmitri? Is that you?"

"Da," Eric replied. Then he made a retching noise and stumbled toward the bathroom, hurling himself inside and slamming the door. He made more retching noises as footsteps sounded outside in the hallway.

"You will throw up your organs," Ivan's voice commented.

Eric just groaned and flushed the toilet.

"Don't pass out in there, eh? I have to pee."

"Piss in the sink," Eric said, muffling his voice through his hand. "Piss anywhere you want. Just go away."

Ivan chuckled. "You sound terrible."

A few more fake retches and his footsteps finally retreated. McDougal breathed a sigh of relief and then quickly dug the necklace out of its makeshift pocket in the old cornice board. He slipped it into his jacket and then eyed the tiny square of glass with some misgiving.

He had no choice but to go out the window.

Kelso called right as McDougal landed headfirst in a bed of what looked like kale and turnips outside the restaurant's bathroom.

"Unbelievable," he muttered as he got to his feet, shut the window behind him, and lurched forward into a getaway run. He took the precaution of diving into some bushes fifty yards away before answering.

"McDougal."

"Why, Eric, how are you?" said Disney's Donald Duck. *Eh-wic.* Kelso communicated out of the ether, usually via text but sometimes using electronically altered voices.

"Fine, sir, and you?" McD resisted the urge to reply in Daisy Duck's dulcet tones.

"You sound out of breath." *Bweth.* Jesus, this was surreal.

"Just made an exit via window, sir. A very small window."

"Good, good," Donald Duck said genially. "Glad to hear it. Listen, I've got some excellent information for you. High-voltage stuff, so be judicious in how you apply it."

"Yes, sir."

"Are you someplace private?"

McDougal raised his eyebrows and peered out from under the bush. "Sure."

"All right. Here goes. Turns out that your Suzdal is a pretty nasty guy. No surprise there, right? He's made very few missteps in his rise to power with one notable exception. In 2005, it seems that he cooked up a plan to have Vasily Somov, his former mentor, assassinated along with his heir apparent so that Somov's faction would be vulnerable to takeover. Suspicion did turn on Suzdal when the plot failed, but he managed to convince Somov that the danger came from another source. To prove his 'loyalty' to Somov, Suzdal even took this other man out by murdering him in his bed as an early Christmas present."

"Nice," said McDougal.

"Oh, very. Word is that he presented the man's terrified wife as a holiday gift, too. She was still wearing lingerie splattered with her husband's blood."

The hair on McDougal's arms stood up. "Sweet Jesus."

"Indeed. I'll spare you the details of how she was found later."

"I appreciate that."

"Suffice it to say that she is now living in the U.S. under a blanket of terror and an assumed identity."

"I see. She provided the information?"

"Some of it. Mostly she corroborated intel mined from a source inside Suzdal's organization. At any rate, she'll live in fear for the rest of her life. But you can use this secret of Suzdal's to—"

"Blackmail him," McDougal said flatly. "Neutralize him. Get him off my back for good."

"Your back, or Natalie Rosen's?" Donald Duck asked slyly.

"Both." Mother of God! Did *everyone* in the company have to know his personal business?

"Be careful. It's advisable that you have copies of this info with ARTemis and your lawyer before you go near Suzdal."

"Oh, you can bet on that, sir. Thank you. Thank you very much. I think you've just saved my ass."

"I haven't saved it. I've just given you the right tool, Eric. Stay in one piece, you hear me? I have no desire whatsoever to go to your Scots-Irish wake and sing 'Danny Boy.' "

McDougal emerged from the bush, found his borrowed car once again, and drove it back to where it belonged. This time he left enough money inside to cover a tank of gas. He locked it back up again and sauntered away, whistling.

A quick gander at the entrance to the Savoy two blocks over told him that his Russian honor guard was back, and he was thankful that he'd soon be rid of them, courtesy of Kelso.

He dodged away and found a café, where he ordered some steaming chai and sat for a moment to think. He would give the necklace back to Nonnie, and damn the $200,000 commission. Within the next year he'd probably get an assignment or two that would be just as lucrative.

The important thing was Natalie. He loved her. She evidently returned the sentiment. But did he have it in him to stay loyal to her?

Across the street, a long-legged blonde moved gracefully down the sidewalk, and McDougal eyed her over the rim of his cup. *Loyalty, you bastard. Do you have it in you?*

He admired the blonde's curves, her fitted clothing, and the fall of her hair down her back. But she didn't stir him like the sight of Natalie with wet hair and a fresh-scrubbed face and an oversize man's sweater hanging down to her thighs did.

The blonde wouldn't laugh like Natalie did, or say the wry, funny things that she did.

Wow . . . Chivalry is not dead. It's been run over a few times; it's diseased and dirty; it's hooked on Boone's Farm and meth . . . but holy cow, it's still stumbling along in rags, raising its ugly head just when you least expect it—or want it.

How could he not love a girl who thought, much less said, things like that?

I know perfectly well that I'm drunk, she'd told him indignantly outside Reif's. *Do you think I'd do this sober?*

He grinned, and just like that the blonde turned her head. Thinking that he was smiling at her, she grinned back. She flicked her long hair over her shoulder in a practiced maneuver, hesitated as if she were thinking of coming over to talk to him. He averted his gaze, dismissing her, and with a little shrug she strutted away.

He took another sip of the hot chai, and as it burned down his throat he came to a realization. Loyalty wasn't something that was organic. It was a decision, like the resolve to be happy.

Loyalty to a woman didn't have to mean that he was blind. He could still appreciate female beauty. He could still wink at a gorgeous girl. But at the end of the day, loyalty meant coming home to someone who understood him, could laugh with him, and saw him as he really was, flaws and all.

Loyalty wasn't a leash—it wasn't a rule. It was a commitment you made because you wanted to. He could have great sex with any number of women, but at the end of the day sex was just sex . . . with no meaning, no intimacy.

Loyalty meant deserving someone who could forgive him. It meant trusting the woman in his life as she trusted him. It meant a commitment to not hurting her. It meant putting her needs and desires ahead of his own.

McDougal closed his eyes and thought of all the times he'd seen his mother's tearstained face, the hollows under her eyes and the betrayal in them.

He saw his father's weak, beery shame and then the anger that chased it and drove him back out of the house to repeat the cycle again.

Both of them had made decisions about their own behavior that they'd then blamed on others. Mom had gone the miserable-martyr route, blaming everything on her husband. And Dad had embraced booze and other women because he couldn't "make" her happy—rationalizing that therefore his cheating was her fault. She "drove" him to it.

No. That's all a load of crap. I don't know why it's taken me thirty-odd years to figure it out, but it has.

Asking if I can stay loyal to Natalie is a cop-out. It's like saying that I move on autopilot with my cock at the helm. If I can't control my own cock, I am one weak, spineless son of a bitch.

McDougal's arm brushed against the bulge of the necklace in his jacket as he finished the cup of chai. He left a little money on the table and got up to leave.

I may be a deceptive, ruthless, often sacrilegious jerk

with a twisted sense of humor. I may not be anyone's idea of a gentleman. But I am not weak, and I sure as hell am not spineless.

About a block down, on the opposite side of the street, an old woman was setting up her wares at a kiosk. She had the standard Russian souvenirs: Matryoshka dolls, the hollow wooden figures that stacked inside each other; painted and shellacked wooden eggs with icons on them; brightly colored wooden bowls and spoons; bright woolen shawls; Soviet memorabilia; and hand-painted trays and boxes.

He strolled down to the kiosk and looked at what the woman had to offer. The intricately painted Palekh boxes were exquisite, if expensive. One of them in particular pictured a couple, male and female, standing before a great castle in the background. Next to them was an old woman in a sort of shack—she reminded him a little of Nonnie, who had essentially brought him and Natalie together on this strange journey.

McDougal purchased the box. It was exactly the right size to hold the St. George necklace. The old lady wrapped it in paper for him and "accidentally" gave him back the wrong change.

Ordinarily, he would have argued with her and demanded the correct amount back. But he was in a forgiving mood, so he counted the change, made it clear that he knew exactly what she was up to, and looked directly at her. Then he winked and shook his finger, amused to see a blush climb to her cheeks.

He walked away, leaving her puzzled and staring after him. On the way back to the Savoy, he bought another copy of the *Moscow Times*. Then he strolled right in the front door, giving a little wave to the man across the street who had the hotel under surveillance. The creep couldn't touch him because of the bevy of doormen, porters, and security guards who went about their duties as a group of businessmen arrived for a breakfast.

Funny, the asshole just talked furiously into his phone and didn't wave back.

Thirty-six

Natalie rolled over sleepily as Eric came in. As quietly as possible, he removed a package from inside his jacket and slipped it into a drawer of the nightstand on his side of the bed.

"Eric?" she mumbled.

He straightened quickly. "Good morning, sweetheart."

"Morning. Mmmmph." She dragged a hand over her face. "You've been out already?"

"Yeah, just went to get an English paper." He turned on a low lamp across the room and held the *Moscow Times* up for her to see, making no mention of whatever it was that he'd put in the nightstand.

The necklace? He'd claimed not to have had it on him yesterday. Had he snuck out early this morning to retrieve it? But Natalie played oblivious, closing her eyes again as if she might drift off.

"Listen, Natalie . . . ," he began. He paced across the room. "There's something I have to do today, alone. And I just want you to promise me that you'll stay here, that you won't do anything risky. If all goes well, then we won't have anything to fear by tonight."

Queasiness slid around in her stomach like a glob of mercury. Eric might be a liar and a cheat, but he'd also been her lover, and she didn't want him in danger. Perversely, she wanted him alive and well so that she could slap his face on her way out of his life. "What is it that you have to do?"

He shook his head. "I can't tell you."

She sat up in bed and pushed her hair out of her face, tucking it behind her ears. "Well, then, I'm not making any promises to you about staying in this room."

He sighed. "Natalie, please—"

"Don't you 'please' me, Eric. Come clean. I'm sick of your lies and dodges." She turned on the bedside lamp and eyed him implacably, folding her arms under her breasts.

"Okay," he said. "The truth is that I'm going to meet with Pyotr Suzdal, the head of the Mafiya branch that's out to get us."

"You're *what*?"

He came and sat on the bed next to her, so close that the sleeve of his leather jacket touched her bare leg. She inhaled the musky scent of the leather, the faint essence of sex that still clung to his skin from the night before, and a peculiar smell of . . . dirt? Greenery?

"I have acquired some information that I can guarantee he won't want to get out, so I'm going to track him down, have a chat with the man, and make him see that it's in his best interests to forget about us."

"He'll kill you!"

Eric shrugged and took her hands, just as she discerned that there was mud in his hair. "He might. But quite frankly, that's better than him killing *you*."

If she hadn't seen the mud, if it hadn't been for the mysterious package in the nightstand, she might have fallen for the light of concern in those Newman blue eyes, the warm pressure of his hands squeezing hers, the leap of her libido at his proximity.

But Eric hadn't just been out to get a morning paper. He was still hiding things, still playing her. And she was tired of being his personal violin.

"No," she said. "No, no, no, no." The idea of his death might just be growing on her.

He had no way of realizing that she was talking to herself and not him. "I'm not going to let him kill me, Nat. I have too much at stake. Your grandmother's safety, yours, and . . . the promise of a life together."

She stared into those blue lagoons of deceit framed by angelic golden lashes. Again, the silly side of her that believed in fairy tales mourned. Why couldn't he be for real? What cruelty for him to taunt her this way, for him to impersonate a hero when he was the worst kind of villain. An old-fashioned word, *villain*, but the shoe fit.

As little as two days ago, she would have thrown herself into his arms and let him sweep her off her feet. She would have ridden off into any sunset, anywhere in the world, with this man. Tears warred with anger inside her, but she cloaked both with deceit of her own.

"A life together," she whispered. "You and me?"

He nodded, stroked her cheek with the back of his fingers.

"Yes, if you'll give me a chance to make you happy."

She bowed her head over their clasped hands. Eric wasn't going to meet with this thug today in order to blackmail him. He was almost certainly going to meet with the man to see if he could get more money out of him for the necklace than ARTemis would pay him in commission for bringing it back.

Give him a chance to make her happy? Simple: He could make her happy by lying down on a highway in front of a semi. She pictured him with tire tracks down his back.

He freed one hand to stroke her hair, and she shivered half in disgust and half in pleasure, since her idiotic body still hadn't figured out that he was the devil incarnate.

He rubbed her back, and she forced herself not to move away from him, not to spit in his too-handsome, lying face.

"So," he said, "will you promise me that you'll stay here today? I won't be able to think on my feet if I'm worried about you."

She raised her head and looked into his charismatic, calculating face, which had achieved an expression of sweetness that was so convincing . . . she almost bought it in spite of everything she knew about him.

"I promise, Eric," she said. "I promise."

"Thank you," he said simply, and kissed her. Before she knew it, she was making love with the bastard again. But she insisted to herself, even stark naked and deliciously impaled by him, that it was only so that he wouldn't become suspicious.

Natalie waited until he'd disappeared into the bathroom and she heard the rings of the shower curtain slide along the metal rod before taking action.

She scrambled over to the side of the bed Eric slept on and eased open the drawer of the nightstand. Inside was something wrapped in paper. She pulled it out and unwrapped a colorful hand-painted box. She shook it; something heavy and metallic rattled inside. She lifted the lid, and there, winking back at her under the lamplight, was the St. George necklace.

Without conscious thought, she snatched it out of the box, hopped naked out of bed, and scurried over to drop it into one of her boots. It slid down to the toe, and she stuffed a sock after it.

But what to put in place of the necklace, so that if Eric were to pick up the box to take it with him, he wouldn't notice immediately that it felt lighter?

She thought quickly, then ran to her purse and pulled out a handful of coins—quarters and rubles for the most part. She went to the bag of fabric scraps next and chose a remnant of cloth that she didn't particularly need. She spread it on the floor, put the coins in the middle, and tied the corners together diagonally. Then she did the same with the two remaining corners. The pouch wasn't so tight that the coins didn't chink against one another at all, but it was snug enough that the sounds were subtle, in keeping with the rattle of the necklace.

She placed the bundle of coins into the lacquered box, wrapped it back in the paper, and carefully replaced it exactly as it had been inside the drawer. Gently she pushed it closed and then rolled back to her side of the bed—and not a moment too soon, since Eric emerged seconds later with a towel wrapped around his waist.

"You gonna get up, lazybones?" he teased her.

She yawned. "Why? If I'm staying in the room all day, what's the difference?" She pulled the covers up to her chin and snuggled sideways into her pillow.

"I guess you have a point," Eric said. He dropped his towel on the end of the bed and stepped into a pair of boxers while she enjoyed the view of his impressive nudity for the last time. The tattooed Mona Lisa smiled smugly at her from the cheek of his ass.

She'd miss the eye candy. She'd miss the way he made love, always seeing to her pleasure before his own—or making sure she was right there along for the ride. She'd miss her brief glimpse of the high life, staying in hotels like this that easily, in Moscow, cost $1,200 a night—probably more.

But she would not miss the fear, the violence, or the lies.

Eric put on a gray cashmere turtleneck and dark trousers. He sat on the bed to pull on dark socks and slip his big feet into black leather lace-up shoes that looked wickedly expensive. She'd never seen him in clothing like this.

"Getting dressed up for Mr. Thug?"

He cast a quick glance at her. "This is serious business, negotiating for our lives. Jeans or khakis don't feel right, under the circumstances."

"Ah. Of course it's important to be well-groomed for a prospective executioner. I should have thought of that."

He poked his tongue into his cheek, got up, and stood looking down at her, his hands fisted on his hips.

"Sorry," she said. "I guess fear makes me flip."

He shook his head, ran a hand through his hair, and rubbed the back of his neck. "Nat," he said quietly. "Look, if anything goes wrong . . . if anything happens to me . . . contact Avy Hunt. She'll have information that you need. And don't check out of the hotel until you've talked to her, okay?"

Under the covers, her body began to tremble. Unbelievable schmuck that Eric McDougal was, she couldn't think of him truly hurt or dead, despite her brief highway fantasy. "You can't let anything happen to you, Eric." God, her voice was shaking.

"Yeah, I won't. But just in case . . . Natalie, I love you."

She threw off the covers and ran to him, pressing her naked body against his, the cashmere of his sweater soft against her breasts. She wrapped her arms around him—this was good-bye. *Good-bye, fantasy man. End of story.* Finito, *you idiot. Kick his ass on his way straight to hell.*

She lifted her face for a last kiss, which was gentle and masterful and achingly erotic.

God help me. Why can't I control my own emotions? Why?

"I love you, too, Eric," she whispered. Once again, she wasn't lying.

But Natalie dove for the phone as soon as the door closed behind Eric. She dialed the number of her grandmother's hotel and asked for Mrs. Ciccoli's room.

"Nonnie? It's me. I have St. George . . ."

They all made an effort to disguise themselves this time, just as a precaution. Nonnie wrapped herself to the eyebrows in a cobalt blue scarf with a red floral design on it. Natalie jammed her hair up underneath a stretchy wool cap of Eric's, also swiping a pair of his sunglasses and a jacket. Without too close an inspection, she could pass for a teenage boy wearing his older brother's clothes.

While she guided Nonnie, the colonel stayed out of sight on his own, alert for any sign of trouble.

They arrived at the Cathedral of the Assumption without any trouble, and Natalie located a priest in the sacristy. Nonnie spoke quietly to him in Russian while he pursed his lips and stroked his beard. At first he shook his head.

Nonnie spoke further to him, her tone earnest and insistent. His expression went from negative to skeptical.

Finally, Nonnie gestured to Natalie and told her to show him the St. George necklace. Natalie had brought it wrapped in her sock, and she pulled it from her pocket. She upended the sock, and the piece slid out and into her hand.

The priest stared at it, his eyes wide. He nodded, raised a hand as if to ask them to wait, and hurried off. He disappeared into a hallway and they waited, Nonnie taking a seat in the pews.

Natalie wandered, gazing at the scenes from the life of Metropolitan Peter on the south wall, taking in the white stone Patriarch's Seat and the gilded czarina's throne adorned with its double-headed eagle. The cathedral was a historical, religious, and architectural marvel and had been the most important in Moscow from the early fourteenth century.

She could imagine Catherine the Great in this place, sweeping through in her grand brocade coronation gown and her crown with its five thousand gems, wielding the magnificent Orlov Diamond at the top of her scepter.

Slow, deliberate footsteps claimed her attention from

the image. Natalie turned to find an archbishop with a long gray beard in full vestments approaching. She quickly went to Nonnie and helped her to her feet, guiding her out of the pew.

The archbishop spoke in Russian. Nonnie bowed her head, and Natalie did the same out of courtesy.

Then Nonnie murmured words to him, tears welling in her old eyes.

He nodded and asked a question.

"Give him St. George, my dear," Nonnie told Natalie.

So she did.

The archbishop took the necklace into his hands and traced the outline of the little sculpted saint on his horse. He closed his eyes and said a prayer over the piece. Then he turned and gestured for them to follow him.

They descended deep into the belly of the church, the air growing cooler as they went. The damp got increasingly pervasive, and the whole atmosphere supported a cloying melancholy.

After the third set of stone steps, they turned down a dark passageway that was little more than a tunnel. Small chambers lined it on either side, and in the chambers were tombs much smaller than the ones that lined the nave of the church on the ground level.

The archbishop counted as they went along, stopping at the ninth chamber. He gestured them inside, and while Nonnie could stand at her full height, he and Natalie had to bend and bow their heads.

The tomb inside looked small to Nat, but then, the date on it was 1798, only two years after Catherine the Great herself had died. People had grown much larger in the two centuries since then.

Natalie was half afraid that the archbishop would unseal the actual tomb, but instead he went to the head of it, where there was a stone structure that looked a lot like the headboard of a bed. He tugged hard at the double-headed eagle that adorned the apex, and to her surprise the top section of it moved, groaning with the scrape of stone on stone. It slid off like the lid of a box.

The archbishop reached inside the body of the box and lifted out a bundle wrapped carefully in layers of hide. This he presented to Nonnie before moving the heavy stone lid back into place.

Nonnie clutched it to herself and murmured a prayer. Then she turned to Natalie. "Open it, Natalya. Please."

The archbishop had brought with him an old-fashioned oil lamp, and she used the light from it to see.

There were three layers of soft suede leather. As she unwrapped them, Natalie could barely breathe.

Under the final layer were several items. "A Bible, the Old Testament," Natalie said aloud for her grandmother's benefit. "A handwritten journal."

"Both my mother's," Nonnie said. "Go on."

"There's a book of recipes."

Nonnie smiled. "My grandmother's. Glory be."

"A manuscript? Something like that . . ." Natalie leafed through it carefully. The signature on the last page made her heart stop. "Signed Natalya Goncharova, 1832," she said faintly.

"Ah. I wondered if that still existed. You know who she was?"

"Alexander Pushkin's wife. He's Russia's most famous poet!"

"Yes. Unfortunately, he died in a duel over her. She

was a cousin of ours. Of course no one suspected she was a writer herself."

"Is this manuscript any good?"

"I don't have the foggiest notion," Nonnie said. "I was five when we left, remember? But even if it isn't, I should think it has great historical value. Now, what else is there?"

"Three packets of letters. An embroidered cloth with military medals pinned to it. A lace collar . . . no jewels, though, Nonnie. Not the treasure you were expecting." Natalie looked up at her grandmother's face, afraid she'd be upset.

Instead, she wore an expression of utter nostalgia and content. She smiled gently. "No treasure? Why, what do you call this? These things are the keys to our family history, and what could possibly be more valuable than that?"

Nonnie reached out, took Natalie's hands, and stood on tiptoe to kiss her cheek. "Gold, emeralds, diamonds—they're like peacock feathers. They merely show us who we *want* to be: perhaps more important, more glamorous than we deserve.

"The tokens of our ancestry: letters, journals, portraits, recipes—these show us where we came from and who we really *are*. Now, I ask you, which is more precious?"

Thirty-seven

"Hi," said McDougal as he walked right up to the scowling man posted outside the Savoy. In disbelief, the Russian actually dropped his crackberry onto the sidewalk.

But not all his reactions were slow. Within half a second, something ominous tented his coat pocket, and it was aimed way too close to McDougal's heart.

"Well, golly jeepers," he said, raising his eyebrows. "Is that a gun, or are you just happy to see me?"

When the man just stared at him, nonplussed, McD switched to Russian. "Take me to your boss, Suzdal. I have a business proposition to discuss with him."

"I have business proposition, American pig. I shoot you and throw you in the Moskva."

"That's not business," McDougal explained kindly. "That's just a mundane, garden-variety assassination. You get no ROI in that maneuver. Understand?"

The man just squinted his pouchy little eyes.

"ROI. Return on investment. I can offer your boss some great terms, I'm telling you."

"Necklace?"

"This does concern the necklace, yes."

"You have?"

"I have," McDougal assured him. "But not with me."

"You get."

"All in good time."

"You get now, or I shoot."

McDougal sighed and shook his head. "I can see that the art of the deal is lost on you. Now, let me explain something: You kill me now, you will never get the necklace. You take me to your boss and you just might. So where are you parked, you ugly waste of oxygen?" He said the last words in English with an I'm-your-best-buddy grin.

The man had picked up his crackberry, and he now hit a button and spoke into it, explaining what McDougal wanted to the man on the other end. Evidently Suzdal was curious enough to see him, because his lackey ended the call and said, "You have gun? Knife? Bomb?"

"Fresh out," McD said in sorrowful tones as he shook his head. "Left 'em in the rented dacha along with your naked, willing wife."

Oblivious to the insult in the English words, the man said, "Walk." They went several blocks before they came to—no kidding—a late-model Saab that looked all too familiar. While Eric bit his lip hard to keep from laughing, he submitted to a full pat-down so the guy could be sure he had no weapons.

"You want to look in my shorts, too?" he asked.

Again, no reaction. The man unlocked the doors of the Saab, they both climbed in, and they headed northeast, out of the city. In about half an hour, they pulled up to a grand country house in the classical style with a circular porch delineated with Ionic columns.

As the car doors slammed, a well-dressed, dark-haired man with a cigar came walking forward and studied McDougal casually. Judging by his driver's deference, this was Suzdal.

Adrenaline skated down Eric's spine, but he remained cool outwardly—even knowing that the man probably didn't intend to let him live. He didn't look like a vicious mob boss—he had large, liquid brown eyes that gave the illusion of warmth and humor. And that was just plain creepy.

"Mr. McDougal?"

He nodded.

"I have bad habit of smoking," Suzdal said, waving his cigar in a self-deprecating manner.

You have a lot of bad habits, buddy. Murder, theft, smuggling, money laundering . . .

"My son, he is allergic. So. You object to walking outside on the grounds?"

"Not at all." *Easier to scrape my body off the snow than off an expensive rug, is it?*

"How are you enjoying your stay in Moscow, Mr. McDougal?" Unbelievably, there was not a trace of irony in his voice. He could have been a cultural attaché making small talk at an embassy party, which was even creepier than his luminous, kindly eyes.

McDougal raised an eyebrow. "Aside from the surveillance, the kidnappers, and the brutal assault on my girlfriend in our hotel room, we've had a grand old time."

Suzdal said nothing. He slanted a quick, dark glance at his guest and produced a creditable imitation of a welcoming smile, a cobra offering a bunny an aperitif.

"Other than that, Moscow is a beautiful city with a great sense of history."

"Yes," Suzdal said. "You have been to the Kremlin? The Pushkin Museum of Fine Arts? The Tolstoy house?"

"Oddly enough, we've had very little time for sightseeing," Eric said. "You know, because of fearing for our lives. That can suck a lot of the joy out of a vacation."

Suzdal ashed his cigar into an urn and evaluated him. His fleshy lips clamped around the cigar again and he drew in on it until the tip glowed red. "You do not seem to fear for your life at this moment, Mr. McDougal. Perhaps you should."

"Oh, please call me Eric. And no, I'm not afraid for my life right now." A lie, but it rolled easily off his tongue even as unease spiraled through his gut.

He was alone here. No backup. Nothing to protect himself but his mouth and his powers of persuasion.

"I'm not afraid, because once you've heard me out I think you'll be happy to chauffeur me back to the Savoy and perhaps even pick up my dinner tab."

"Indeed?"

"Indeed."

"I must say that I am intrigued. What is this business proposal you have for me, Eric?" Suzdal's tone was avuncular, almost fatherly.

This was it. This was the moment where McDougal took his life into his hands and waved it, like a tasty little mammal, inches away from the mouth of the unpredictable cobra. Had the reptile eaten his fill just this morning? Or did he have a raging and vindictive appetite?

McD swallowed. "The proposal, as you call it, is all

about information. There are certain documents filed at the ARTemis offices and with my lawyer, documents which attest to the fact that in 2005, you may not have had your friend and mentor Vasily Somov's best interests at heart."

Suzdal stopped in his tracks and took a deep drag on his cigar. "Go on," he said, his voice suddenly frostbitten.

"Now, I'm as sure as you are that these documents contain only the most vicious and unfounded lies . . ."

Suzdal exhaled the smoke slowly, as if it were poisoned gas, into Eric's face. "Of course."

"But we all know that rumor and innuendo can easily ruin a man, especially if his friends are given to paranoia and violence. I would hate to see such a long and . . . er . . . productive friendship ruined. I'm sure that Somov's companionship and trust mean everything to you."

Suzdal tossed his cigar into a snowy bush. "What do you want?" he asked flatly, his gaze flicking up toward the roof.

McDougal saw the telltale glint of a long black scope and had no doubts at all that the bridge of his nose was in the crosshairs of a sniper's rifle. His mouth went dry and his guts slid greasily.

"I want you to leave us alone," he said. "I want you to forget that the St. George necklace ever existed. And I want safe passage out of this country for myself and every one of my associates. That's all."

He stood for a long agonizing moment, wondering whether his face would blow apart; whether the cartilage of his nose would burst through the back of his skull;

whether his head would just split like a melon. Whether he'd ever see Natalie's face again.

Would he feel pain, or would it be over too fast?

Would they put his body through a wood chipper?

Dissolve it in acid?

Suzdal's voice broke into these pleasant musings. "I want the documents in return."

McDougal threw back his head and laughed, even though he felt a lot more like pissing himself. "No way. No way in hell." Good. His voice wasn't shaking.

"I will not leave myself open to future blackmail."

"I'm not a blackmailer, Mr. Suzdal. I'm just a simple thief. And I'll keep the papers safe as long as you keep us safe."

A muscle jumped in Suzdal's jaw. He said nothing. He glanced upward again. Several long, very long, moments ticked by.

Ask for the close. Ask for the goddamned close, McD, before your head gets perforated. McDougal unstuck his tongue from the roof of his mouth. "Do we have a deal?"

Suzdal turned his back on him and walked toward his house. "Yes, damn you. We have a deal."

Relief shot through McDougal like vodka on an empty stomach. Giddy. He felt giddy. He pushed his luck just to celebrate the fact that he was still alive. "How 'bout that dinner tab?"

"Go and fuck yourself," Suzdal said crisply. "Now, get off my property before I call dogs on you."

McDougal didn't need to be told twice, but he wasn't about to hike back to the city center. Too bad the man who'd driven him here was nowhere to be found.

With a shrug, Eric did his best to saunter on his rubbery legs over to the trusty Saab. He opened the driver's-side door and collapsed into the seat. Then, with shaking fingers, he 'jacked the car again. This time he didn't bother to leave gas money inside.

The Do Not Disturb sign was on his and Natalie's room at the Savoy, but McDougal figured that was for Housekeeping's benefit, not his own.

Adrenaline still pulsed through his veins, mixing with relief that he'd secured Natalie's safety . . . and the tumultuous anticipation he felt. He would finally present her with the St. George necklace as proof of his loyalty to her. Proof of his apology. Proof of his love.

He couldn't decide how to stage it, or whether it was a gesture that should be staged. Perhaps he should just be casual—go to the nightstand, pull out the box, and toss it into her lap.

Or maybe he should get down on his knees.

Should he order a bottle of champagne for the occasion?

As usual, he hated indecision. But his feelings for Natalie made him feel like a teenager again, trying to pick out a corsage for the prom. He had no experience with anything like this. His confidence had always come from knowing he wanted to leave a woman, not knowing that he wanted to stay around.

And even though she'd told him that she loved him, he sensed that she was holding something back. He sensed something dark, even tragic behind the words . . . something threatening.

McDougal took a deep breath and slid his key card

into the door. The room was dark, with the curtains drawn. "Natalie?"

No response.

He flipped on the light switch closest to the door, which softly illuminated the place. She wasn't in the bed. Nor was she in the bathroom.

"Natalie?" His heart fisted in his chest and tried to punch its way through his rib cage, again and again.

She was gone.

Holy Mother of God, she was gone.

A million horrifying scenarios poured into his mind like sewer water from a broken main.

Natalie beaten.

Natalie strangled.

Natalie raped.

Was she suffocating in the trunk of a car? Buried in the frozen ground? Floating facedown in the Moskva River?

Had Suzdal lied through his teeth, sending someone here for her even as McDougal walked with him and his damned cigar? A hefty bribe could have gotten a man past security.

Hands shaking again, Eric went to the drawer of the nightstand and slid it open. The lacquered box, in its wrapping, was still there. He pulled it out, shoved it into his jacket pocket, and, knees trembling, sat down hard on the bed.

If Suzdal had sent men for her, they would have turned the place upside down in search of the necklace. It wouldn't still be here. The only reason Eric had left it in such an obvious place was that he'd known—or thought he'd known—that Natalie wouldn't be leaving the room.

He forced himself to take deep breaths and focus as he looked around. There was no sign of a struggle at all. Her purse was gone, as were her coat and boots. Her suitcase was still on the floor; her toiletries still sat on the bathroom counter.

Natalie had most likely left of her own accord, against his explicit instructions, and in defiance of her promise not to do so. While fear still clawed at his throat, blood, red and angry, began to beat a tattoo at his temples. He got up and paced back and forth, a tiger in a cage.

By all that's holy, I'll kill her myself if someone else hasn't. I'll wring her slim white neck.

He turned and kicked her suitcase, but it didn't make him feel any better. Where was she? Would the concierge know? Should he go out and search for her? Or should he wait right here until she returned so that he could . . . could . . . What? Shake her till her teeth rattled?

I'll teach her a lesson, by God, I will.

Then it occurred to him, like a slap in the face, that he already had. He'd taught her how to break promises. He'd taught her how to lie. He'd taught her to deceive.

Was that the dark thing he'd sensed behind her words? It was. Natalie no longer possessed that bright, unspoiled quality, that droll naïveté that had pulled him up short when he'd first met her. There'd been something sad in her eyes when he'd left her in bed this morning, but he'd been so preoccupied with the coming face-off with Suzdal that he'd dismissed it.

You stupid bastard. You've ruined things for her. The girl who believed in fairy tales, in happy endings, is gone.

Thirty-eight

McDougal had his hands together and his fingers steepled when the hotel room door opened to reveal Natalie. He was praying for the first time since his release from his Jesuit tormentors at St. Joseph's more than a decade before.

Even more humiliating, he had actual tears in his eyes, eyes that had always been dry and wicked and reflected unholy glee—a source of great pride.

McDougal had also always been fairly articulate, but at this moment so many words threatened to blurt from his mouth that he sounded strangled, like a cat choking on a fish.

Sweet Jesus, you're safe!

I'll kill you myself for scaring me . . .

I love you more than life itself!

You crazy bitch, how could you risk your neck by leaving?

He lunged at her, seized her despite her shriek of alarm, and wrapped his arms around her. He buried his face in her neck and spun around like a lunatic top. "Thank God, thank God, thank God . . . ," he repeated.

"Eric," she squeaked, "I can't breathe!"

"Neither can I." But he set her down. He held her by the shoulders and drank in her features, the dazed navy eyes, the sprinkling of freckles on her slightly pug nose, the gorgeous cheekbones, the pale pink of her bolster-like lower lip.

Then he set about kissing her properly, which took some time, because he had to do a safety check on every square millimeter of her mouth. He would have double-checked, but the silly girl kept trying to speak to him.

"I am *furious* with you," he told her as he unwrapped her scarf, pulled her sweater awry, and buried his face between her breasts.

"Er . . . you are?" She sounded breathless.

"Enraged. I don't think I'll ever forgive you."

"Uh . . ."

"Thank you, God. She's wearing a dress," were his next words. He sat down on the bed again, slid his hands up under her skirt, and ripped her panties by the seam at each hip as she squeaked again in shock.

"Eric! What are you—"

"Please," he said thickly. "It's not just sex. I need you. I thought I'd lost you . . ."

Wordless, she looked down at him, tears gathering in her eyes. Good tears or bad tears? He didn't know.

"Please let me in. Please, Natalie—I need to be inside you."

She hesitated. Then she took his face in her hands, bent down, and kissed him.

That was all the permission he needed. He freed himself from his pants, pulled her on top of him, parted her, and thrust into her.

"Ohhh."

He held her by the hips as his eyes damn near rolled back into his head, moving in and out of her tight, wet heat. She came first, her head collapsing on his shoulder, and he wasn't far behind.

"Um," she said when she could catch her breath. "Will you get mad at me more often?"

McDougal let out a ragged groan. "Don't ever scare me like that again."

"I won't. I promise."

He brought his head up and looked straight into her eyes. "Would that be a promise that you'll actually keep?"

"Depends," she said coolly.

"On?"

"Whether you keep yours."

"I do." He was still wearing his jacket, even if his pants were around his ankles. How dignified. He reached into the inside pocket and withdrew the lacquered box. He placed it into her hands. "This belongs to you, Natalie."

To his surprise, her whole body stiffened. She slid off his knees and pulled her skirt down. "Wh-what is it?"

He straightened his own clothes. Not a man alive could look sexy naked from the waist down and wearing black shoes and socks. Not even a certified chick magnet like him. "I think you know what it is, sweetheart."

She put a hand to her mouth and shook her head.

"It's the St. George necklace."

"Oh, no." Her eyes filled again, overflowed, and tears rolled down her cheeks. "No," she said brokenly. "It's not."

He was puzzled by her reaction, to say the least. "It is. Open the box."

She did open it, with shaking fingers. "I'm so sorry that I didn't have faith in you, Eric," she said.

"What?"

"But you've been a little hard to trust."

In front of his disbelieving eyes, she pulled out a bundle of fabric that he'd never seen before, and tossed it into his lap.

He untied the corners and stared down at a jumble of coins.

"I . . . um. I repossessed the necklace, Eric. We took it to the cathedral this morning and made the exchange for my family's belongings. That's where I've been."

His mouth opened and closed.

"I'm sorry," she said again. "But I didn't think you'd give it back to me—you've taken me for quite a ride."

He took a moment to absorb the shock.

Natalie had stolen the necklace right out from under his nose. It was poetic justice.

It damn well served him right, but he didn't know how to react. "You—," he said, then shook his head. "You didn't." He pulled a hand over his face. "You're not the type—"

Finally, McDougal hung his head between his knees and laughed until his ribs hurt.

"I do love you, Eric," she said uncertainly. "Even though you're an asshole and I've been really, really pissed at myself over the whole thing. I can't help but love you."

"Natalie," he said, lifting his head and mopping at his

own streaming eyes with his sleeve. "I don't know what to say."

He looked at that sweet, straightforward face of hers. "I love you, too. You have no idea how much. But I was afraid you were way too honest for me, sweetheart."

She lifted her shoulders, then let them drop again. "Guess not," she said sheepishly.

"Come 'ere." He grabbed her hands and kissed her. "I may be a thief with a permit. I may enjoy a good con. But you can trust me on this, at least: My heart is one hundred percent yours, and nobody else will ever repossess *that*."

Thirty-nine

Natalie, Eric, Nonnie, and the colonel stood at Poklonnaya Gora, Moscow's monument to World War II. In front of it was a massive granite slab displaying the year 1945.

Beyond that, on a raised pedestal, was the monolithic figure of a dragon, its mighty head severed from its scaly body. St. George, his cloak rippling in the breeze, sat astride a rearing horse, which trampled the dragon's body while the saint's great spear fatally pierced it.

Natalie described the monument for Nonnie as they walked closer to it and ascended the stairs so that she could touch it, run her old hands over the gigantic sculpture.

"There's a huge obelisk behind St. George, Nonnie, and it seems to reach all the way to the sky. On the four faces of it, soldiers emerge from the stone, men who fought bravely for Russia and its territories during the war. Their courage is immortalized for everyone to see."

"Men like my father," the old lady murmured. "Before he forfeited his right arm."

"Yes."

"You know he would have gone back to fight, Natalya? He just wanted to see us to safety. He was no coward."

Nat slid an arm around her grandmother's shoulders and squeezed. "I never thought he was."

"St. George," Nonnie said, reverently. "Hero on a mythical, religious, and symbolic level. The dragon at this monument stands for the Nazis. St. George is Moscow." A smile crossed her face.

She touched the new, sparkling ring on the fourth finger of her left hand, then turned her old blind eyes toward Eric with a coy expression. "St. George also operates on a personal level, eh, Natalya? He has brought us love in spite of all odds."

"Yes, he does." Natalie squeezed Eric's hand and he flushed. "My knight in—"

He shook his head. "Lady, I keep trying to tell you—I'm no knight!"

"—tarnished armor. I think it's beyond tarnished, actually. It's creaky, kind of rusted out, truth to tell, so it's a good thing I have contacts in the restoration business."

"Hey!" He poked her in the ribs, and she batted at his hand.

"Be serious, children," said Nonnie. "I have a question to ask you."

They waited.

"Will you come with me on my next quest?" she asked. She groped and found Ted Blakely's hand, while he gazed at her fondly. "All of you?"

"What quest would that be?"

"I'm going to find Wiemar von Bruegel, the Nazi

bastard who killed my father and many others. Inside the necklace was a safety-deposit key. Inside the safety-deposit box was proof of his true identity and of his crimes. He's been living under an assumed name, right here in Moscow! And I will hunt him down if it's the last thing I do."

"Er," Eric said, rubbing the back of his neck. "Mrs. Ciccoli? His assumed name is Oleg Litsky, and my co-workers already have him in custody. They 'repossessed' him for the World Court. Someone will probably be calling you soon so that you can confront him and testify at his trial."

Nonnie stared sightlessly at him, her eyes filling and her mouth working. Then she threw her arms around him and kissed him on both cheeks. He could feel himself blushing, probably borscht red.

"See, Natalya?" her grandmother said. "What did I tell you? That necklace has mystical qualities. It calls forth the true spirits of those who handle it. Your young man and his colleagues were sent by St. George himself."

"Of course they were," Natalie agreed wryly. "Was there ever any doubt?" And then she leaned over to kiss Eric deeply.